'Raven is a superb storyteller' – *Los Angeles Times*

'Enjoy this as an excellent piece of storytelling, crammed with comedy, suspense and action, which gives an alarming glimpse of the iceberg beneath the James Bond playground' – *Daily Mail*

'The glimpses of hell and a continuously sinister undertone in the book are quite real and quite frightening' – *Spectator*

'Probably the finest book he has written' – *The Scotsman*

Simon Raven

The Sabre Squadron

Panther

Granada Publishing Limited
Published in 1967 by Panther Books Ltd
3 Upper James Street, London W1R 4BP
Reprinted 1972

First published in Great Britain by
Anthony Blond Limited 1966
Copyright © Simon Raven 1966
Made and printed in Great Britain by
Cox & Wyman Ltd,
London, Reading and Fakenham
Set in Intertype Plantin

Contents

ALMS FOR OBLIVION will be a series of ten novels (of which The Sabre Squadron *is the third) to cover the English upper middle class scene since the war. The series is not planned as one long saga; each volume will present an independent story. But the ten major characters are all loosely connected with one another by birth or upbringing. If there is one theme which will dominate the series it is that human effort and goodwill are persistently vulnerable to the malice of time, chance, and the rest of the human race.*

Part One

IL PENSEROSO

'KAFFE, bitte. Schwarz,' said Daniel Mond.

The waiter bowed and shuffled off over the terrace. From a little lower down the hill a drowsy bugle called from the British occupied barracks. On the ridge above, the summer woods of rustling green and scented pine spread away to Daniel's right and swerved down as far as the formal park which skirted this side of the town. Then there were the suburbs prettily ranked; and then Göttingen itself, like an eighteenth century pastiche of a medieval city, ordered, polite and yet perceptibly Gothic, its three towers flickering in the haze of high afternoon. A seemly place, thought Daniel as he looked down from the terrace on the hill; serene, civilized and seemly.

The waiter shuffled back along the terrace, set down the coffee, and, for an instant, gave Daniel that look, quick, guilty, aggressive, which he had seen in so many faces during the last three months and which, even now, stirred a light chilly tremor in his gut. Ah well, he thought, reassuring himself for the thousandth time: we're already well into 1952, over seven years since it all stopped, very soon now they'll forget, they must forget. A brief glance must not be allowed to spoil an afternoon like this. In a few minutes he would start over the meadow and down the hill, would meet and follow the wall of the oddly elegant barracks which the Nazis had built in 1935 (nothing to fear now, surely), would veer away to the right through the cool woods; in half an hour he would be back in Göttingen, would greet the statue of the Goose Girl in her little courtyard and turn down the narrow street, past the den where the Germans played *skat*, to his lodgings in the house with the crooked white front. There he would settle to the work which waited; he would trace the manuscript pages of graceful symbols which must surely reveal, before much longer, the truth which he sought, his truth, pure, formal and ascetic, yet alive with the stuff of romance and even fantasy, with mysteries which lay beyond itself. Later, much later, exhausted and so for a few hours appeased, he would stack his sheets, say good night to them aloud, and walk out through the friendly alleys to dine.

A brilliant afternoon in late July, a gentle walk down hill into a peaceful and pleasant little town, several hours ahead of a congenial and absorbing search. No; not a prospect to be easily spoiled by one glance from an elderly waiter still rancorous at his country's well earned shame. And yet that glance reminded him of so much else that he would wish to forget. It reminded him that this evening, as always lately, he would dine alone; that for weeks now there had been something – he could not quite say what – something sly, something treacherous about the behaviour of the symbols and series to which he would shortly return; that there was, too, something wrong in a wider sense, something which included his loneliness and the threat posed by his symbols and yet transcended these, something which, as he sat warm and well fed on the sunny terrace above Göttingen, seemed suddenly to settle all about him like air from a tomb.

Back in January, soon after Dirange, his research supervisor, had first suggested that he should spend some months in Göttingen, Daniel had discussed the matter with Robert Constable, the College Tutor.

'Why Göttingen?' Constable had said.

'Dirange thinks there's some stuff there which will help me. Unpublished dissertations, some manuscript papers . . .'

'I thought they were best known for physics at Göttingen. Max Planck, for example: Atomic Theory and so on. As I understand it, your research is concerned with the purest of pure mathematics.'

'Physicists often develop new methods which are of interest to us. In the same way . . . regrettably . . . as our formulations often turn out to be useful to them.'

'Regrettably?' said Constable, who, an economist himself, resented the airs and graces of 'unapplied' men.

Daniel shrugged miserably. Of all things he hated the line of argument which he knew to be coming, the bellicose assertion of the benefits conferred by science, the patronizing reminder that, while the pure mathematician might indeed be 'of value' in himself, he must not be too proud to assist in practical ventures. But he had brought it on himself by one careless word, and now, for what seemed the millionth time, he must see it through.

'I mean,' he said carefully to the affronted Tutor, 'that physicists aren't always very delicate in the use they make of our help. The Atom Bomb . . .'

'Perhaps. But doctors? I'm told that Bio-mathematics is proving a great help in developing new cures for diseases of the blood.'

'By the application,' said Daniel, 'of elementary theories of Chance to the behaviour in motion of the corpuscles. A child could do it.'

One of Daniel's troubles was that he so often, out of sheer nervousness, said either much more or much less than he meant. If the former, he was apt to sound petulant (rather than arrogant), if the latter, to appear as grovelling (rather than discreet). As things were just now, he had allowed himself to be irritated into a piece of peevish inaccuracy, and he awaited Constable's retort with horror. Fortunately, however, the telephone rang.

'Tutor, Lancaster College,' Constable said, and listened for three minutes with growing impatience. 'I'll see him tonight,' he snapped into the receiver: 'if he doesn't pay in seven days, he can pack up and go home.'

He turned back to Daniel, his eyes raw with distaste.

'Contemptible,' he said. 'He comes up here and pretends he's rich, champagne parties and hired cars, causes all kinds of resentment among the poorer undergraduates, and then won't pay his landlady.'

Constable pronounced the word 'resentment', Daniel noticed, as though it were a commendable and even ennobling quality of mind.

'He can either pay up or get out,' Constable went on, his

indignation at once cheapening and sharpening his idiom. 'We're through with that sort of lark. I will not tolerate extravagance,' he said, reverting to general issues as his anger began to subside, 'even in those who can afford it. Where were we?'

'Dissertations and papers at the University of Göttingen,' Daniel said. 'In particular, Dirange thinks, the Dortmund papers.'

'What's so special about them?'

'When he died in 1938, Dortmund was working on a new type of matrix. His idea was that the symbols should be arranged in a rectilinear framework, not just of two dimensions as before, but of three dimensions, thus greatly increasing the variety of relations between them.'

'Like three-dimensional chess?'

'Quite a good comparison,' said Daniel, trying not to sound condescending. 'The trouble was, though, that it all had to be expressed on paper, so that he needed an entirely new notation – to put in the third dimension, so to speak.'

'Couldn't he,' said Constable, tense and admonitory, 'have fixed up three-dimensional frameworks – modelled them in wire or something – and then used bits of cardboard with the symbols written on? Clipped them in place?'

'He could have. Perhaps he did. But that wouldn't have been much good when he came to publish. I mean,' said Daniel, feeling exceedingly silly, 'he could hardly send little cages of wire all round the world with symbols dangling all over them. So he devised this new notation for representing what he wanted on the page. And died before he had explained it to anyone.'

Constable said nothing, a sign of his qualified approval.

'His widow,' continued Daniel, 'gave all his papers to the University. The Nazis were curious at first, but when they were told that his work had no obvious scientific bearing they lost interest. The point really was, though, that no one at all could decipher the new symbols which Dortmund had invented. There were some good men at Göttingen and they called some more in from outside, and still they couldn't crack the code . . . so to speak. But Dirange thinks,' said Daniel, cringing like Uriah Heep, 'that I might be able to ... disentangle it all. This would mean that I could understand Dortmund's matrices, and these in turn might give me some help I'm looking for in my own line of investigation.'

'*Might* give you *some* help,' Constable insisted.

'Even if they didn't, the work would be worthwhile. Dortmund was never quite in the front rank but he was an important man. What he did in those last years ought to be understood and made available.'

There was a long silence.

'So what it comes to,' said Constable kindly but firmly, 'is that you want the College Council to give you leave of absence to go to Göttingen, there to undertake an ambitious task which has defied senior men for years and which, even if accomplished, may take you no further in the line of research which you proposed to us when we awarded you your Grant.'

'Dirange—'

'—Dirange may be a big man in the Faculty of Mathematics but he is not a member of this college, still less of the College Council. The Council has to take an official view. You were elected to a Post-graduate Studentship,' said Constable, his prim, boyish face knotted in conscientious caution, 'in July of last year – 1951. This means we expect the first draft of your Fellowship Thesis by Christmas 1952 – *this* Christmas. Supposing your work at Göttingen turns out to be a side-track – no matter how interesting? You'd never have time to get back on your proper course and turn in a thesis by Christmas. This,' said Constable, 'the College Council would find very displeasing. It is, after all, a matter of contract.'

'I'm ready,' said Daniel snivelling, 'to take the risk.'

'You may be. But you are *our* investment. As I just said, if senior men have failed with the problem ever since 1938—'

'—Then it's possible the problem needs a younger man with a fresh approach. The whole point is,' said Daniel, beginning to honk, 'that in pure mathematics you do your best work, your creative work, as a *young* man. So if you think you see your way – and it's bound to be a bit of a gamble – you've got to follow it up at once. After you're thirty there's nothing left for you except consolidation.'

'And you are . . . how old?'

'Twenty-two.'

'Leaving you eight more years.' Constable looked inquiringly at Daniel, picked at some of the spots which marred his cherubic complexion, and then let his face go absolutely blank, a signal (to those, like Daniel, who understood him) that he had reached a final decision. 'Eight years. Not long, really. So let us hope,' said Constable, facetious and energetic, 'that your summer in Göttingen will not be wasted. For I shall recommend to the College Council that they accede to your request, so I think you can take that as settled. But there is surely,' he said, 'one other problem to be thought of, Daniel?'

'I know,' said Daniel: 'I think of it all the time.'

The 'other' problem he had discussed a few days later with his contemporary, Jacquiz Helmut the historian.

'It's not as if the Germans can *do* anything to you,' Helmut had said, looking placidly along the Backs from Lancaster bridge. 'For the time being at least they've been tamed.'

'But how would you feel about going there?'

'It's different for me.' Helmut's eyebrows, which normally met in the middle, seemed to part for a moment in polite protest. 'I'm the real thing, you see. You're only Jewish on your father's side, and therefore not a Jew at all by a strict reckoning.'

'The Nazis took a different view.'

'The Nazis have gone for good.'

'No, they haven't,' said Daniel; 'that's just my point. The uniforms have gone, but the mass of the men that wore them are still there. In every shop, every restaurant, walking along the street . . .'

'They're too busy just now to bother with you,' said Helmut, suave and dismissive. 'They've got their living to make. A whole country to rebuild. I grant you, they're rebuilding it just a little too quickly for comfort, but there's work to keep them out of mischief for some time to come.'

He turned from the balustrade of the bridge, clasped his hands together in front of his groin, and indicated to Daniel by a slight nod that it was now his pleasure to walk. They progressed in silence along the avenue and towards the Fellows' Garden, Daniel, as usual, being sadly embarrassed by the difficulty of matching his stubby legs to the august stride of his six-foot-six companion.

'For someone wholly Jewish,' said Daniel crossly, 'you've no business to be so tall.'

'Among the Jews as elsewhere height is a sign of aristocratic descent.'

It was not always easy to know whether Jacquiz Helmut's remarks were intended seriously or not. Silent once more, they approached the gate of the Fellows' Garden. Helmut prodduced a key on a golden chain and let them in.

'No one's given me a key,' said Daniel resentfully.

'You only have to ask at the Porters' Lodge. All resident graduates are entitled to one.'

'I did ask. Mr. Wilkes said they'd run out.'

'That was what Wilkes said to me. I told him,' said Helmut with a twitch of his cardinal's nose, 'that unless I was given a key within twenty-four hours his slackness would be reported to the Bursar.' He looked round the deserted garden with condescension. 'Uninviting,' he said, 'but at least there is privacy. Now we can be serious about your little problem.'

'You've just said that there is no problem.'

'Superficially, none at all. To start with, you don't look particularly Jewish. Small and dark, yes, but without that distinguishing facial structure. You, my dear Daniel, could be anything. And even if the whole of Göttingen knew of your paternity, even if they discussed nothing else from morning to night, you are still under the protection of His Britannic Majesty, their conqueror, who will not allow them to whisk you off and turn you into soap.'

Helmut paused in his walk and surveyed the Judas Tree with growing annoyance, as though it had been that kind of joke which, excellent at first hearing, turns out to have tactless and grating undertones.

'However,' he continued, 'there *is* a problem, if only because you feel there is.'

Then he fell silent and began, with both hands, to stroke the fur collar of his overcoat. Although his manner was still composed, his eyes were uneasy and even furtive.

'There has recently been an elaborate and scholarly book,' he said at last, 'written by a Jewish historian with whom I am in occasional correspondence. It purports to prove, beyond any further question, that the Romans were exclusively responsible for the execution of Jesus Christ.'

'*Exclusively?*'

'You have taken my point. Everyone knows that the Romans must bear a share, a substantial share, of the blame, but no one in his senses could pretend that the Jews were wholly innocent. And yet this is just what my correspondent, apparently a sane and erudite man, wishes to maintain. What does this suggest to you?'

'That we are a self-righteous people.'

'And what else?'

'That we are a self-deluding people . . . in some matters at least.'

'Come on, Daniel. More still.'

Helmut's tone was not hectoring, like that of a rugger coach calling for greater effort.

'We are . . . a self-loving people?'

'All peoples are that. We are worse than self-loving, Daniel: we are self-obsessed.'

His eyes cleared again. Delivery of this judgment had evidently restored his ironic good humour.

'Hence to your problem,' he said. 'You feel, to put it crudely, that in Germany you will be surrounded and contaminated by the murderers of your kin. Every time you show your ticket on a train – and on German trains one is *always* required to show one's ticket – you will imagine that same conductor herding thousands of Jews into cattle-trucks. In other words, you are thinking only in one set of terms: you are – or will become, if you are not careful – self-righteous, self-deluding, self-loving and self-obsessed.'

'Self-deluding?' said Daniel after a long pause.

'Yes. You delude yourself into thinking that the Nazi massacre of the Jews is the only thing which counts, almost the only thing which ever happened, in the whole history of Germany. Try thinking of something else for a change. Try thinking of Arminius, Goethe, Theodoric or Dr. Faustus . . . anything you like, but just forget for once in a way about Adolf Hitler.'

'You think . . . we should just behave as if it never occurred? All that death . . . the deliberate planning . . .'

'Listen,' said Helmut. He wagged a reproving finger at the Judas Tree and stalked on towards the summer house. 'Listen to me, and you shall hear my very last word on this tedious topic. The crime you talk of can never be wiped out. But you are going to Göttingen of your own free will, and the work you have there is important. If you want to do it properly, I suggest you will find it easier to think of yourself as a mathematician first, as a visitor in a foreign but well ordered country second, and as a Jew, if at all, a long way third. After all, half of you's solid Anglo-Saxon.'

'That's just the trouble. It would be nicer to be complete. One way or the other.'

'Nonsense,' Helmut said. 'We're all very pleased with you as you are.'

In the end Daniel had accepted and profited by Jacquiz Helmut's advice. He had insisted to himself that he was a scholar doing research work in a foreign university, nothing more and nothing less. True, this did not prevent him from noticing the sullen and suspicious looks which often came his way in public places, but he reminded himself that in a poor and defeated country any stranger, comfortably fed and dressed, must provoke resentment. Since the Germans, as a whole, were already well on the way back to prosperity, Daniel was not being strictly logical in this; but then his had never been a problem which could be solved (for all Jacquiz Helmut's calm good sense) by strict logic. It was necessary to cheat a little, and Daniel felt sure that the flexible Helmut would, on balance, have approved the slight shift from the letter of his instructions.

Despite the mild apprehensions he retained of anonymous Germans in the mass, Daniel found no difficulty whatever in his private dealings. His landlady, a huge, resigned woman who had seen better days and walked with a waddle, performed her duties punctually and unobtrusively; while the only other German on whom he must depend to any extent had treated him with a blend of professional courtesy and personal indifference which he found entirely reassuring. This was Doktor Aeneas von Bremke, to whom he was recommended by Dirange and whom he had visited promptly after his arrival in early April.

'The Herr Doktor Dirange has, of course, written to me,' von Bremke said solemnly. 'It is my pleasure and privilege to be of assistance. Will you care to come with me?'

He had led the way down a high, bleak corridor on the top floor of the building until they came to a door on which was a printed card:

HERR DOMINUS DANIEL MOND

'Dominus,' said von Bremke, his stern face becoming, for a moment, flaccid with satisfaction: 'that is the correct title of an English Bachelor of Arts, is it not?'

'I suppose so ... I mean, yes indeed,' said Daniel, trying to look impressed.

'Very good. Then this room we have put aside for you to work. Most of the Dortmund papers, you understand, cannot leave this building. But the Herr Curator will be pleased to place them at your disposal in this room.'

'You're very kind.'

'Please ...'

Von Bremke tested the desk-lamp and inspected a bust of Archimedes which stood on the window-sill.

'Naturally,' he said, as though addressing Archimedes, 'we are honoured that a learned and proficient young gentleman, from so ancient and remarkable a university, carrying the esteemed recommendation of the internationally regarded

Herr Doktor Dirange, should be coming here to examine the Dortmund remainders. But please do not hope for too much. I too, some years ago—'

He broke off like a record from which the needle has been lifted without warning.

'There is dust on this filing cabinet,' he said.

'Never mind, Herr Doktor.'

'I do not mind. It should not be there, that is all.' He took out a handkerchief of fine linen, dusted the top of the cabinet, and then dropped the handkerchief into the waste-paper basket. 'I too, some years ago,' von Bremke said, as though the gramophone needle had been suddenly replaced, 'examined the Dortmund relics. Our national calamity interrupted my work, but I had already done enough to know that I could do no more. This is all that I am trying to tell you: do not assure yourself of success.'

'I realize the difficulties.'

'No, you do not.' There was neither rudeness nor aggression in this, Daniel noticed; just a flat statement of fact. 'You know, as we all know, that Professor Dortmund invented a novel notation. This notation, we say, was necessary in order to convert an ordinary matrical method into one much more complex, occupying three dimensions. This was the Professor's object, this must be our clue: relate the notation to its function and the way of its working must sooner or later become apparent. You agree?'

Daniel nodded.

'Then why has it not become apparent? Through nearly fifteen years?'

'Because so little is known about the function to which it must be related.'

'Precisely, Herr Dominus. And then suppose that we knew even less. That Professor Dortmund was not always devising his novel notation for what we would be thinking but for something else. That he transferred himself, at some stage, from his three-dimensional matrices to a different, even more complicated field – related, very possibly, but *different*. What then, Herr Dominus?'

'We are agreed,' said Daniel slowly, 'that the nature of the Professor's work in his first field – little as we know of this – could give us the clue to the notation. Perhaps the notation, in turn, could give us the clue to this later field . . . into which, as you say, he transferred himself.'

'Perhaps,' said von Bremke, turning a poker face on Archimedes. 'But no one has yet accomplished even the first step. As for the second, when the Professor started to change his field to work towards another object, in many ways he also changed the notation. So you have not only one notation to decipher, but also a later variant. And for what this was intended we have no possible—'

Again he stopped in mid-speech without warning.

'I should have wished,' he said, 'that my wife could receive you in our house. But she has been ill.'

'I'm sorry.'

'Do not concern yourself. We cannot receive you; that is all. At this time there are no compatriots of yours here – in the University, that is to say. But there are the British soldiers up on the hill.'

'I don't know much about soldiers.'

'You did not do – what is it you say? – your Government service?'

'I was excused National Service. As a child I suffered from—'

'—It does not matter. You need not excuse yourself to me. For the rest, there is an American, an Herr Earle Restarick, so he calls himself, who studies modern history. He has heard that you are coming and will make himself introduced. Is there anything more you wish to ask?'

'Yes,' said Daniel, who had taken in very little of von Bremke's social information and was still considering what had been said about Dortmund. 'This second step, this second field which you say Professor Dortmund strayed into—'

'—He never "strayed" into anything, Herr Dominus. A most disciplined man.'

'Progressed into, then. Surely you must know *something* about it. Or at least have made a few guesses.'

On the face of a man less dignified, Herr Doktor von Bremke's expression would have been called a pout.

'No thing,' he said, keeping the two words deliberately separate. 'But you, Herr Dominus?' He now seemed anxious to shift the ball into Daniel's court. 'What are you looking for in the end? Doktor Dirange tells me that if you solve the notation then Professor Dortmund's work may help you with your own. What is your own?'

'An Englishman called John Wallis,' said Daniel, deliberately oblique, 'wrote a book, nearly 300 years ago, called "Arithmetica Infinitorum". It is often said to have contained the germs of the Differential Calculus. I think it may have contained the germs of something even more surprising. Something exceedingly delicate, in working on which I shall need a very precise and sensitive method. Both Dirange and I were hoping that Professor Dortmund's matrices would provide that method.'

'But first you must solve the notation,' von Bremke said gently. 'Allow me to wish you good fortune and to offer any assistance, of an administrative kind, that I can render.'

He walked across the room to the door. There he hesitated, then turned.

'There is one more thing I should tell you,' he said, suddenly and unexpectedly diffident in tone. 'When Professor Dortmund died he had been ill for some time. A ... *krebs-bildung* ... a cancer of the bowel. Whatever else those symbols stand for, they signify a man in pain. Please do not forget that. You must be ... worthy.'

As Daniel opened his mouth to reply, Doktor von Bremke raised a hand to silence him, bowed elegantly and was gone.

Within two days Daniel found that the room prepared for him by von Bremke was unsuitable to work in. Quite why he could not have said, for the furniture and fittings were admirably if economically contrived: the drawers of the filing cabinet ran smoothly, the desk-lamp gave a generous light, his chair was exactly angled (or so the Curator from the library told him) to ensure that he sat in a healthy posture.

Even the view from his window (south-west over placid suburbs and rolling corn-fields) might have been arranged for its theraputic qualities, relaxing and reassuring yet too dull to invite delay.

Perhaps this was why Daniel found the room so disagreeable: he had a sense of being bullied, of being compelled to sit in a healthy posture, forbidden to look at the view for more than five minutes in every hour. Although he was in many ways a methodical man, he resented discipline imposed, however discreetly, from without. If he was to work properly, there must be, as there always was at Cambridge, at least the possibility of self-indulgence and disruption, there must be some temptation to resist. But the only temptation in his room on the top floor was to break the smirking bust of Archimedes, and this was almost certainly made of some efficient German material which could withstand a steam-hammer. No, whichever way he looked at it the accommodation so courteously provided by von Bremke was intolerable; he would work in his lodgings instead, slumped in an arm chair as crookedly as he pleased, constantly delighted and distracted by the grotesque church tower with the phallus tip which bridled over his window as if about to violate it at any moment.

This decision led to difficulties over the Dortmund papers. As von Bremke had observed, many of them were not allowed to leave the building, and the Curator, a friendly little man in most ways, had a Teutonic relish for regulation. However, there was nothing to stop Daniel making copies; and he found that if he spent one hour a day doing this, usually in the early evening when his room on the precincts was least objectionable, he could take away enough material to occupy him over the next twenty-four hours, and at the same time ease his conscience with the reflection that he was, after all, making some use of the amenities which von Bremke had been at pains to proffer. There was also, he later found, a further advantage in this system: the act of copying Dortmund's manuscript required an attention to detail which not only made for a thorough introduction to the matter before him but also began to lend him a limited yet real insight into the working of the mysterious symbols, as though he had acquired by his devout imitation a certain affinity of spirit. On several occasions he found himself supplying the next term in a series before he had referred to the original; and although he was still ignorant of the meaning which lay behind the notation, it was no small encouragement that he was beginning to understand how to operate it.

One way and the other, then, he started to look forward to his evening hour in the otherwise detestable and antiseptic apartment over the Library. At this time of day Archimedes, his back turned to the sun as it declined over the cornfields, lost his smugness in the shadow which obscured all but his noble forehead; at this time of day there was a light, elusive whisper, which found its way even into these prim confines, of pleasures and excitements (albeit they were not for him) held in store by the coming night; and at this time of day, some two weeks after he had arrived in Göttingen, Earle Restarick the American had bowed himself into Daniel's life, a tall, silent figure, slipping through the door without knocking, confronting Daniel with a bland, seductive smile, as though he were about to remark that the pleasures hinted at by the vespertine whisper were readily available in the next street and that he would now take Daniel by the hand and lead him to them.

Instead,

'Herr Dominus Daniel Mond?' Earle Restarick had said, in a deep voice and entirely without irony.

'Yes . . .?'

'Earle Restarick. They told me you were coming, but I've been out of town.' He frowned as though he had been caught picking his nose. 'Away from Göttingen,' he emended, and again his mouth curved into the inviting and mysterious smile which seemed to promise so much but which, once more, heralded only the flabbiest piece of social commonplace.

'I called at your lodging,' he said, 'and the old lady said you might be here.'

'I often work here for a little in the evening.'

'You're sure I don't disturb you?'

Earle Restarick put his hands in his pockets and leaned companionably against the door. Americans, Daniel reflected, even educated ones, did not respect privacy. 'You're sure I don't disturb you?' was not really a question but an affirmation, not only on Restarick's behalf but his own, of the American belief that no sane and moral man could prefer an intellectual occupation to human company, however dull or ordinary. Indeed, the more ordinary it was, the more a sane and moral man was expected to prefer it. If this new acquaintance was to be pursued, Daniel would have to find a way of establishing that meetings could take place by prior agreement only. But for this once, well, Restarick had taken trouble to seek him out, the least he could do was to show good will, and he was more relieved than he would have expected to find himself, after two weeks, talking to someone who approximated to a fellow countryman.

'Not at all,' he said: 'you don't know how glad I am to see you. Just let me finish this off.'

He lowered his head to his page. Restarick raised an eyebrow and lounged over to the window.

'Nice view,' he said, as if complimenting Daniel on a piece of personal property.

'I suppose so . . . I shan't be a moment.'

'Nice piece of sculpture. They gave me Thucydides. That's because I'm an historian.'

Dear God . . . 'Sorry, but this bit's a little complicated.'

'Nice cabinet,' persisted Restarick. He opened and closed each drawer in turn, announcing aloud what he found each time, which was nothing.

'Nothing here either,' he said, slamming the last drawer to and turning reproachful eyes on Daniel. 'It's a shame not to keep something in such a nice cabinet.'

'I keep my stuff at home . . . Just this last line.'

'At home? But that can't be. Your home's in Bri – England.'

'My lodgings,' Daniel said and gritted his teeth. Perhaps he needn't trouble to be friendly after all? Perhaps he could say he suddenly felt ill? He looked up from his finished work to see Restarick smiling at him. After the inanity of everything

the man had said, the smile still promised something well out
of the ordinary. An invitation, as it were, to Xanadu, or a taste
of the Golden Apples. Something, at any rate, which was
certainly not to be rejected out of hand. You must come with
me, the smile said, and see for yourself. Very well, thought
Daniel: this once at least I will.

'Sorry to be so long,' he said, surprised by the eagerness of
his own voice; 'it's all done now.'

In the street outside, and blocking it, was a 1935 Mercedes,
the sort of car in which German generals cavorted about
(smoking cheroots and making cynical remarks to handsome
aides-de-camp) in war films. A German policeman who was
hovering looked hard at Restarick and then stalked resentfully
away.

'Still an occupied country,' Restarick had commented, 'but
only just. This time next year he'll want an apology, and the
year after he'll try to make a charge. Peaked caps are reappear-
ing, if you've noticed.'

Both the car and the observation Daniel found indicative,
the first of a stylish and individual taste, the second of an
articulacy which Restarick had suppressed hitherto. There
was, furthermore, something slightly sinister about his remark,
an uncritical acceptance of authority, whether his own or that
of the peak-capped policeman who must in time supplant him,
which Daniel was still nervously trying to analyse when, five
minutes later, they emerged from the last of the suburbs along
a lumpy road to the south-east.

'Dinner,' said Restarick: 'we'll go to Bremke.'

'Dinner with Doktor von Bremke? But has he asked us? He
told me he couldn't receive people. His wife—'

'Not him ... though I dare say there's a connection.
Bremke is a village about fifteen k's away. There's an inn
which will give us a beautiful meal. Veal steaks stewed in milk.
You're not Orthodox, I take it?'

'No. I'm not Orthodox.'

'Lucky for you. These steaks are not to be missed. And first
we might take a look at the border – to give us an appetite. For
I don't suppose,' Earle Restarick said lazily, 'that many people

in East Germany will be having veal steaks stewed in milk
for their dinner tonight.'

'I didn't realize the border was quite so close.'

'You climb a hill above this gasthaus of mine and there it
is. Just over the next valley.'

And so they had climbed the hill to see the border.

A dispiriting sight (as Daniel was to write to Robert Constable at Lancaster a day or two later), a high barbed-wire fence
of several thicknesses with watch towers every quarter of a mile
standing a short way back on the other side. It was evening when
we saw it, so that the valley which lay between us and the ridge
along which it ran was in deep shadow, while the fence itself
was still visible in every detail and so appeared to be the only
clear-cut reality in a world of shades. Not only that, but the sun,
flashing along the strands of wire, gave the impression that the
whole network was alive with some malignant current which
would leap out and consume to ashes any living thing which
came near.

Most depressing of all, however, was a small village which was
a kilometre or so the other side. You see, at first sight it might
almost have been the same village in which we had just left the
car and ordered our dinner. The same grassland all round it, the
same little hills above it, the same friendly houses with their off-
white walls and red roofs, with their barns and stables and yards;
and yet, because of some accident of war, because of a tactical
decision taken seven or eight years ago and perhaps at a very
junior level, the village on the other side was condemned and for-
saken, and became a region beyond the Styx where *they*, the pale
and bloodless ghosts, must drag out their weary days for ever.
And indeed if there are still inhabitants in the village they
can only be ghosts; for a second look reveals that it has long been
deserted, presumably because it is too near the border for official
comfort. The grassland is wild, the hills bare (trees give cover
from watch towers), the red roofs pitted and gashed, the yards
derelict.

'Cold comfort farm,' said my American friend.

At first I thought this was one of his callous jokes, for he had
already made two or three of them in the single hour he had
known me; but when I looked at him I saw that he was very

much affected, that his face was tense with outrage. This was a
very understandable reaction, yet there was something about the
jut of his chin which made me uneasy, suggesting that here was
not so much sorrow or indignation, but contempt. However, I
didn't think much of this at the time because I was trying to reas-
sure myself, to tell myself and my battered left-wing conscience
that it couldn't really be as bad as all that. Since the scene was
peaceful and the brutal fence was getting harder to see in the dark,
I had almost persuaded myself; no doubt they're really quite
happy over there, I thought, all this about slavery and starvation
is just propaganda, how foolish of me just now to think of them
as damned.

'Look,' I said to Restarick, fatuous with hope, 'the lights are
coming on over there. Just like everywhere else.'

'The lights are coming on all right,' he said: 'in the watch
towers.'

And he pointed up at one of them from which a searchlight
suddenly stabbed out towards the ruined village and then swept
back in a slow arc picking out, yard by yard, the eastern ap-
proaches to the wire.

Every day, Robert, East Germans in tens, scores, hundreds
risk their lives to cross the border in this area. Refugee camps have
been established; there is a large one not far from Göttingen to
which Restarick has promised to take me one day soon. He says
that they are already horribly overcrowded; it is easier to escape
from an old life than to be admitted to a new. Yet still they pour
in from the East, dodging beneath the cruel searchlights, rip-
ping their flesh on the wire.

You must tell our friends this. There must be less of the facile
pretence that everything over the border is (more or less) well.
Socialist hypocrisy is even more vile than the right-wing kind,
because we claim moral integrity, whereas they can always plead
a pragmatic tradition . . .

But for all the doubts and emotions raised by the barbed-
wire fence the evening at Bremke had been a success. The food
was as good as Restarick had promised, and there was a brisk
red wine, served from a barrel in jugs, which was locally
famous, Restarick said, for loosening both tongues and bowels.
The service was casual yet prompt; and the room in which
they dined was snug and friendly, disposing them to confidence.

Although it was not Daniel's habit to say much about himself until he had known a person for some time, he found himself, over the third jug of wine, telling his companion something of those fears which so far he had discussed only with Jacquiz Helmut.

'My father's parents were Jews ... from Hannover. They had the sense to get out early, in the late 'twenties. But you see, Earle, Germany is my country in a way ... and also the country which has rejected me.'

Restarick considered this.

'You know German?' he said.

'Only a few words from the phrase book. My grandparents both died when I was four, and my father refused to have the language spoken in his house. He gave away most of my grandfather's German books. The rest he burnt.'

'If you don't speak German,' Restarick said, 'this isn't your country.'

'Even so I have a sense of returning ... returning to a place which has expelled me ... so that I am more afraid of it than if I were simply coming here for the first time.'

'But you are simply coming here for the first time,' said Restarick doggedly. 'However long your ancestors lived in Hannover or any other damned German place, you were born in England, you hold an English passport, and you have never in your life set foot in Germany until sixteen days ago. These people have nothing on you, nothing at all.'

'They know different.'

All the same he found this unsubtlety oddly comforting.

'The English,' Restarick persisted, 'they didn't intern your father in 1939?'

'No. They found him work in the Ministry of Information.'

'And your mother – you say she wasn't German nor Jewish either?'

Had he said that? He couldn't remember, but it was true enough, so he supposed he must have. This wine was rather confusing.

'She was the daughter of an English schoolmaster. Strictly

old style he was – a housemaster at a big public school. I never met him. My mother's parents didn't like the marriage, you see, and neither did my father's. They weren't strict, mind you, but they kept the main Jewish festivals. I can just remember my grandfather standing at the head of a table and saying, very gravely and sweetly, "Next year in Jerusalem". He didn't mean it, of course, and in any case next year he was dead. A little later my grandmother died . . . and then my mother.'

'She must have been very young.'

'An accident on the river. Near Staines, of all places. I was never really told the details, and somehow I didn't like to ask. Sometimes I wonder—'

'—You wonder too much. Your trouble is,' said Earle Restarick, 'that you're too polite to ask straight questions, so then you get to torturing yourself by making up your own morbid answers.'

Daniel was pleased with this diagnosis. So true, he told himself; and indeed I've been sitting here all through dinner talking about myself without a single attempt to find out about Earle Restarick.

'Tell me, Earle,' he said; 'what are you doing in Göttingen?'

For a moment Restarick looked startled and even affronted.

'You did suggest,' said Daniel, 'that I should start asking questions.'

'Sure I did. Only I thought you knew the answer to that one. I'm an historian, like I said, a modern historian. You've heard of a guy at Oxford called Trevor-Roper? An expert on the top brass of the Nazi Party and what happened when things started to break up? Well, I'm following up a few little hints from him.'

'Then you've been at Oxford?'

'No . . . I came straight from Harvard. But I know this Trevor-Roper's work.'

'But surely,' said Daniel, much interested, 'Göttingen is hardly the place to go into all that. A peaceful academic backwater.'

'A lot of stuff drifts into backwaters,' said Restarick sharply: 'you never know what you'll find among the rubbish.'

Daniel opened his mouth to comment on this proposition but Restarick was before him:

'Besides,' he said, 'there's a family connection. An uncle of mine, he studied here back in 1910. Mother's side of the family – the Boston side.'

He paused to see whether the significance of this remark had been taken. Daniel, who was not strong on American social distinctions, merely nodded non-committally.

'Father's people really come from Boston too,' said Restarick with a frown, 'but they moved to Connecticut some time back.'

'How long have you been in Göttingen?' said Daniel, rather confused by all this topographical insistence.

Again Restarick looked startled and affronted.

'Since early this year . . .'

It was said almost furtively. But then Earle Restarick looked at Daniel and smiled his smile. After the wine it promised even more than before; it promised Helen of Troy, the Treasure of Minos, the Tree of Life.

'I've been very lonely, Daniel,' he said. 'I'm so glad you've come . . . a friend?'

It was both an appeal and an offer, modest, sincere, irresistible.

'Call for more wine,' said Daniel: 'the best.'

For a month and more after that evening at Bremke Earle Restarick and Daniel Mond were together nearly every day, dining, walking, making excursions in the 1935 Mercedes. Daniel need not have feared that Earle would disrupt his work. On the contrary, his new friend was at great pains to discover exactly at what hour each day it would best suit Daniel to meet him or be picked up, and never once intruded on him before that time. So far from distracting Daniel, Earle seemed to regard himself as responsible for rationing his amusements.

'I'm not sure that you ought to have the day off,' he would

remark, à propos of some projected expedition to Hannover or the Harz.

'But it's only for once in a way.'

'That's just the kind of excuse which can become habit-forming . . . particularly with a weak character like yours. '

For it was Earle's contention that Daniel had an all too malleable nature which must be both stiffened and protected. Daniel, who liked being mothered, enjoyed this concern for his welfare, the more so as it was little needed. For his work was going steadily and well; and indeed if anyone required to be kept up to the mark it was Earle himself, who had no routine and seldom seemed to settle to his research.

'What did you do today?' Daniel would ask at dinner.

'Messed about in the car . . . Read that novel of Anthony Powell's you lent me. I didn't realize you English could be so oblique.'

'Don't you ever do any work, Earle?'

'It'll all come right in time, you'll see. Just now I'm waiting for a line. No good starting off until you know which way you're going.'

'Surely it's up to you to decide that.'

'In this case – no.'

And then the topic would be changed.

They seldom tried to say anything of intimacy or intellectual depth to each other, remaining happy with light comment on whatever they were doing at the time. Daniel, whose mental energies were fully taken up by the increasing complications of the Dortmund papers, found this triviality of intercourse easy and restful: to Earle, on the other hand, it did not apparently occur that any other way was either possible or desirable. 'No point going too far into it just now,' he used to say whenever their conversation touched on some serious subject: 'only find trouble.' And although at another place or time Daniel might well have considered it his moral duty to 'find trouble', it seemed that Earle's company acted on his conscience as an anodyne, persuading him to sink back in his seat and enjoy, for so long as the drug should last, the peace of mind which it bestowed. Perhaps, he sometimes thought,

Earle was right about his character: it lay wide open to corruption of whatever kind.

If Earle eschewed profundity, he evinced, on one occasion at least, a disquieting turn of logic. This was on the day when they visited the refugee camp for East Germans. They had been introduced to a Professor of Art History recently fled from Dresden, a snowy and, despite his sleasy brown battledress, distinguished old gentleman, who was convinced that the only proper recompense for his sufferings was the immediate offer of a chair in England or America. Although Daniel thought the Professor was too shrill and presumptuous in this claim, he nevertheless felt that something handsome should be done for him by the scholarly fraternity of the free world, and later, as they walked past the seedy Nissen huts towards the Mercedes at the gate, he expressed this view forcibly to Earle.

'You know his record?' Earle said.

'Only that he's been at Dresden for many years.'

'Too many years. He's been sitting there since 1930, and never once, before, during or after the war, has he been in the smallest trouble with authority of any branch or persuasion. What do you deduce from that?'

'That you are remarkably well informed.'

'It cuts across my subject, you might say. What do you deduce about the Professor?'

'That he is of amenable disposition.'

'Too true.'

Earle looked with displeasure at a family of gipsies who were brandishing rusty billy-cans on the steps of a cook-house.

'They make their way up from Greece,' Earle said. 'They get everywhere. No money, no passports – and no stopping them . . . This Professor you're so steamed up about. He's been sitting in Dresden being amenable, as you call it, for over twenty years. He's all of sixty; so why does he stop now?'

'He's finally seen too much.'

'He never saw a thing he didn't want to see in this whole life. And just suppose he *was* in trouble at last, or that something *had* happened to hurt that plasticine conscience of his, he didn't have to come all the way to Göttingen to make his crossing. It'd have been half the distance north to Berlin or south to Coburg. He came to Göttingen, Danny boy, because Göttingen marks the beginning of the British Zone, and it was therefore the nearest place he could be sure of being interned by the British and not by the Americans or the French.'

'A compliment.'

'In a back-handed way, yes. The French hate the Krauts so much they'd have starved him to death, and the Americans are so hot on security they'd have cracked his cover to pieces. It's only you British who are soft enough to feed him and believe him both. He's a plant, Danny; a good old-fashioned plant . . . Not that it's his fault. They just got fed to death with him stitting there in Dresden as smug as a new banknote in the middle of all that Art, and they said, "Now, comrade, your big chance to serve the cause has come at last. You get off your arse and escape like hell to the British. And when they've set you up in a nice big office in the British Museum, our representative will call around to tell you what to do next." '

'Poor old chap. What will happen?'

'Our intelligence boys will tip off your lot. Your lot will think it's all ungentlemanly American hysteria, but they won't want to cause offence because of all those dollars you're short of, so they'll just see that he stays where he is and rots. And sooner him than me.'

They both turned to look at the lines of Nissen huts. From the cook-house, which had now absorbed the gipsies, rose a column of yellow smoke. 'Stays where he is and rots,' thought Daniel.

'And if he's genuine?' he said.

'Too bad.'

'You seem very sure of what you say.'

'I'm a student of modern history,' Earle replied, 'and this is just what most of my subject's about.'

Other excursions had been more cheerful. The weather, uncertain in April, had changed in early May and yielded a long succession of Arcadian days, warm and breezy, green against blue. They drove into the Harz Mountains, to

Paderborn with its strange barn-like cathedral (ancient scene of
God knew what theological excesses), to Osnabruck, to Hameln,
to Minden, to the walled brothel quarter in Brunswick, to the
sandy heath round Luneburg, and, one week-end, far to the
south, where the pretty spa-towns had once more been taken
out, so to speak, and dusted, like expensive toys which had
lain packed away during the season of danger.

Of all their journeys Daniel most enjoyed this last, because
it was the only one on which there had not been the constant
sight of British Army uniforms. Since these were still a familiar
enough spectacle even in England, it was hard to say why he
found them so oppressive here. Explaining himself to Earle
in their usual light terms (and therefore telling something
less than the truth) he deposed that he was bored by the dowdy
battle-dress, that if there must be soldiers round the place they
might at least dress the part with style.

'Then you'd feel more inferior than ever,' Earle said. 'Because that's what you really mean. You resent the military
because you've never been in the Army yourself.'

'It's more than that ... Those officers we saw dining in the
Alte Krone the other night. It wouldn't have been so bad if
they'd shouted or smashed the place up. What I couldn't bear
was those quiet, level voices which assumed automatic
obedience.'

'They must have come from the barracks on the hill. The
Wessex Fusiliers, I'm told. Know anything about them?'

'I know nothing about the Army.'

'My informant said they were "undistinguished". In your
Army, that apparently means an ordinary regiment of the line
which has fought bravely in every action since Blenheim but
only has middle-class officers.'

Daniel considered this piece of expertise.

'Your ... informant?' he said at last.

'American I met in Kassel. And that reminds me. Tuesday's
out. I've got to go to Kassel then instead of Thursday.'

Every Thursday Earle had what he called 'my jaunt to
Kassel'. Daniel understood that there was an American centre
there, of a vaguely cultural kind, and that Thursday was an

'at home day' attended by the handful of American civilians in the area and sometimes by American Army officers from Bad Hersfeld and further south. In Göttingen there was a similar British institution, called Die Brucke, which housed an English library, many pamphlets about the British Way of Life, and a pleasant Scottish Director who occasionally got up a play-reading or a debate. But Earle's centre in Kassel – he never told Daniel what it was called – seemed somehow more formidable; from the deference with which Earle referred to it and the absolute regularity with which he attended its Thursdays, Daniel had concluded that he was under an obligation to report himself, as though to some consular agent or to someone appointed by Harvard University to keep an eye on him. For Americans, Daniel knew, were always on a leash which stretched back to America. One thing at least was clear: if Earle had been summoned to Kassel next Tuesday Earle would go, and this was disappointing, as they had arranged to drive into Hannover for a concert.

'Why have they changed the day?' Daniel said morosely.

'Important visitor . . . Don't get upset. There'll be other concerts; we've all summer.'

But Daniel continued to sulk. Eventually Earle turned the car off the road and stopped on a track which led through a grove of fir-trees.

'Come on, Danny,' he said: 'it's too good an evening for that.'

'I'm sorry. You're right, of course.'

And indeed, Daniel thought, there could not be so many evenings like this in a life-time, evenings passed with a friend in a little wood under a darkening but kindly sky, still warm from the sun. A soft floor of pine-needles to walk on. A car to retreat to the moment the first chill of night crept through the trees, hinting deliciously at atavistic terrors, and gave warning that it was time to be gone. How many more such evenings? There was all summer, Earle had said. But Daniel belonged, if only in part, to a race too ancient and too wary to trust in any promises of future seasons.

And as it turned out there were to be no more evenings in

T—B

pine-woods, no more journeys to the south. When Earle returned from his Tuesday jaunt to Kassel, he had changed. He was like a man who, assured of a great inheritance, is suddenly told that he has been discovered to be illegitimate and must content himself with a pittance, even that being given him only by charity of the true heirs. He was angry, disillusioned, trapped. At first Daniel assumed that he had at last been rebuked, by whatever authority dwelt in Kassel, for his laziness, had been told to amuse himself less and settle to his work; for this would explain why he no longer suggested drives or excursions, and indeed would only meet Daniel every third or fourth day. But it was soon obvious that something must have occurred far more serious than a mere telling-off. People told to work harder are still permitted to meet their friends and dine at leisure from time to time; but Earle would no longer dine with him at all, confining their meetings to a sparse half-hour at lunch time or to a brief afternoon walk. This Daniel would have been prepared to accept, on the ground that his friend had received a nasty shock and must have time to recover, had it not been for Earle's palpable hostility. This not only wounded him deeply, it was beyond any possible explanation: for while he could readily understand that some unlooked for reverse might make Restarick bad-tempered and inattentive, he could find no excuse for naked malignity directed straight at himself. Unless of course he, Daniel, was in some way to blame for whatever had happened; but how could this be?

After this state of affairs had continued for nearly three weeks, Daniel decided to ask Earle what was wrong. He was reluctant to do so because he sensed here something that it would be unwise to probe. But after all, it was Earle himself who had recommended, when they first met, the virtue of straight questions; and the fact that Earle still met him at all, however disagreeable he was while they were together, must mean that there was still something between them which could be rescued and preserved.

And so, as they walked silently along the city wall in the heat of the day, Daniel red and sweaty in his heavy sports jacket,

Earle smooth and aloof in a suit of gaberdine, Daniel took his friend by the elbow and said:

'What's the matter, Earle? Have I done anything?'

Earle stopped, moved his arm slowly and deliberately from Daniel's grasp, and then walked on, keeping three or four paces ahead and talking straight in front of him.

'You just don't know, do you? You just don't know what you're doing. Every day you stick your face into a pile of papers which nobody up till now has understood, and you work six, seven, sometimes ten hours, hoping to find the answer. But what happens if you do? Have you thought of that?'

So that was it. Earle, who had always seemed so solicitous about Daniel's work, was in truth jealous of it.

'Of course I've thought about it,' Daniel said to the blank expanse of gaberdine moving before him. 'If I find the answer, I shall go back to Cambridge and make use of it, if I can, to help me finish my research. What else would I do? I'll be sorry to leave Göttingen, sorry to leave you, I shall miss those drives we have – used to have—'

'—You just don't know, that's what. You work away on those papers, trying to put life into symbols that have been dead fifteen years, and in the intervals you're happy because you've got a tame chauffeur to drive you around. But do you have any idea what those symbols may do if you call them up from the grave? Of course you don't. You don't even have any idea where your tame chauffeur's driving you. When he says, "We're going to Bad Harzburg today", you just sit back with a smug smile on your face and look forward to a nice, cosy ride. But for all you *know* he might be planning to drive you straight to Hell.'

'I don't understand you,' said Daniel sadly to the gaberdine back. 'I'm sorry, Earle, if I seemed to take you for granted, but I thought—'

'—Pardon me, that's just what you haven't done.' Hitherto Earle's voice had been one of peevish anger: now it took the bleak tone of one who, though he has abandoned hope, nevertheless tries for the twentieth time to explain a simple proposition to a backward child. 'You haven't thought at all,' he said.

'You've got your priorities all wrong. You're so full of imaginary fears that you don't see the real ones. You worry so much about whether or not to take an umbrella when you go out that you forget what you're going out for. Or take that socialism of yours: you fuss yourself sick about whether some bloody labourer should get another shilling a day, and meanwhile you don't notice that your whole country's going bankrupt ... Or you're scared that everyone hates you because you're a Jew. They don't give a rap, most of them, what you do with your bacon; what bothers them is the way people like you parade your consciences round the world, yapping and squealing about morality and justice and making trouble where there was peace and quiet before.'

'But with you ... I've kept quiet about all that ... because I knew you wouldn't care for it.'

'It was there all the time in your face. Wherever we went, whatever we saw, there was that great oozing conscience of yours hanging out to dry.'

Two large tears appeared at the inner corners of Daniel's eyes.

'If you felt like that, why didn't you say so before? Instead of letting me believe you liked me, wanted me with you. And why did it have to be so cruel? One day the same as ever, the next this horrible, silent hate.'

At last Earle turned to face him.

'It isn't hate. It's fear. I'm afraid of you, Daniel.'

'Afraid of *me*?'

'Afraid of what you might do ... without meaning it, without knowing it even. I'm afraid of that patient, subtle mind of yours, caressing those dead symbols into life. Why can't you let them stay dead, Daniel?'

'But you ... you always encouraged me.'

Earle looked carefully round, as though to make sure they were unobserved. 'Listen, Danny boy,' he said, almost into Daniel's ear. 'Leave Göttingen. Put those symbols back into the tomb where they belong, tell everyone in a loud, clear voice that you can't do anything with them, and then go home.'

'Not now. I couldn't. I'm just beginning to understand—'

'—You understand nothing,' Earle hissed at him. 'You won't even listen when you're told.' He touched Daniel in the crook of one arm. 'Go home before it's too late,' he hissed; 'just go home.'

And then he walked away very fast along the wall.

That had been in the middle of June, and Daniel had not seen him since. After that there had been only work.

This became daily more fascinating, and he thought that he was now near to an important breakthrough. If this were so, then the problem of the Dortmund notation, in its first stage, would soon be solved, and he would be able to understand at any rate the earlier matrices. His trouble would then lie, as von Bremke had warned him, with Dortmund's shift in usage, which seemed to correspond to a shift in purpose, or rather, to a more rigid definition of purpose. That problem was for the future, but Daniel had looked far enough ahead to form a general hypothesis. Dortmund, he considered, had at first developed the matrices, together with the notation through which they must be expressed, without any particular purpose in view; he was forging a mathematical instrument and that was all. However, at some late stage in the process it seemed to have struck Dortmund that this instrument would be very well suited, provided certain rather complex adjustments were made, to one definite form of investigation. This, of course, was very much what von Bremke had suggested, but in one respect Daniel had advanced further: he now had a shrewd idea what particular investigation Dortmund had decided on; and this, if he was right, was related more closely than he had dared to hope to the investigation which he himself wished ultimately to pursue.

So there had been work, on balance very good work; but work was not enough.

I can't tell you (he wrote with defensive suavity to Jacquiz Helmut) how dreary it is in Göttingen now. The German summer seems to scorch the life out of everything. I had never realized before what it meant to live on an island, never to be more than an hour or so from the sea.

My American chum has disappeared. He started to sulk in June, I never knew why, and finally blew himself up into a remarkable fit of pique and vanished for good. It was very odd. I thought at first that it was all caused by jealousy of the way I worked – for poor Earle never seemed to come to terms with his own work or even to know where to start. But thinking it over since I've decided that jealousy is not in character. I've an idea he was irritated because he thought I was wasting my time on something too difficult, and that even if I did solve the problem the answer would be no good to myself or anyone else. . . . (This, thought Daniel, was something less than a candid assessment, but for the time being it was as much as he cared to tell Jacquiz) . . . Even so, it's hard to see why be behaved as he did; he went on at me as if I were practising black magic or hunting for the Philosopher's Stone. I'm sure there's some simple but entertaining quirk of trans-Atlantic psychology here which you will at once explain to me when we meet again.

I wish this could be soon as it would be pleasant to talk to someone. My landlady has been so well trained over the years to efface herself that there can be no communication there. Herr Doktor Aeneas von Bremke, whom in any case I have hardly seen since I presented my credentials, has withdrawn to a summer fastness up in the Harz. Even the Librarian, who used to tell me how he visited Lancaster before the war, has left for his annual month by Lake Konstanz; and his assistant is a sour, self-pitying youth with technicolour spots. To crown everything, my favourite restaurant has closed its doors for three weeks.

It would be nice if you could come here for a few days. I know what I've said in this letter can hardly be much inducement, but Göttingen is really an attractive little town, just what a university should be . . . if only it offered the sight (or even the hope) of a familiar face.

But I don't suppose for a moment that you can leave Cambridge just now. You must be working very hard on Garibaldi, and of course the Long Vacation is always right for work – the college half empty, just a few friends to ensure a little discreet gaiety when needed. In Göttingen there is no gaiety, so I think of you often, of what you might be doing at this hour or at that.

By now, I imagine, the Summer Festival is in full swing. In March the talk was that the Marlowe would do The Family Reunion in July, not my favourite play, though I like that bit

about the clock stopping in the dark. Have you been to see it? If
you have, do let me know if Toby had a part (he was very anxious,
I remember) and how he got on; I always enjoy the way he
gangles so shyly on to the set and then upstages everyone without meaning to.

I long so much to be back. But the work I have will take at
least two months more, even if everything goes as well as possible, and it will be late in September before I can hope to be
finished . . .

He thought of this letter now, as he sat with his coffee on
the sunny terrace of the restaurant on the hill. He had written
it two days ago, feeling at last that he must send some signal,
to those who might care enough to read it right, that all was
not well with him; but although he had told Jacquiz as much
as he dared of his loneliness, he had told him nothing of his
fear: the fear which now rose in him every time he sat down
again to the Dortmund papers ('Put them back in the tomb
where they belong'), and the other fear, even vaguer yet even
more ugly . . . 'go home before it's too late'.

Daniel laid a note on the bill in front of him and added some
coins from his purse. Then he walked to the edge of the terrace
and looked carefully down at Göttingen. A seemly town and
surely innocent: there could be nothing to fear except the
oppression and the heat. Once again, a bugle sounded from
the barracks below; he did not know what the call meant, but
it spoke somehow of an afternoon far advanced. It was time to
walk down the hill, to return to Dortmund's dead symbols that
he might bring them life.

Part Two

THE BAND NIGHT

ONCE across the meadow which lay beneath the Gast-haus where he had been lunching, Daniel followed a tall wire fence through bushes and scrub for two hundred yards and then emerged on to a road by the main gate and guard room of the barracks. The meadow he always enjoyed; but the barrack fence posed a disagreeable mystery and the barrack gate a positive threat, suggesting a Kafkaesque nightmare which tormented him every time he passed . . .

'*You there, come inside at once. Yes, you.*'

'*Me? There must be some mistake.*'

'*On the contrary. I have a warrant here with your name on it. "Daniel Mond," it says: "posted for National Service" – and high time too.*'

'*I'm exempt.*'

'*So you keep telling everybody. But we know better, don't we?*'

'*I assure you—*'

'*—Sergeant-Major, have this man arrested and taken inside. Cut his hair, burn his clothes, take his money, and just to be on the safe side give him a new identity. We don't want any of his left-wing friends making trouble . . .*'

'Hey, YOU. You there outside the gate.'

A clatter of boots. And a roaring noise in the background. Keep calm, he can't possibly mean you.

'Not so fast.'

A large man blocking his way. Two stripes on his arm. A corporal? (*Habeas corpus.*) A black band above the stripes with the red letters 'R.P.'

'Come with me . . . sir.'

'Sir'? Ironic, obviously. '*Because you've got what is laughingly called a degree, Mister Mond, we're officially compelled*

to let you serve your time as an officer . . . in name only, of
course . . .'

'I'll do no such thing. Who do you think you are, shouting
after people like that?'

The large man sighed and looked as if he were going to
burst into tears.

'No harm intended,' he said in the thick accents of the west
country. 'It's *'im.*'

He pointed back towards the gate. Daniel turned to see a
plump freckled face hung round with earphones and supported by a torso which had been clumsily crammed, like a
swollen cork, into the turret of what he took for a small
tank.

'*Daniel*,' said the face, splitting juicily in welcome.

''Im,' insisted the large corporal, bending gently and
lugubriously over the terrified Daniel.

The cork eased itself out of the turret with a plop to reveal
a pair of bright pink thighs. At first Daniel assumed these
must be naked (something to do with the heat inside the tank?),
then he realized, as calves followed thighs into the open,
that he was looking at a pair of elegant and unusual trousers.
These, though intriguing, could not help him to identify
their owner; but then the earphones were whisked off like a
wig, and the raddled and receding fair hair above the young
face suddenly recalled a score of happy and unedifying
evenings.

'Julian . . . Oh Julian, is it really you?' Daniel called, while
the large corporal melted with pleasure. 'But I thought . . .
You said when you went down that you were going to sell
wine.'

'National Service first. Didn't want to upset your sensitive
feelings by telling you . . . Hat,' said Julian to the side of the
tank.

A hand appeared out of the turret holding a huge peaked
hat of khaki felt which was fronted by a silver device of a grinning skull that wore an earl's coronet. Julian put on the hat
with care and then trotted towards Daniel.

'Cornet J. James of the 49th. Earl Hamilton's Light

Dragoons,' he said saluting smartly. 'Thank you, corporal. Pray dismiss.' The corporal did several very noisy things with his hands and feet, and lumbered off.

'Sorry if he gave you a fright just now, Daniel. These west country boys are really as soft as butter but the Fusiliers will teach them to bang and shout.'

'Fusiliers? I thought you said you were a Dragoon?'

'The barracks are occupied by the First Battalion of the Wessex Fusiliers. I belong to a squadron of armoured cars that's been sent here for special training with them. We only arrived last week. What about you?'

'I've been down at the university over three months.'

'Lonely . . . after Lancaster.' The assumption was immediate. 'Yes.'

'Well, now you've got friends.'

'I'm not sure that Dragoons are quite in my line.'

'We're a very jolly lot, you'll find. The Fusiliers now, they're rather stiff and gloomy, but you needn't meet any of them. Dinner this evening?'

'Just you, Julian?'

' 'Fraid not. There's two of my crowd I've asked and the doctor. You'll like them, I promise.'

Daniel hesitated.

'Come along, my dear. It's been over a year and I want all the Lancaster gossip.'

'Your friends . . .'

'. . . Will enjoy it as much as me. It is perfectly respectable, Daniel, for an intellectual to mix with the military. Or have you forgotten Proust and Doncières?'

At first, as he set out for the restaurant Julian had named, Daniel was full of misgivings. After all, Julian was little more than a pleasant acquaintance, associated with frivolous dinners and summer afternoons in punts, never received (nor wishing to be received) into moral or intellectual confidence. Although he was intelligent (he had taken a good idle second in the Classics), he was light-minded, sceptical of aspiration, and politically unconcerned to the point of callousness. To Daniel,

Julian was an agreeable reminder of good days rather than a
man of value in himself; he was an acceptable bit-player
'to swell a scene or two', peripheral and slightly suspect; so
that a year in bad company might well have brought out displeasing tendencies towards philistinism and reaction which
had always, Daniel thought, been lurking beneath the amiable
neutrality of his Cambridge persona. And the possible corruption of Julian was only one of Daniel's worries. How was he to
talk to his friends? 'A jolly lot . . .' What did that imply?
Fornicating redcoats from Farquhar? Bumperizing and melo-
dious Magyars? One thing it did not imply (thank God) was
the even speaking and self-satisfied officers (presumably
Wessex Fusiliers) whom he had seen dining some weeks ago
and on whom he had commented to Earle. But would it not be
even worse if Julian's companions turned out to be Regency
rakes who expected him to introduce them to some prodigi-
ously gilded brothel or stake his entire year's income on a
single card at Faro?

The event was reassuring. Julian's guests were dressed in
unpretentious civilian suits, had long if well cut hair (unlike
the remembered officers of the Alte Krone, who had all been
cropped), and spoke in mild, friendly voices. Much of the talk
was of what they hoped to eat, as it seemed that Julian had
elaborated his expertise, already evident at Cambridge, as a
gastronome; while for the rest the conversation consisted of
informed and articulate gossip, which ranged from the current
state of ante-post betting on the St. Leger to the Earl Marshal's
preparations for the coronation the following summer.

All present were so easy and unassuming that it took Daniel
some time to sort out their official precedence and functions –
a task to which, with typical perversity, he had at once
addressed himself. In the end, it appeared that a quiet, shambling man, who looked like an over-nourished version of
Douglas Fairbanks Junior, was called Major Giles Glastonbury and commanded Julian's squadron of armoured cars.
Then there was a bright, nervous youth in his mid-twenties,
who had a girlish but ravaged face and dazzling auburn hair;
this was Captain Fielding Gray, second in command to Major

Glastonbury. Daniel gathered that besides these two and
Julian James there were two more officers in the squadron, both
of them subalterns and both expected for some unspecified
entertainment later on; but the only other guest at dinner was
a certain Lieutenant Motley of the Medical Corps, who was
doing his National Service as Battalion doctor to the Fusiliers
and who spoke with a high-pitched Liverpool-Irish accent.
Before Daniel could puzzle out what Motley was doing in this
particular gallery Julian led them to table, where Daniel was
placed on his host's right with Captain Gray to his own. A
pattern of exchange was soon established: Julian was too concerned about the service of dinner to talk to anyone except
waiters; Motley and Glastonbury settled to an expert discussion of National Hunt courses in the Midlands; and Daniel's
entertainment was left entirely to Captain Gray. Perhaps this
had been previously arranged; for Gray, as one about to try
a prepared but perilous gambit, breathed deeply and said:

'I was interested to hear that you were at Lancaster with
Julian. I was to have gone there myself.'

'Was?'

'A squalid misunderstanding. Please tell me what I have
missed.'

'Where should I start?'

Gray smiled narrowly.

'What I should really like to be told is that I have missed
nothing. If you could tell me that I would have been frustrated
by second-rate pedants and sickened by callow undergraduates,
it would be a great relief to me.'

'Not everyone cares for it, certainly.'

'But would *I* have done?'

'I don't know you well enough to say. In any case, the question is too theoretical to bother with. As things are, you have
your own place' – Daniel gestured lightly over the table – 'and
your own friends to share it.'

'Not,' said Gray intently, 'the ones I would have had at
Lancaster. The kind I used to have when I still thought I was
going there. It is as though my . . . rejection . . . paralysed, or
even killed, some faculty within me.'

Daniel shuddered. Much given to self-pity himself, he was always revolted by its ugliness in others.

'Short run in,' rumbled Glastonbury from the other side of the table, his face turned towards Motley but his eyes settled on Daniel and Gray.

'No worse than Uttoxeter, Giles,' said Motley.

Glastonbury appeared to wink at Daniel, then switched his eyes back to the doctor.

'U'xeter,' he said.

'Pay attention, chums' – this from Julian – 'and for what you are about to receive may the Lord make you truly grateful. Lobster Lucullus. I particularly want you to notice the white truffles.'

For a while there was general chat about the Lobster Lucullus. Then Captain Gray, who was clearly tenacious of his thread, leaned close to Daniel and said:

'I've told you what I have because it is my nature to worry a sore place until it is gangrenous.'

'A dangerous habit.'

'I know. But there's one more thing I must ask. Julian tells me you are the friend of a man called Robert Constable.'

'Our Tutor.'

'Your Tutor. It was Constable who was ultimately responsible for refusing my entry to Lancaster. What kind of man is he?'

Daniel studied a truffle.

'A just man,' he said at length.

'A Christian?'

'No.'

'So not a man of charity?'

'I suppose not. He angers easily. He's a powerful hater. He is kind to honest failure, but merciless to indifference.'

Gray flinched.

'That explains a lot,' he said wearily. 'A committed man . . . He can't have had much time for Julian then?'

'Oddly enough, he rather liked him. He used to say that no pilgrimage was complete without Mr. Worldly-Wise-Man. A rationalization, of course. Like the rest of us, he just enjoyed Julian's charm.'

'You know,' said Gray, who seemed unaccountably cheered by this remark, 'Julian is an excellent officer. He encourages people to underrate him. He puffs and pants and simpers until his opponents are right off their guard, then he comes whipping back and ties them in knots before they know it.'

'His opponents?' Daniel was glad of this opportunity for a decisive change of topic. Gray's obsession for conjuring the ghosts of a past which he had never had was making him increasingly uneasy. 'Julian's opponents?' Daniel persisted. 'Surely he's in a peace time Army and serving among friends?'

'He is a resourceful man,' said Gray. 'He thinks of short and easy ways of doing what tradition prescribes should be long and toilsome. This is never popular with senior men, who feel more secure when people are safely occupied. So they find Julian immoral and subversive.'

'Major Glastonbury thinks that?'

'Major Glastonbury is a civilized man in a civilized regiment. He favours intelligence and good will. Most regiments still work the old way – blind obedience and bloody-mindedness. Our hosts, the Fusiliers, are an excellent example.'

'I'm rather intrigued by this *animus* you all seem to have about the Fusiliers.'

'The animus is more on their part. We,' said Gray, not without irony, 'are the 10th Sabre Squadron – old titles die hard – of Earl Hamilton's Light Dragoons. Our motto is "*Res Unius, Res Omnium*", which implies more concern for private loyalties than the public service. We wear decorative trousers of a deep pink because Lord Hamilton was in his rose garden when he received his commission; and we call them "cherry" out of deference to William IV, who had the story wrong and thought it was a cherry orchard. In the winter we wear riding cloaks lined with silk of the same colour and trimmed with collars of white fur, to buy one of which absorbs the whole of an officer's uniform allowance for about ten years. So you will not be surprised to hear that most of our officers, though not myself, have substantial private incomes, or that Giles Glastonbury, to take only one instance, has connections which might be called princely. All this, as I think you will agree, adds up to amplitude.'

'Whereas the Fusiliers' – where had he heard this? – 'are middle-class and jealous?'

'Worse. The Fusiliers are not only tortured by lack of money and incessantly nagged by their discontented and snobbish wives: they are also so afraid of losing even what little they have that they allow themselves to be bullied hysterical by superiors who are in much the same case. From their Colonel down to the newest joined Second Lieutenant they are hagridden by precedent and precedence. They hardly dare let their wretched soldiers out of their sight for fear of what may go wrong. And here we have the most significant and injurious difference between us: we can afford to speak our minds and treat our men liberally, while the Fusiliers cannot.'

'Then why have you been sent here . . . if it means such an uneasy alliance?'

'We were the only cavalry squadron available that was properly equipped for the role.'

He was about to expand on the statement, Daniel thought, when they were distracted by noise from over the table.

'What you don't understand,' Major Glastonbury was saying to Doctor Motley, in a voice far too loud to suit either his personality or the sentiments expressed, 'is that steeple-chasing is not merely a public circus. There is a tradition; there are standards to be kept up. If you make the Grand National course easier, then the standards will drop with the height of the fences.'

'And what you don't understand,' said Motley, 'is that these days the public – the paying public – insists on inter-fering. The public wants the fences lowered out of kindness to the horses.'

'Kindness kills standards,' remarked Julian with satisfaction. 'To get a Strasbourg pie you must be cruel to the goose.'

'That is why public opinion is against Strasbourg pies.'

'No, it's not. It's because the public can't afford them. Envy.'

'Wrong,' said Glastonbury. 'It's because the public mistrusts perfection. To appreciate and deserve perfection, you need a trained palate, a trained eye, a trained mind – superior taste, in short. And this of course is an offence to popular notions of equality.'

'It's not so much that,' said Daniel, unhappy and conscientious. 'The general feeling, to adapt Julian's image, is that starving children should be fed before trained palates are titillated with Strasbourg pies.'

Glastonbury and Motley both nodded, at once sincerely conceding the point and thanking God that Strasbourg pies were still smooth on the tongue.

'Pure mathematics,' said Captain Gray, 'is a Strasbourg pie if ever there was one. On your own showing, you ought to be advancing the general nutriment with technical inventions.'

Julian grinned with affectionate malice and turned to harrass the waiters. Glastonbury nodded once more, as though indicating to some distant colleague that all danger had now passed, and resumed his quiet duologue with the doctor.

'You must excuse all that noise and smoke,' said Gray to Daniel. 'Giles interrupted because he thought I was about to be indiscreet.'

'Indiscreet?'

'Tell you what we're doing here. It wouldn't do for every public busybody to know about it.'

'I'm sorry if I've given that impression. I'm told I let my feelings show.'

'On the contrary, you've reassured him. You entered your protest honourably but with civilized reluctance. With proper consideration for the company.'

'I'm not sure I feel complimented.'

'You can feel trusted,' said Captain Gray. 'That is much rarer.'

Two almost indistinguishable young men, both of them having weak chins, jelly-fish eyes and braying voices, now greeted Julian and sat down at the end of the table. Daniel was introduced to Jack Lamprey and Piers Bungay. Both smiled limply; both turned to a hovering waiter to order coffee and cognac without reference to their host.

'Both Troop Commanders, like Julian,' Gray explained. 'A sabre squadron consists of three sabre troops, a Headquarters, and in our case a more than usually elaborate technical section.'

He waited for Daniel to ask the obvious question; but Daniel was considering Lamprey and Bungay, and wondering how it was conceivable that a bicycle, let alone a 'sabre troop', should be entrusted to their care.

'The technical section,' said Gray in a lecturing tone, 'is because we must be self-supporting. Very important in our line of business. I must tell you about it,' he insisted, 'now that Giles has approved of you.'

'I'm not very interested in all that. I prefer the social details.'

'They become more piquant if you know the military ones. A few facts of life for you, Daniel.'

'Don't patronize me, Captain Gray.'

Gray's face sagged slightly.

'You misunderstood. I'm the one who's asking favours. You'll see why when you hear what I have to say.'

'I'm still not sure I want to listen.'

'Not now anyway . . .'

For now everyone was suddenly stirring. Julian was flipping through a pile of bills, signing some and waving others away. Glastonbury and Motley were ponderously gesturing each other towards the lavatory. The lately arrived subalterns were on their feet, draining their glasses and shooting their cuffs, in anticipation of immediate action.

'Tomorrow,' continued Gray, 'I'm up in the Harz for reconnaissance. You know the Jagdhof in Harzburg?'

'I think so.'

'I'll meet you in the bar at twelve.'

'I work in the mornings.'

'Suit yourself. I'll look for you in case.'

Gray followed Glastonbury and the doctor to the lavatory. The subalterns looked at Julian, fawning slightly like greedy dogs uncertain of their master's continued indulgence. Julian looked back, feigning indifference, finally and deliberately relenting.

'All right, boys,' he said. 'The Schwarzer Keller. Come along, Daniel.'

'I don't think—'

'—We shall be very hurt if you leave us now. Shan't we, boys?'

The subalterns nodded eagerly.

'It was a lovely dinner, Julian, but I think I'd better go home.'

Daniel became aware that Glastonbury and the doctor were standing on either side of him.

'Do come,' said Glastonbury quietly and unrefusably; 'we've hardly had a single word.'

Nor did they have many in the Schwarzer Keller, which was dominated by the strains of a small cinema organ. But with the lack of conversation the evening achieved a shapeless but cosy gaiety of a kind new to Daniel. It was, he supposed, 'the spirit of the Mess'. Whatever it was, it promoted, after one and a half bottles per head of the best hock, a feeling of friendliness and solidarity (even with the chinless subalterns) which persuaded Daniel that all of them were somehow in league against an undefined but common enemy. The blaring organ became, as it were, the band behind which they marched; and later on, when it broke into selections from 'The White Horse Inn', he found himself banging his glass in time on the table and bellowing out, with the rest, his intention to join the legion and face the foe.

Only Fielding Gray had not come on to the Schwarzer Keller.

'He goes home and reads,' as Giles Glastonbury explained to Daniel, 'reads and drinks.'

'Unfriendly,' said Doctor Motley (Mick), and downed a bumper of Rhenish.

'Oh no. He's friendly enough in his way. But he can't stand noise.'

'Funny he should be in a tank regiment,' Daniel opined.

'Armoured cars ... I suppose so. He says it's human noise he really can't bear because men have no excuse.'

'I see his point,' said Daniel, already rather ashamed of his contribution to the singing.

'I don't know. Not a bad thing to change the air in the old lungs from time to time.'

A medical exposition in support of this thesis now followed from Mick Motley but was swamped by the organist. As he watched the doctor's mouth noiselessly open and shut, Daniel was reminded for a moment of Dortmund's symbols in their ordered yet still almost meaningless succession. This increased his guilt at the time he was wasting; until a grin from Julian, as he lifted a bottle from an ice bucket to refill Daniel's glass, once again restored the warmth of the occasion and drove out doubts as to its worthiness. It was so pleasant simply to be accepted, to belong, to be a christian name among christian names (Giles, Mick, Piers *et al.*). And then the mindlessness of it all was so reassuring. Undeniably 'the spirit of the Mess' had something to recommend it: it shut out the questions which one did not wish to answer, it made one feel safe and loved; and this, he supposed, was the reward offered to soldiers in return for risking their necks. For even while they sat here drinking happily in Germany, were there not wars in the East which might claim them at any moment? Fighting men, he had read, were jealous in the bestowal of their company; he now began to realize why, and to count it a privilege, if not a wholly desirable one, that he should be so courteously admitted.

His great moment came when he was invited to help carry the unconscious Jack Lamprey out to Giles Glastonbury's car.

'I expect he'll be sick on the way up,' Glastonbury confided, 'but these little outings do them good. Good night, old chap. See you soon.'

'Good night,' echoed other voices all around him: 'see you soon.'

* * *

In the morning, Daniel was divided between pleasure in

having been kindly received by the unfamiliar men and irritation at so easily allowing himself to feel flattered. A combina-
tion of drowsiness and light-headedness, which from second
to second disrupted his work, at first made him nervous and
even more irritable but at length resolved itself into a euphoric
excitement which induced him to declare holiday. He would
go to Harzburg and meet Fielding Gray. This decision was
reached less from curiosity to learn what Gray wanted to tell
him than from a novel and collective affection for the whole of
the cavalry group, as a representative of which rather than as
an individual Gray at this stage still appeared to him.

Finding the bus service incommodious, Daniel engaged a
taxi and was still irresponsible enough, on arrival at the
Jagdhof, to pay out ninety marks without noticing. Although
the time was only ten minutes to twelve when he entered the
bar, Gray was already waiting.

'You're early,' said Daniel blithely.

'In the Army, to be punctual to the second is a punishable
offence. One must be ready five minutes before the stated time
of parade. A prudent man allows ten.'

'Meeting me isn't a parade.'

'It is an engagement which I have undertaken . . . I've got
lunch for us both in my Land Rover, and I'm very glad you've
come.'

He looked at Daniel with gratitude, then led the way outside
to a yellow Land Rover, the bonnet of which carried the regimental device, prominently executed in deep pink, of skull
with coronet. A grinning soldier, whose acne flared as bright
as the insignia on the bonnet, was formally introduced to
Daniel as Trooper Michael Lamb and then helped them both
into the vehicle with warm, well chewed but very clean hands.

'Where to now?' the grinning soldier said.

'The Warlocks' Grotto.'

'Righty.'

'You know,' said Gray as they drove off, 'you made a very
good impression last night. I had to hear about it when they
all got back.'

'I enjoyed myself.'

'That's what pleased them. They thought you'd find them crude. Instead of which you joined in. The doctor said the same thing over and over again – "Nice chappie for a brain-box, worth bloody ten of you." '

'How aggressive of him.'

'Just drunk. The doctor's a devout Catholic but intelligent enough to know it's all a load of rubbish. The trouble is that family pressure's too strong to let him escape, so he drinks his way out every night and feels unworthy of the Virgin every morning. Then he has a good crying jag to make him better and gets nicely tanked up at lunch.'

There was no attempt, Daniel noticed, to keep any of this from the driver. Gray simply spoke as if he wasn't there – or so it seemed until suddenly he acknowledged the man's presence by inviting his opinion.

'You've met the doctor, Michael?'

Trooper Lamb screwed up his face in thought, not as one who wishes to be tactful but as a free agent whose view will be heeded and even valued. Daniel was reminded of his own feeling the previous night, that he had been admitted to fellowship on equal terms. 'We band of brothers', he thought reluctantly: *res unius, res omnium.*

'I've met the doctor,' Lamb said, 'and liked him. It's true what you say about his drinking, but he's got a way with illness.'

They turned off the main road along a track which climbed steeply uphill through pine-trees.

'Take Johnnie Burden,' Lamb continued as he went smoothly down through his gears. 'Captain Joyce back at the Regiment said he was just constipated and gave him a pill. But when he first gets here a few days back and goes sick to Mick Motley, he's in an ambulance in ten minutes and has his appendix out before dinner. Another few hours and it would have bust wide open – and Captain Joyce none the wiser, though he's a regular and all.'

'I know,' said Gray. 'You'll find that Captain Joyce won't be there any longer when we get back to the Regiment.'

The sentence was somehow the more sinister, Daniel

thought, for being so vague. Trooper Lamb shook his head, regretting but acknowledging the mutability of human fortunes, and deftly changed the subject.

'And when shall we be getting back then?'

'Immediately after Apocalypse. It came through yesterday.'

This apparently explained everything. Lamb nodded thanks for the information, took them in a quick spurt up a steep rise ahead, then slowed almost to a halt before nosing down a sandy bank.

'The Warlocks' Grotto, gentlemen.'

The uphill track had ended on the rim of a perfect natural bowl which was entirely surrounded by pine-trees except for the narrow entrance through which they had driven in the Land Rover. The bowl itself was open to the sky, and all of it except for one small corner was flooded with sun. At its centre, which lay perhaps ten yards lower than the circumference, was a rectangular slab of grey rock, six feet long by two feet wide by one foot visible depth, the rest being embedded in the soil. The surrounding pine-trees were very close along the rim; and behind them was circle upon circle, the trees in each of which, evenly spaced, guarded the gaps left by those in front, so that beyond a few yards their ranks were impenetrable by the eye and for all one knew might stretch away to the ends of the earth. It would not be wise to leave the sunny bowl for the forest.

'Who told you about this place?' said Daniel.

'We found it the other day. Lamb named it.'

Lamb smiled modestly and started to unload a hamper from the back of the Land Rover.

'In the shade, Michael . . . You see,' said Gray, 'I've been up here a lot lately, planning a little exercise for the Squadron and the Fusiliers. I thought this grotto would make a good Rehabilitation Centre. Nice and remote.'

'What have you to do with rehabilitation?'

Gray took Daniel by the arm and led him over to where Lamb was spreading the lunch: rough pâté, cold chicken and mayonnaise, a bottle of hock.

'Imagine,' said Grey, 'that the enemy is concentrating his forces in this area. Then imagine that you've fired an atomic shell to wipe the whole lot out.'

'I didn't know,' said Daniel turning cold, 'that there was such a thing.'

'There probably isn't. But there very soon will be, or something similar, so one fine summer morning you pull a lever – and crunch . . . The next thing you've got to do is move into the devastated area, take it over and tidy it up. That's what this exercise is about. The tenth Sabre Squadron and the first Battalion of Wessex Fusiliers are being sent in to practise tidying up. Food.'

All three of them sat down together. Lamb took his share of the dainty provisions, including a glass of hock.

'So,' Gray went on, 'the cavalry arrive first in armoured cars, having first taken precautions against radio-active contamination. Everything is a complete shambles for miles. We burn the dead where they lie, along with their equipment. Then we see whether there are any survivors, soldier or civilian. These are suffering from obscene injuries caused by flash or blast, they are out of their minds with shock and horror, and they have absorbed massive doses of radiation; they will die very soon in any case, and can only be a nuisance until they do. Logically we should shoot them down and burn their bodies on the spot. But it has been decided that we must make a civilized gesture. Instead of killing the survivors straight away, we must herd them together and take them to a "Rehabilitation Centre", where there will be a medical unit to make every effort on their behalf. In practice, Mick Motley tells me, "every effort" can only amount to filling them up with morphine and, once more, burning the bodies as soon as possible. By this time the Fusiliers will have moved up on foot to join us, so that will probably be their job. We shall be too busy getting ready to go on to the next devastated area. Some chicken? More hock?'

'So this is your . . . your role,' Daniel said, accepting food and drink automatically. 'This is what Major Glastonbury thought public busybodies shouldn't hear about.'

'There's a lot more to it than Captain Gray's told you,' said Lamb, who showed no doubt of his right to share in the dissertation. 'We're responsible for mapping out the area – it'll need a new map, see – so that when the Fusiliers come up they can take over as guides for the main body of the Division.'

'I should have thought,' said Daniel, appalled but fascinated, 'that the main body would have kept as far away as possible. Moved forward by another route.'

'Ideally, yes,' said Gray. 'But we've got to prepare for a situation in which the whole length of the front has been contaminated in this way. In that case, a section must be cleared for the advance to proceed. So each division is to provide itself with what is called a Courier Team, which will consist of one highly mobile squadron of armoured cars and one battalion of infantry to bring up behind. Hence our connection with the Fusiliers: between us we're atomic couriers to our division.'

Daniel stared into the infinity of trees beyond the grotto. Up till now academic interest had outweighed repugnance. It was time for morality to reassert itself.

'And here,' he said, 'you're to have a Rehabilitation Centre for poisoning people to death.'

'The most permanent and comfortable form of rehabilitation which the circumstances will permit ... In August,' Gray continued in a firm expository voice, 'there are to be two preliminary exercises, Broomstick I and Broomstick II, to practise us in our new function. We shall assume the devastation of the entire area between Bad Harzburg and Goslar inclusive. Broomstick I will concentrate on the procedures involved in re-mapping and re-planning the area: Broomstick II on ... adminstrative measures ... in the remains of towns and villages.'

Daniel began to feel rather sick.

'And then in late September,' Gray went on, like a museum guide running efficiently through his stale repertoire, 'there will be a large-scale manoeuvre, code-name Apocalypse. "This manoeuvre will comprise two British Divisions, two American Divisions, one French Division, one Belgian Brigade, and

Dutch and Danish Units to be later specified. Present as observers will be general officers designate of the West German Army, currently re-forming. Apocalypse will presurmise an invasion of West Germany from the Communist occupied territory of Czechoslovakia; and will consist of a massive counter-attack delivered in a southerly direction against the flank of the invading army by the Allied Forces enumerated above. It will be posited that both sides have a limited number of tactical atomic weapons at their disposal; and the prior objects of the manoeuvre will be: (1) The Exercise of Senior Commanders in the use of such weapons; (2) The Exercise of All Ranks in the procedures peculiar to this type of warfare; and (3) The Exercise of the newly formed Atomic Courier Teams in clearing passages through areas of nuclear devastation." You see,' said Gray, offering the hock and reverting to his normal tone, 'what is being cooked up?'

'*Why did you want me to know?*'

'Because I want you to understand our position. I'm telling you, before you can find out from elsewhere, just what is going on, and asking you not to hold it against us . . . not to abandon us, Daniel, before you really know us.'

Trooper Lamb looked anxiously at Daniel, associating himself with the appeal.

'It will only be exercises, Mr Mond,' he said. 'Practice, like. Not a hair of anyone's head will be hurt.'

'And if the day comes when it's all real? This Rehabilitation Centre with the rest?'

Daniel looked slowly round the bowl in which they sat.

'It's just a little clearing in the woods,' said Fielding Gray, 'Like many others. The odds are a million to one that nothing – nothing out of the way – will ever happen here.' He glanced at the central rock. 'You know, you scholars are an odd lot. There's so much you refuse to acknowledge. How often, for example, does anyone admit that the famous Athenian democracy was nothing of the kind? That it was a minority assembly of superior citizens, who built their priceless civilization on the bodies of aliens and slaves? Or take yourself, an aspirant mathematician. How often do you care to remember where the work of other mathematicians has led? Which is straight to Broomstick and Apocalypse.'

'I know that well enough. I aim to keep my own work entirely pure.'

'There's always someone,' said Fielding Gray, 'who comes along and spoils things. However pure the intentions, there's always someone – he used to be called the Devil – who finds a way of perverting them. I wanted to be a scholar too, Daniel. But the Devil caught up with me before I'd even started. He took hold of my beautiful intentions and persuaded the world they were obscene, and there was an end of that. He'll catch up with you in time, and then you'll be doing the same as the rest of us. Looking through the woods for quiet grottoes . . . to rehabitate people in.'

There was a long silence.

'Funny,' said Daniel at last. 'Until a few weeks ago I would have laughed at what you've just said. If I hadn't been too indignant. But since I've been in Göttingen . . .'

'*What* since you've been in Göttingen?'

'One or two things have happened . . . never mind what . . . to make me suspect that you could – just *could* – be right.'

For a moment both Gray and Lamb looked unmistakably relieved. Then,

'So that's settled,' Gray said lightly. 'Now you can get to know us better. The day after tomorrow there's a band night in the Mess. It's the Fusiliers' show, but we'll all be there and you can come as my guest. You've got a dinner jacket here?'

'No.'

'Then you can borrow Bungay's. He's about your size and cut, and he'll be wearing uniform like the rest of us . . . Time to go.'

Lamb busied himself with the remains of the picnic. Daniel and Gray walked across to the slab of rock.

'You think it's a good thing, that I should come to this . . . band night?'

'Yes. You'll see how we justify ourselves. Or rather, how the Fusiliers do, but it comes to much the same.'

'I thought you were so different from the Fusiliers.'

'In many ways. But at bottom we all suffer from the same guilt, so we use the same mechanics for self-deception ... We'll drive you into Harzburg to pick up your car.'

'I haven't got a car. I came by taxi.'

'Did you now?' said Gray with a quick flush of pleasure. 'Then it will be our privilege to take you home ... if you can put up with a little of my reconnoitring first.'

At six o'clock on the evening of the Band Night Trooper Lamb called at Daniel's lodgings with the Land Rover to take him up the hill to the barracks. The main body of these consisted of three rows, ranged one above the other, of white three-storey blocks, each row having a terraced parade ground just beneath it. The officers' mess was the furthest block of the bottom row, and thither, after some altercation with a sergeant at the barrack gate, Daniel was driven. Fielding was waiting for him outside.

'Fusilier Sergeant at the gate making trouble,' said Trooper Lamb. 'Said no civilians allowed in without proper authority.'

'Mr. Mond has my authority.'

'I told him Major Glastonbury's to make it simpler.'

'Well done.'

'He said it should be in writing. He's going to report the matter to his C.O.'

'You see?' said Fielding as he led Daniel on to a sloping lawn that lay beyond the officers' mess. 'Fusilier pride. They're so convinced of their own importance they think you might try to spy on them.'

'I'm sorry if it'll cause trouble.'

'None at all. Giles will get a chit from their adjutant requesting an explanation. In order to annoy them he'll say you were a barber specially ordered from Götingen to shave him, or something of the sort.'

'His Jewish money-lender?'

'I beg your pardon.'

'Just a pleasantry. Very impressive,' said Daniel, surveying a large swimming pool at the bottom of the lawn: 'for the common use?'

'The men have their own. And the Sergeants. And the Corporals.'

As they approached the swimming pool, three scrawny women called their scrawny children out of the water and hurried them away into a line of tented cubicles.

'Fusilier officers' wives,' commented Fielding. 'They're in a bad temper this evening because their husbands will come home drunk after the band night.'

'What exactly is a band night?'

'You're here to see for yourself. But I'll give you a hint. It's the military equivalent of Holy Communion.'

It was said with irony.

'What are you doing in the Army, Fielding?'

'I like closed institutions. They protect one. They demand conformity, but in return they offer security and privilege. They impose a routine, which makes the days pass smoothly. Best of all, they leave no one in doubt as to his place.'

'One could say the same of a college, I suppose.'

'Precisely.'

The three scrawny women, clutching their children fiercely by the hand, trailed away up the lawn giving Daniel and Fielding resentful backward glances. From somewhere not far off a French horn sounded a beautiful and melancholy phrase of music.

'Officers' Dress Call. I've got Piers' dinner jacket ready for you in my room.'

'Why was it so sad . . . that call?'

'This is essentially,' said Fielding, 'a lugubrious occasion.'

The force of this judgment was not at first apparent, for when Daniel entered the ante-room with Fielding half an hour later he found every colour in the spectrum deployed for his pleasure. The Fusiliers, to be sure, were nothing out of the way in their dark blue tunics and trousers; but the five Dragoons, who wore skin-tight cherry overall trousers, sky blue tunics with black bandoliers from left to right (each containing twelve live revolver cartridges), ornamental daggers slung on the outside of the left thigh, and highly polished mess boots with gilded spurs, made a very remarkable sight indeed. Daniel, who could neither approve of anything so insolent nor disapprove of anything so beautiful, resolved his difficulty by examining the other diners. Although there was no one among them as splendid as the Dragoons, there was much else to catch the eye: the gold order at the throat of a General (the guest of honour); the scarlet mess jacket of his A.D.C.; chain mail on the shoulders of an Hussar (Giles Glastonbury's guest); and the elegant dark green of a small group identified by Fielding as visiting Riflemen. The Fusilier servants, far grander than their own officers in regimental liveries of deep yellow piped with purple, passed and repassed with chased silver trays on which were Victorian decanters of hideous yet massively opulent aspect; and the Colour Sergeant of the Sutlery (for such, Fielding said, was his title), when he marched in to announce dinner, carried a halberd which he thumped three times upon the floor:

'May it please Your Royal Highness to dine.'

'You see,' explained Fielding, 'their Colonel in Chief is Prince Charles, and on Band Nights he is considered symbolically present.'

Further comment was drowned by a blast of bugles just outside; all present made way for the Fusilier Colonel and his guest of honour; and as the two of them stepped out of the ante-room, there commenced a colossal roll of drums. When he followed a little later with Fielding, Daniel saw that the long corridor down to the dining-room was lined, on either side and at intervals of five yards, by scarlet-coated drummer-boys, who kept up their rapid beat until the last diner was standing behind his chair. The Colour Sergeant at the dining-room door then raised his halberd, and at the exact moment at which he brought it down on to the floor, with a crash that made the table quiver along its length, the now almost intolerable tattoo ceased, to be succeeded by absolute silence for twenty seconds clear.

'God grant that we may rise as many as we sit,' an egg-shaped chaplain intoned.

'A reference to the plague in Hong Kong,' said Fielding. 'One night three of them fell dead at dinner.'

Once seated, Daniel started to absorb the strange spectacle around him. Tears, laughter, delight, denunciation – he did not know which was the most appropriate and was in turn inclined toward all four. At the top end of the dining-room ('hall' would have been a more apt description) the wall was decorated by a pair of crossed flags, banners or standards, as he supposed, beneath which hung a large photograph in colour of the infant Prince Charles, who was playing with a woolly ball. On the floor under the photograph was a kind of wigwam of piled drums; and huddled inside this, at the head of the table, sat an unimposing major in Fusilier blue, who, to judge from the periodical twitch which shook his entire frame, was responsible for the management of the affair. The table, which was without a cloth and polished jet black, stretched forty yards down the room and so gave ample space for the twenty-five officers on either side of it, these being served by liveried waiters under command of the Colour Sergeant, who directed them, from his station to the left of the wigwam, by a code of signals performed with his halberd.

All of this, though novel, did not grossly exceed Daniel's expectation: what moved him to something near hysteria, however, was the triple-ranked array of ornamental silver, which occupied every spare inch of the table from one end to the other. The middle rank, which made a kind of watershed down the centre, consisted of the tallest and most contumacious pieces: six sets of candelabra in the form of casuarina trees, a minutely detailed reproduction, two feet square by four feet high, of the Edwardian keep in the Regimental Depot at Shepton Mallet (or so Fielding vouched), a model airship ('They shot one down with rifle bullets at Dover during the '14 war'), and, half way down the table and opposite the guest of honour, a silver mountain complete with woods, tracks, châlets and Fusiliers of the late eighteenth century stalking beaver-hatted Americans.

Parallel with the centre row and on either side of it were two lines of lesser offerings, such as loving cups, miniature

howitzers, statuettes of horsemen and cricketers; and in addi-
tion to all these, each guest had a small object placed for his
private admiration to the immediate right of his cover. Daniel's
was a silver-gilt snuff-box of the early nineteenth century,
perhaps the only piece in the whole display which approximated to seemliness but not enough by itself to remove the
impression that he was in some nightmare of Freudian fantasy.

'Where on earth did they get hold of all this?' he asked
Fielding when he had resumed control of himself.

'Mostly presentations from retiring officers. But some of it's
loot. That snuff-box was pinched when they sacked the White
House in 1812. And there's a silver-mounted bidet somewhere
which an ensign lifted from Napoleon's bedroom for a bet
when they were guarding him on Elba.'

'This was the lot that let him escape?'

'Oh no. They were relieved long before that. Whatever the
Wessex Fusiliers have in hand,' said Fielding with grudging
respect, 'they do it thoroughly.'

This observation was now borne out by the appearance,
in a small mistrel's gallery at the bottom end of the hall, of
a squad of Fusilier Bandsmen, who let fly with a selection of
Italian arias. The effect, even more bloated than usual, which
these produced when rendered by brass instruments, com-
bined with the sheer expertise of the performance (for some
score and a half of bandsmen were contriving to play in a
gallery large enough for ten), nearly reduced Daniel to hysterics
once more. To fight these off he distracted himself with a more
careful survey than he had yet attempted of those present.

Moving in a clockwise direction from the harassed major
under his canopy of drums, Daniel's gaze slipped over three
elderly and wooden-faced Fusilier captains, all of whom were
eating for dear life, to Giles Glastonbury, who was talking
past his guest to Doctor Motley. The latter was sweating
heavily, drinking water out of a tumbler and, as Daniel
watched him, waving away a plate of roast beef; the fact that
it was Friday, along with heaven knew what deposits of guilt
and acid from the previous night's activities, might be held to
account for this abstinence. Some four places down from

Motley, to the right of the guest of honour, was Julian James.
A vague facial resemblance between Julian and the General
explained his proximity but clearly blood was all they had in
common, for the General, who was listening with strained
politeness to an anecdote of Julian's, was also inspecting the
latter's liberal paunch with disapproval, and winced hectically
when a gay and gallic gesture from Julian concluded his story.

The fusilier Colonel, to whom the General now abruptly
turned, was a long, lean gentleman with a long, lean face which,
in repose, was blank to the point of imbecility. However, as
soon as the General began to speak, which he did with a slight
nod back at Julian and with obvious reference to the impro-
priety of his conversation, the Colonel's face came alive with
an almost baroque anguish, this causing it to change colour
and expand laterally, as though a limp and yellow sausage-
balloon had suddenly been further inflated and become a big
red round one. And filled with gas at that; for the Colonel's
head bobbed furiously on his shoulders, as though in dynamic
compensation for not being able to take off vertically, and
eventually gave a fierce accusatory flip in the direction of
Lieutenants Bungay and Lamprey. These were sitting some
way down to his left and helping one another to a double mag-
num of champagne, which was clearly out of order as everyone
else was being served with a fruity red burgundy by circling
waiters. Daniel decided that the Colonel, inspired by com-
plaints about Julian, was issuing a collective indictment of the
Dragoons: an indictment which woefully miscarried; for a
bald and white-tied German civilian on the Colonel's immediate left conceived that the latter's stare of rebuke was somehow intended for himself, and bridled like a sexually rejected
gorilla. As Daniel watched this peculiar exhibition of temperament, it was unexpectedly accounted for by his own neighbour
on the left, to whom he had not yet spoken.

'That Kraut is dead nervous,' a dry, rather grinding, voice
said to him: 'as a young major he once commanded a train
carrying political prisoners to a labour camp near Erfurt. He's
terrified it'll be brought up against him and his new appointment cancelled.'

Turning towards the voice, Daniel found two square feet of silver portcullis, through which, as through a grill, his informant continued to address him.

'He's to hold an important staff appointment in the new Kraut Army. He *says* that he thought the train was carrying voluntary workers. In which case why did it need a major and a whole company of troops to control it? Luckily for him the official records have disappeared.'

'Who told you all this?'

'An uncle who has knowledgeable friends ... My name's Percival, Leonard Percival.'

Percival pushed the silver portcullis from between them. Daniel saw a young man of about twenty-four with a face like Mr. Punch's, at first sight knowing rather than intelligent, the pointed nose of which seemed almost to meet the up-turned chin; scant dark hair emphasized the ascetic pallor of the forehead, while behind aggressively mounted spectacles were the eyes of a paranoiac scholar. Beneath this interesting ensemble was the dowdy blue tunic of the Fusiliers, decorated by a lieutenant's two pips on either shoulder and, on the left breast, by a single medal, which hung from a green and purple riband overlaid by a silver oak leaf.

'You're Julian James's mucker from Cambridge,' Percival prompted, patient under surveillance.

'Sorry ... Daniel Mond.'

'Glad to know you. I'm flattered to sit next the only educated man in the party.'

'Oh no,' said Daniel, fatuous and disingenuous; 'there's Julian ... and what about Captain Gray?'

'I'm afraid I haven't seen enough of them to say. We tried to be friendly with the Cavalry boys, but they stood off from the start.'

'I've been told that there are ... differences of outlook.'

'You've been told, I suppose, that they are men of taste who exercise a quiet, well-bred authority, and that we Fusiliers are a lot of squealing martinets.'

'Something of the sort, yes.'

'You could see it that way. Or you might find, if you looked closer, that they are selfish and lazy men who leave most of their work to cleverly selected N.C.O.'s.'

'That I wouldn't know.'

'Well, I would. I've watched them at it. "Carry on, Sergeant-major" ' – he mimicked the breathy neighing of Messrs. Lamprey and Bungay – ' "I'm off for luncheon now and I shan't be back this afternoon. Or tomorrow morning either." '

'Perhaps,' hazarded Daniel uneasily, 'soldiers have more regard for their officers if they don't see too much of them.'

'That's easily said. But it puts too much strain on the N.C.O.'s.'

'If they're intelligently chosen, as you imply . . .?'

'It's still wrong. I know what you're thinking,' said Percival; 'you're thinking that here's a busy little man who breathes down his soldiers' necks all day long, until he's become thoroughly worn out and unpopular and jealous of people who have a lighter touch.'

'I wasn't thinking anything of the kind.'

'Oh yes, you were. But understand this. That Sabre Squadron, as they so grotesquely call it, consists of eighty per cent regular soldiers, mature and reliable and intelligent men, because they only accept above-average entrants for armoured regiments. But the poor bloody infantry, who don't have glamorous clothes to show off in and have to walk everywhere on their flat feet – we have to take anything we're sent. Most of them are clod-hopping west country boys, under twenty and as sick as mud because they've been called up for National Service just when they'd found some silly slut to drag into the bushes every night.'

'Country copulatives?'

'With a sprinkling of small-town delinquents. They can't even keep themselves clean, half of them, unless there's someone to stand over them sixteen hours in every twenty-four. Every time they go out of barracks, they get drunk on raw spirits or pick up a dose of clap from some old whore who's been here since Bismarck. What would you do with a crowd like that?'

'I should tell myself,' said Daniel, 'that they were very young and lonely men in a strange country.'

'All right. But what would you *do*?'

'Try to educate them.'

'The Army isn't a finishing school. We're short of men — even the kind they send us — and there's a lot to be done.'

'This Atomic Courier Team?'

The moment the words were out of his mouth, Daniel realized that he had made a bad mistake. Percival's nose seemed to grow an inch and his spectacles flashed like morse lamps.

'Who told you about that?'

'I . . . I read about it.'

'No, you didn't. It's still on the secret list. One of your cavalry friends has been opening his mouth, that's what it is. Flagrant breach of security — but of course they wouldn't understand that.'

'Surely, everyone will know about it when they have this manoeuvre in September?'

'So you've heard about that too? You're a mathematician, Mond, or so they tell me. But you seem to need reminding that between now and the end of September is a good seven weeks. For obvious reasons, the Army Council is anxious that nothing should be known about Apocalypse until as late as possible.'

'Afraid of public disapproval?'

'In a way. Afraid that public disapproval could be used in political circles to stop the exercise. This,' said Percival, who now ceased to cark and assumed a manner cool yet earnest, 'would be a grave pity. Because Apocalypse has been devised in response to certain known and concrete realities.'

'Some of us think that a different response is needed. Protest. Your Apocalypse is a form of acceptance.'

'Of preparation. That is our job. There are plenty of people left over to do the protesting.'

'People whom you despise,' said Daniel, angered by Percival's smug and quizzical expression. 'Like those National Servicemen of yours. *You're* going to decide what's best for them and for all of us, whether we should be clean or dirty, whether we should be allowed out of barracks to risk getting clap, and *we're* not going to be consulted in case we make trouble. In case we get drunk and open our mouths and kick up such a rumpus in the whorehouse that the whole world gets to hear of it and puts a stop to this obscene game you propose to play in September. You couldn't bear that, because for all your talk of duty and preparation you relish the thought of playing at Atom Bombs with the whole of Europe for an arena. You'll be the big man then, the one who burns our bodies or hauls us off to Rehabilitation Centres to supervise our death. You'll be God, Percival, and you can trample all over the long-haired students and the smelly, malingering workers until there's nothing left of them but a vast desert of radio-active dust.'

'You have a point,' said Percival, blinking slightly behind his lenses, 'but I don't think you're being very polite or very clever. You've been taken in, Mond; you've been had. When your nice friends in the Dragoons were so foolish as to tell you about all this, did you accuse *them* of wanting to play God? Of course you didn't. Because they put on their little act. Because they were apologetic and cosily confidential. But all that means is that if ever *they* had to fire an Atomic missile, they'd say it was work unfit for a civilized man – and make the corporal press the trigger. I'd have the guts to press the trigger myself, or I hope I would. You see, I don't believe in fudging issues and to you that apparently makes me a maniacal killer. I'm disappointed in you, Mond. You're a bigot.'

And with this Percival pulled the silver grill back between them.

By this time the pudding plates had been removed and preparations were being made for dessert. Space was found, not without difficulty, for several large bowls of oriental design and unexciting content (mostly apples and bananas), and before each diner were set three separate port glasses.

'One for the Queen,' said Fielding, 'one for Prince Charles, and one for later. The port, for a miracle, is quite decent:

they've had a standing order with a firm in Lisbon ever since the Peninsular War.'

'I'm afraid,' said Daniel, 'that I've been indiscreet. My neighbour strongly resents my knowing about your Courier Team. He says it's a breach of security.'

'I told you. These Fusiliers are so pompous they think everything they do is top priority and top secret. Though Leonard Percival, from what little I've seen of him, is shrewd enough to know better.'

'That's what I thought. Do you suppose he was putting on some kind of act?'

'Fusiliers don't put on acts.'

'And he certainly seemed sincere . . .'

'I expect he's been indoctrinated like the rest of them. You have to be quite strong-minded to resist all this.' Fielding gestured up the table towards the piled drums and the crossed colours. 'And I understand that their speciality has still to come.'

The port now made its appearance in five decanters, each placed on one of five trucks which were attached to a silver model of Stephenson's Rocket. This was driven by slow clockwork; and the trick, apparently, was to lift a decanter, fill your glass, and replace the decanter in the correct truck without stopping the train.

'You don't think that *this* is their speciality?'

'Heavens no. It'll be something altogether more alarming. Something to do with the toasts, I expect.'

The Queen's toast at least was drunk without much elaboration – beyond the fact that they all had to remain standing, with glass held high, while a pink-cheeked band boy carolled three verses of 'Here's a health unto Her Majesty'. Nor did the toast to Prince Charles, as Colonel-in-Chief, produce anything sensational, although the convention that His Royal Highness was symbolically present involved everyone's bowing low in the direction of the wretched major at the head of the table, who twitched so much that he nearly dislodged a drum. After this, during a pause while the clockwork train went its round for the third time, Daniel felt expectation in the air; on his left beyond the grill Leonard Percival was smiling thinly but happily, rather as though he were about to pull a switch which would release naked ladies from under the floor-boards, and even the three wooden-faced Fusilier Captains at the top end of the room were giving off mild palpitations of excitement.

'It's coming now,' he whispered to Fielding.

As indeed it was.

The Fusilier Colonel, his long face undulating like a tooth-paste tube that someone was squeezing from the bottom, rose to his feet; the Colour Sergeant's halberd crashed to the floor for silence; the electric lights were switched off; and a liveried corporal with a huge set of bellows passed down the table puffing out the candles on the six sets of candelabra. When the room was in total darkness,

'Absent friends,' the Colonel croaked.

'Absent friends,' came an answering murmur from round the table; and suddenly, to the right of the piled drums, a tall figure was seen, holding up a single candle and so casting a dim light on its uniform, which recalled to Daniel a long forgotten plate in his first history book.

'Captain Thomas Keyne,' said Percival, in a soft but clear voice, obviously intended to be heard by all in the room: 'in the Forlorn Hope at Minden. A sword-thrust through the heart.'

'Captain Thomas Keyne,' came the low murmur from the invisible diners.

For perhaps ten seconds the figure stood silent and motionless, while little noises of clinking and sucking down the table told Daniel that glasses were being raised to the dead Fusilier. Then the figure stirred and passed its candle, as it went, to another figure in uniform of a later date.

'Fusilier Joseph Sutton,' said an Officer's voice from somewhere down the table, in the same tones as Percival had used: 'to save a fallen comrade at Saratoga. A bullet in the throat.'

Again the murmured toast. Again a change of figure and another voice.

'Sergeant John Upwood. In the rear-guard action at Corun. Of multiple sabre-cuts.'

'Major Rupert Forsdyke. Leading the charge at Waterloo. A bullet in the brain.'

'Ensign David Rory, Guarding the Colour at Balaclava. Trampled to death.'

'Fusilier George Bates . . . Calcutta . . . Regimental Sergeant-Major Adam Roberts, Victoria Cross . . . a bayonet thrust . . . Mafeking . . . Mons . . . Ypres . . . Distinguished Service Order . . . a shell-splinter . . . gas . . . the Somme.'

And now a figure in the battle-dress and beret of the 'forties.

'Second Lieutenant Conrad Stern, Victoria Cross, the Normandy Landing. Leading a detachment of—'

But his figure elected to speak for itself.

'Daniel Mond,' intoned the figure in a low, sarcastic wail, 'what are you doing with the soldiers? Stay away from the soldiery . . . Jew Mond.'

And that was all (as Daniel wrote to Jacquiz Helmut some days later), but quite enough to upset their little pageant. There was much scrabbling about and calling for lights, the band suddenly struck up with a march, and everyone shuffled off to the 'ante-room' and started to drink a lot rather furtively. The colonel was full of apologies. It must have been, he said, some crude form of joke. He explained that the silent figures who appeared in fancy dress were all corporals or sergeants, among whom the office is held to be an honour, and that the brief epitaphs were spoken by selected officers. 'Conrad Stern' had certainly been on the agenda: he was one of several Jews who held commissions in the Wessex Fusiliers during the last war (a brother, oddly enough, of your publishing chum Gregory) and was killed by a land-mine on the Normandy beaches. Appropriately, they'd found a young Jewish lance-coporal, who's doing his National Service, to impersonate Stern in the procession of *imagines,* but he'd been injured while on training that day, so they'd decided to leave Stern out. The epitaph-speaker had been duly notified, but when he saw 'Stern' appear after all, he assumed all was well and started it with his piece – only to be interrupted as I've described. Obviously, the colonel said, someone had taken the lance-corporal's place, perpetrated this little 'jape' (the colonel's word), and then disappeared in the confusion. The colonel seemed entirely satisfied with this version, despite all the questions it left unanswered, though a general who was there as a guest looked very put out indeed. I must say, it was a peculiar thing to happen.

And there was something else I thought distinctly curious, though by no means so bizarre. After all the apologies, Gray persuaded me to stay on for a while, in order as he said, to show there was no ill will. Would I care to play a game called Cheminder-Fer? Giles Glastonbury was getting up a table . . . not without difficulty, as the Fusiliers disapproved of gambling and always celebrated these occasions with an extraordinary rite which consisted largely of forming themselves into rugger scrums and whooping. So while the Fusiliers, who were by now recovered from the Stern fiasco, capered round the Mess like Red Indians, I settled down with the doctor, the five dragoons and a visiting hussar at Giles's gaming table, where for a full hour we played a childish and mechanical game dependent solely on counting the number of pips on one's cards. Upon my soul, I don't know which party was the more stupidly employed; and to make matters worse I was embarrassed by beginners' luck winning a large sum mainly from the doctor, who had abandoned his earlier abstinence and was making up to the tune of one double brandy every ten minutes. Clearly, I should have to stay put until I lost at least some of it back; and what with the blinding tedium of the game, the cacophony still making all around us and indigestion brought on by the coarseness of the food and wine, I began to feel very unhappy. However, rescue came from an unexpected quarter, in the form of Lieutenant Percival, my neighbour at dinner, who now arrived as herald to the second oddity of the evening. Percival, who had taken no part in his companions' antics, suddenly appeared through a side door and asked Glastonbury to release me, as the colonel wanted to speak to me again. This request was ill received but unrefusable, so I was lead away by Percival, through the side door and into a narrow corridor.

'It's not the colonel, it's Pappenheim,' said Percival, naming the German guest. 'He's anxious to meet you.'

Since I'd have been happy to talk to the Minotaur so long as it let me out of that dreary game of cards, I followed Percival down the corridor to a door which said P.M.C. and opened into a smelly little office. Inside it was Pappenheim, a pot of coffee and a bottle of brandy in front of him sitting at a desk. He rose, shook hands, pointed to a chair and poured me brandy, as full of himself as if the whole place had been his own.

'Thank you, Herr Oberleutnant,' he said to Percival, who bowed gravely and left the room.

'A very excellent regiment, the Wessex Fusiliers,' the gratified Teuton proceeded; 'I simply asked that young officer to introduce us, and he arranged all this.'

'Perhaps he's ashamed of the spectacle outside.'

Pappenheim gave this notion serious consideration.

'I think not,' he said ponderously. 'It is a tradition, no?'

'I'm a stranger in these circles.'

'Of course, Herr Mond . . .'

He now started to look very self-conscious and silly, like a man about to propose to a girl thirty years younger, but after nearly three minutes of huffing and puffing and relighting his cigar, he managed to get under way.

'You have interesting work at the University?'

'Very.'

'The Dortmund papers, I hear. How does your attempt proceed?'

Just then I had such a vicious spurt of indigestion that I hardly knew what he'd said, and all he got in reply was a smothered burp.

'Quite so . . . Herr Mond, if ever you are in difficulty . . . I cannot help you with your work, of course, but any other way. What I mean is—'

But at this juncture the door opened and a fat, neurotic officer, the one who'd been sitting at the head of table during the dinner, came reeling in.

'One's own office. I mean to say, a bit much. Strangers drinking one's brandy. A bit much.'

With this he sat down in an armchair and instantly fell asleep. Pappenheim gobbled like an affronted hippo, but he was very quick to follow me out into the corridor, where he made as if to continue our discussion. By this time, however, I'd managed to realize that he was being shady or presumptuous or both, so I gave him a bleak look and went straight back to the ante-room. There I found that Percival had been 'sitting in' for me and had already lost back all but a few pounds of my winnings.

'The game's automatic,' he said, 'so it makes no difference who plays your cards.'

Although he was quite as insolent in his way as Pappenheim, I was too relieved to care. I was beyond thinking of anything except my stomach and how to get home ... whither Percival, aware of my condition, now volunteered to drive me. Gray looked rather conscience-stricken, but it was clear that the game had a fascination for him, so I accepted Percival's offer gratefully enough.

'I suppose Pappenheim was inquisitive?' Percival said when we were nearly in Göttingen.

'Worse. Prying.'

'That fits. I was inquisitive to find out whether *he* was inquisitive, which is why I set it all up. But to spare you too much annoyance, I arranged for old Archie to barge in.'

He seemed to think that no further explanation was required, and that he had been both clever and thoughtful. For my part, I was too far gone to question this. All I remember after that is getting upstairs, being miserably but mercifully sick (a deep red colour) and collapsing into bed.

And so, my dear Jacquiz, ended a memorable if hardly a pleasant evening. At first I thought that the dragoons, whether from guilt or embarrassment, might hold off after what had happened, and I told myself that I didn't care if I never saw a soldier again. But in fact they've simply ignored the whole affair, I've been meeting some or other of them almost every day, and I must say I'm very glad of it. For while their company sometimes makes me uneasy, particularly when I think of this 'Courier Team,' it is also stimulating because totally unlike anything to which I am accustomed; and in any event it is *company*, so welcome after the dreadful loneliness which I was beginning to feel and the effects of which must have been all too apparent in my last letter. Thank God that's over now.

Oddly enough, though Julian introduced me, I've seen very little of him and much more of this Captain Fielding Gray, who is fast becoming my chief friend among them. A melancholy man, interesting in more ways than one. It seems that he had a scholarship to Lancaster some years back, but that Robert Constable was somehow instrumental in having him refused entry. From what I can make out, Fielding has been brooding about this ever since. If you could find out Robert's version of the story, I'd be glad to hear it ...

The real if rather suspect happiness which his new friends brought to Daniel's leisure also had a beneficial effect on his work. In the second week of August he was able to submit to Dirange in Cambridge a series of specimen workings to demonstrate that he had solved the problem of Dortmund's first notation and could now manipulate the first type of matrix. Dirange wrote back that in his opinion the work which Daniel had sent him was sound, and that even if Daniel were to advance no further, he could congratulate himself on a substantial achievement. In time, Dirange observed, this would have to be written up and published; but meanwhile Daniel must proceed with the second stage of his enquiry and find out whether it would indeed give him the help which he hoped for in completing his Fellowship Thesis – which, in such case, promised to be a remarkable document. In all the circumstances, his advice to Daniel was to keep silent, for the time being, about what he had so far accomplished, lest enquiries and correspondence should distract him from making further progress. Academic etiquette, however, to say nothing of common courtesy, required that some indication of his success be given to Doktor Aeneas von Bremke, whose sponsorship of Daniel had made that success possible. In Dirange's view, and although von Bremke had a character for discretion, Daniel should be vague and tentative in his report, expressing qualified hopes and eschewing concrete definitions.

Since Daniel did not look forward to this exercise in evasion, he was relieved to reflect that von Bremke was still away in the Harz and that any such interview must wait till his return. However, it seemed that von Bremke had a sixth sense in such matters; for some two hours after Dirange's letter had arrived from Cambridge a note was delivered by hand to Daniel's lodgings to announce that von Bremke was in Göttingen and would like to see him that afternoon. This meant putting off a drive through the border villages with Julian and Fielding; but despite the brevity of notice Daniel felt bound to comply with von Bremke's request – if only to get a tiresome obligation quickly out of the way.

Were such a thing conceivable of such a man, Daniel would have said that von Bremke was agitated.

'Herr Dominus,' he said as soon as Daniel was seated, 'you have been in Göttingen, a most welcome and honoured guest, for four months. May I ask what you have achieved?'

'Some useful steps,' said Daniel carefully, 'towards solving the first stage of the problem.'

'Useful enough for you to be calling for papers which bear explicitly on the *second* stage. Or so the Assistant Curator tells me.'

So that was it. But why not? Von Bremke had a right to question his own subordinates.

'I've been calling for those,' said Daniel, 'ever since I arrived. I like to look ahead.'

Von Bremke took a clean handkerchief from his sleeve and flapped it open more vigorously than necessary.

'Yes. But now you are calling almost exclusively for such documents. This says to me that for you the first stage is over. Why was I not told?'

'You were away.'

'We have mails in Germany.'

'I would have told you as soon as you were back.'

'I am back now.'

'I don't wish to be over-confident . . . premature.'

'Then please to tell me, Herr Dominus Mond, what you *think* you have established. You speak in confidence; I shall make no claims on your behalf, or on the late Professor Dortmund's until I am so authorized by you.'

This was square dealing. Daniel could equivocate no more.

'Very well, Herr Doktor. I am virtually certain that I understand the earlier notation and the earlier matrices.'

'And to what functions would these matrices lend themselves?'

'To the solution, among other things, of certain abstract problems of motion.'

'You are interested in these problems?'

'No. They are relatively simple and have already been solved by other if more cumbrous methods.'

'And so?'

'And so I am interested, now as ever, in discovering the second method which Professor Dortmund developed from the first.'

'More matrices?'

'Yes. But of an even more elaborate and elusive kind.'

'Elusive . . . or delusive?'

'I beg your pardon, Herr Doktor?'

'Dortmund, as I have told you, was a sick man towards the end. Sick men delude themselves. Sick men of genius – or something near it – could delude others.'

Daniel frowned and remained silent. There was a heavy sweat on his brow which he now mopped at with a handkerchief that seemed very grey when compared with von Bremke's.

'Herr Dominus. Have you ever noticed, in the course of your work here, something . . . wrong . . . about the Dortmund papers? Something perverse. A deliberate rejection of normality, in the notation perhaps, where normality would have served very well.'

'It's funny you should say that,' said Daniel reluctantly. 'At times I have felt something – something very like hostility in those symbols.'

'Ah. Of course, it is a long time since I worked on them, and I did not have the success we hope you have had. But could not this perversity which we have both observed have sprung from the pains of illness?'

'Ill or not, perverse or not, Dortmund did sound work, at least as far as I have followed him.'

'Yes. But later, when the pains of cancer became all but intolerable, perhaps the perversity, the torturing of symbols . . . for the mere sake of continuing to do *something* . . . was all that was left?'

'No . . . no.'

'I said, perhaps. How far, Herr Mond, have you proceeded towards elucidating the second notation?'

'I have established what it has in common with the first.'

'The easiest part of the task. Do you really think, after all the months you have already spent and with all the difficulties that still lie ahead, that it is wise to go on? When all you may find is the nightmare of a tormented mind?'

'Von Bremke's changed his tune,' said Daniel to Fielding the next day.

Fielding was by now in Daniel's confidence, at least where day to day problems were concerned. Daniel had already found that his new friend had a valuable capacity for cross-examining him on general grounds and an intuitive understanding of the human factors involved in an intellectual quest.

'When I first came here,' Daniel continued, 'and on the few occasions when I saw him later, von Bremke took the line that while he would be surprised if I achieved anything he would also be gratified. He would like, he said, to have me do work worthy of the good man Dortmund was. But now, now that something has been achieved, he seems upset.'

'The guardians of the Sphinx are very jealous of its secrets. There were a lot of angry faces, you may depend on it, the day Oedipus answered the riddle.'

'He's certainly rattled, and I've only answered half the riddle, if that. I was given hollow congratulations and advised to drop the rest of it. Dortmund was very ill towards the end; probably, von Bremke said, he didn't know what he was doing.'

'I disagree. If he had the will-power to go on doing it . . .'

'That's more or less what I think, but von Bremke does have a point. From the start there's been something odd about the way Dortmund set all this up. Perversity was von Bremke's word for it. And the further I go the more perverse I'm finding it. So it is at least possible that Dortmund just went to pieces.'

'If you assume that,' said Fielding reluctantly, 'and go back to Cambridge now, would what you have done be enough to win you a Fellowship?'

'Perhaps. It's not what I promised, as they'll be quick to point out, but it's quite a lot and it's important. Dirange will make them see that. But the thing is, Fielding, I can't give up now. Because if we're right, you and I, in thinking that Dortmund's work was valid till the end, then there's something very much out of the ordinary still to come.'

'What sort of something?'

Daniel hesitated. While he was glad to have someone to whom he could give a running report of immediate progress or setback, he was not at all sure that he wished to talk in longer terms. It might be imprudent, even impious, to discuss such mysteries as these before they were finally revealed. And yet, he needed so badly to talk to someone whom he could trust, from whom he could ask sympathy, for his plans as well as his hopes.

'Well,' he said at last, 'what I've disentangled so far amounts to a new and neater way of accounting for motion in spatial fields of various types. All right?'

'You mean spatial field of more than three dimensions? That sort of thing?'

'No. It's all of it three-dimensional space, but complicated by other factors. Curved or otherwise distorted. Subject to more or less rapid processes of expansion or contraction. And so on. Now, what's coming – as far as I can tell – is an adaptation of the method in order to deal with very *tiny* movements, the movements of almost infinitesimally small entities within an almost infinitesimally small compass.'

'Electrons? Things like that?'

'No,' said Daniel sharply. 'Dortmund's entities, and the kinds of space in which they move, are theoretical ... abstract.'

'If you say so. But surely, if Dortmund has already established laws of motion in these different kinds of space, then those laws will hold even on the tiniest scale?'

'Not necessarily. Because as we move towards the infinite on the one hand or the infinitesimal on the other the normal rules become less and less dependable.'

'All right. I'll buy it.'

'Well, in order to investigate what goes on at an extreme level of smallness, Dortmund, at the stage I've reached, is about to postulate a quantity called *zeta*, which is to be the *smallest possible existing quantity* which is not infinitesimal.

A very powerful concept. More powerful than the infinitesimal itself, because it rubs against it, so to speak, yet remains real.'

'*Real*?'

'In the mathematical sense.'

'So what he's after is to see how these little zeta-things, moving on a zeta-scale, get on in various conditions ... if, for example, the overall spatial field they're in were suddenly twisted or inflated or whatever?'

'That's about it ... in crude terms.'

'Hmm,' mused Fielding. 'You're sure that this is the sort of thing Dortmund was up to?'

'Not absolutely. Von Bremke could be right, and it could be a meaningless nightmare. Or ... or he could be right about the nightmare, wrong about it's being meaningless. That is—'

He broke off abruptly and brushed the sweat from his upper lip.

'Yes, Danny?'

But when Daniel shook his head, Fielding pressed him no further. There was a long silence.

'How much time have you got?' Fielding said at last.

'I want to get back to Cambridge by the end of September. But I suppose I could take as long as I want, within reason. Unless there's interference.'

'Constable may summon you back?'

'Pressure of some kind.'

'There usually is. Pressure of hunger just now. Dinner, Daniel. Giles and the doctor will be waiting.'

My dear Daniel (Jacquiz Helmut wrote from Cambridge),

I'm sorry I left your first letter so long – I was away from here when it came, spending a week with the Stukeleys at Crowleigh. But to judge from your second the first has answered itself. I'm delighted you've found such nice friends to play with. Julian was always an amusing boy (albeit rather coarse) and just what you need to take you out of yourself. In every way your new gang seems entirely *comme il faut*. Giles Glastonbury is well worth attention; he's a second cousin of John Dorsetshire's. Even this peculiar Fusilier, Leonard Percival, has interesting connexions: he was brought up, if my memory serves me, by his uncle Rupert – a solicitor in Somerset who is not only a power in the county but also heard with respect in London.

But I don't suppose you see much of a mere Fusilier when you've got all those glamorous Dragoons running after you. Do remember, though, that it is the plain infantry regiments of the Line who *are* the British Army; Dragoons and so on are often merely top-dressing, or so my acquaintance with military history tells me, and not always a credit to the service. During the Peninsular War Earl Hamilton's Regiment was so cluttered up with officers' private baggage that it was known as Hamilton's Carnival: at least three of them 'sold out' and returned to London in mid-campaign because conditions were not to their liking and Wellington refused to let them bring more than one mistress each. There's a long passage in Gronow about it; in his view the gentlemen in question should have been court-martialled at the drum-head and shot for deserting in the field. The Wessex Fusiliers, on the other hand, have never given an inch, except at Corunna and Dunkerque; and on both occasions they put up formidable rear-guard actions. After Waterloo the Duke said of them, 'The dullest officers in Europe and the steadiest in the world.'

Which makes it all the more surprising that such a very odd incident as you describe should have occurred at one of their band nights. In such circles things just do *not* go wrong or get out of hand. So perhaps you should take it as a compliment that it was your persona which inspired this outburst. It seems very strange that no one should have traced the interloper. Conrad Stern, by the way, though one of those Jews who exult in anti-Jewish jokes, had a far more delicate sense of humour, so it certainly wasn't his ghost. But then even you can hardly have supposed that it was. In case you are inclined to hark back to your fears of persecution let me advise you to regard the whole thing as a thoughtless and drunken prank – got up by an officer who fought in Israel perhaps? Forget it.

Jacquiz made no reference, Daniel noticed, to his subsequent interview with Pappenheim, an occurrence which he had come to consider the more important as it was the more palpable. Perhaps Jacquiz felt that his indulgence had already been sufficiently stretched: that one oddity should have taken place during an evening out might be acknowledged, but two exceeded the limits of good taste.

As you requested (Jacquiz went on) I have asked Robert Constable about Fielding Gray. For the first time since I've known him, Robert was a good deal less than frank. It seems that there was some kind of scandal at Gray's school in the summer of 1945, that Robert, as an old boy of the school and a friend of the Headmaster's, was made *au fait* with it, and that on his representations the College Council decided to withdraw Gray's scholarship (in consequence of which Gray opted for the Regular Army). But just what the scandal was Robert refused to tell me; under mild pressure he grew more and more shifty, until eventually he mumbled something to the effect that the whole thing was perhaps a mistake. *What* was a mistake, I insisted: was there a scandal or wasn't there? Oh yes, said Robert, there was a scandal all right, a very nasty one, but it had later appeared that Gray's part in it had probably been misreported. Then why wasn't Gray reinstated? Well, the mistake – if such it was – had only come to light four or five years later, by that time Gray was established in his career, it would have been painful to a lot of other people to dig it all up again ... and so on. Not at all Robert's usual precise and conscientious self. Anyhow, he refuses to tell me any more, so you'll have to have a go at him yourself.

Well, Daniel. I'm delighted you're in good fettle again. Don't spoil it all by drinking too much with your cavalry friends and then imagining things to brood about. I'm glad I'm no longer needed in Göttingen as I have a very full summer of country visiting ahead. Please remember me to Julian and also to Giles Glastonbury, whom I last met three years ago at Harewood.

That evening Fielding Gray said:
'Broomstick's been brought forward. We're off tomorrow.'
'Oh ... For long?'
'Two days for Broomstick I and another three for the second part. Then a debriefing conference at Divisional H.Q. About a week.'
'I'll miss you.'
'It's nice to be missed. I'll be in touch as soon as we're back.'

'Suppose I came up to Harzburg one day. Would there be any chance of seeing you?'

'I wouldn't do that,' said Fielding with a flicker of irritation; 'not if I were you.'

Part Three

REAR-GUARD ACTION

WALKING down the Nikolaistrasse the next morning, Daniel saw the soldiery pull out for Exercise Broomstick. It was not an exciting scene. A few Land Rovers bearing the Fusilier crest, then some three-ton trucks painted a drab green and full of men in denim overalls, then more Land Rovers, then more trucks. A wagon decorated with a red cross on a white background and containing a dazed Mick Motley in the co-driver's seat. More Land Rovers, more three-ton trucks. A small saloon car, of the same drab green as everything else, and the Fusilier Colonel sitting very straight in the back. A few motor-bicycles chivvying. No horses, no band, no banners when a Courier Team went out to war. But where were the Dragoons and their armoured cars?

'Don't bother to wait for your cavalry friends,' said Earle Restarick on the pavement beside him. 'They've gone across country.'

'Earle . . . How very nice.'

'Let's hope so. Take me up to your room, Daniel. Now.'

Five minutes later, when they reached Daniel's room (oddly unfamiliar in the morning light) at the top of the University building, Earle Restarick said:

'So it didn't work.'

'What didn't?'

'I told them it wouldn't. I told them they hadn't understood the English mind. A scene like that, I said, will simply draw them all closer together. A public insult to an Englishman's guest is the one thing to ensure that he'll make a friend of that guest, even if he hated him before, for life. But of course they wouldn't listen. You're only a go-between, they said; you leave this to us.'

' "They"?'

'Well, now they know I was right. Not that I'll get any credit.'

'Earle. Where have you been all these weeks?'

'Waiting. Waiting for you to get so soft with loneliness that when I came back you'd flop at my feet and tell me all they wanted to know. But unfortunately for them you found yourself some new friends. So then they said, "We must break this up. Before he gets happy and well balanced again. Otherwise he won't talk." '

'So . . . "they" . . . put on that act with Stern?'

'The idea was that you'd go off in a huff, and your new friends would say, "What the hell, it's too difficult, we can't be bothered any more." So then you'd be alone and vulnerable again, and *they* could proceed according to plan.'

'That's why you've come back now? Because I've been left alone?'

'Alone, but only for a few days, and certainly not vulnerable. Because you now know where you can turn for comfort. *Their* little trick didn't work, and your friends will be back in the barracks in under a week, and so now *they're* trying something else. No more psychology, no more waiting around for loneliness to turn you to pulp: just a straight . . . request.'

Earle pondered his silver gaberdine thighs with less than satisfaction.

'A straight request,' he said, 'with me as messenger boy. I'm very sorry, Daniel. When I made a friend of you I was only acting on instructions, but in a way it really did take. I got to liking you, for Christ's sake. That's why I'll never be much good in this game, but we won't go into that. I liked you and so I warned you: "Go on home," I said. But you wouldn't listen, and you're still here, and now it's too late.'

'I can go tomorrow if I want,' said Daniel with reflex indignation.

'But you don't want. Because now you're really on to something at last. And that's the reason *they* won't let you go.'

'How would they stop me?'

'Never mind that. Just take my word for it. As long as you seemed to be getting nowhere, like all the rest that have tried, they wouldn't have bothered. They'd have kept on watching, but if you'd packed up and gone back to Cambridge, they wouldn't have lifted a finger. But *now*, Daniel, now that you're on to something . . .'

'I don't know that I am on to anything.'

'They know better.'

'Who told them? Von Bremke?'

'So they're right?'

Daniel shrugged.

'Let's be plain,' he said. 'Who are "they", and what exactly do they want?'

'You don't need to know who they are, Danny. Better not. As for what they want, it's the pot of gold buried underneath the Dortmund papers.'

'If you mean the final answer, I'm nowhere near it.'

'Correction. You're getting warmer.'

'What if I am? What possible good can it be to them? A batch of symbols conveying an abstract idea which will be properly appreciated by perhaps ten men in the whole of Europe.'

'That's just it, Danny. Ten is too many. My employers want it all to themselves. Greedy of them, isn't it?'

'Pointless.'

'That's for them to judge. What shall I tell them?'

'Tell them . . . that if I'm left in peace I may – just may – find the answer. And that if I do, it will be published in the Cambridge Journal of Pure Mathematics, the editors of which will be very glad of "their" subscription. Enquiries c/o The University Press or Heffer's Bookshop, Petty Cury.'

'I'll tell them, Danny. And I'll be back with their answer.'

When Earle had gone, Daniel's first reaction was to observe his own lack of surprise. It was as if he had always known that Earle would turn up again bearing some such proposition, with the result that he was neither frightened nor angry nor even particularly curious – merely irritated, as though a policeman had called with a long expected summons for illicit parking.

His second reaction was more violent. Anger in one direction he certainly felt; anger with von Bremke. He left his room and strode down the corridor like a storm-trooper.

'Herr Doktor, why have you betrayed my trust?'

Von Bremke nodded to a chair.

'Explain please.'

Hotly, Daniel explained. Some persons unknown had been told of his purpose and his arrival in Göttingen, and had been kept informed of his progress since. Though friends of his own had been in his confidence from time to time, no one had been continuously so for the last five months. Only von Bremke had been that; only von Bremke could be responsible for the leak.

A tinge of melancholy came into von Bremke's face.

'I was never in your confidence,' he said.

'You knew I was coming and why. You knew how I proposed to set to work. You were told, the other day, when the first important stage was complete.'

'Professor Dirange, he too knew of this.'

'Dirange? Unthinkable.'

'But thinkable – this treachery – for me? Of course. A stranger in a dishonoured country. It is quite natural.'

'What else can I think?'

'What else indeed? No doubt you believe I was offered money?'

'I didn't say that.'

'Money which I very much need. So perhaps I wish I had been offered money, Herr Mond.' The irony came awkwardly from the stern, ponderous face. 'Perhaps I would have taken it. We shall never know. Who are these inquisitive people?'

'I've told you, I've no idea. All I know is that the American, Restarick, is their agent. He must have been planted here when they knew I was coming.'

'Certainly I disliked him. He claimed to be an American gentleman. But he was . . . *nicht geboren*.'

Daniel's mouth twisted in distaste.

'That's not the point.'

'It is very much the point. He was a pretence, a fraud. If you had noticed that, perhaps you would not have trusted him.'

'Perhaps you should have warned me.'

'You would have ignored the warning. Because you despise me.' Von Bremke smiled voraciously; for the first time since Daniel had known him, von Bremke thought something was funny. 'You consider, like all Jews, that I am a pedantic German, coarse and unsubtle.' Von Bremke began to laugh in great heaving bursts of merriment. 'The Jews, who invented Jehovah, think *others* are coarse and unsubtle. The Jews, with their Talmud and their Torah, think others are pedantic. The Jews, the race of Judas, accuse others of treachery. Oh, Herr Dominus Mond, it is so long since I laugh like this.'

He lowered his head into his hands, snorting and slobbering in his mirth. Mirth? At a certain stage it is not easy to tell between a gasp of laughter and a sob of pain. Daniel, affronted yet guilty, moved silently from the room.

For the next two days Daniel went on with his work, which was presenting neither more nor less difficulty than he had expected, as though nothing had happened. It was, he told himself, the only thing to do. He had no way of finding out who was behind Earle's threat or how seriously this should be taken. It was absurd to think that 'they' could prevent him from leaving Göttingen if he wished; but in any case he had no intention of leaving. Too much had been done, too much was at stake, to give up now. Presumably Earle would reappear. When he did, the situation must be appraised in the light of whatever he had to say: perhaps 'they' could be fed enough advance information – if indeed there was any – to satisfy them, or perhaps he would have to seek help. Either way, this was a free and friendly country in the West of Europe, and really a solution should not be hard to find.

On the third evening after his confrontations with Earle and von Bremke, Daniel was walking along the town wall when a sudden flash of light half blinded him for several seconds. He recovered himself to see that Leonard Percival, his heavy glasses glinting in the setting sun, was standing in his path at some twenty yards' distance. Percival, who had appeared from nowhere, was wearing a double-breasted blue blazer with large gilt buttons and grinning like Mephistopheles.

' "If there were dreams to sell," ' Percival said, ' "What would you buy?" '

'I beg your pardon?'

' "Some cost a passing bell,

Some a light sigh . . ."'

'Thomas Lovell Beddoes. He lived in Göttingen for quite some time, you know. He is reputed to have held orgies here. Perhaps this is where he picked up his pox. For such a pretty little town it certainly has some nasty surprises.'

'Why aren't you on Exercise Broomstick?'

' "If there were dreams to sell,

Merry and sad to tell,

And the crier rung the bell,

What would you buy?" '

'Peace of mind. Why aren't you in the Harz with the rest of them?'

'Rear-guard. Someone has to take care of the barracks . . . An interesting case, Beddoes. He was a doctor but he couldn't cure his own syphilis, so in the end he did himself in. But I'm sure I don't have to spell out the moral to you.'

'You seemed so dedicated to your task,' Daniel said irritably, 'and yet on the very first rehearsal they leave you behind.'

'A good job for you that they did. Because now I can take you to see Pappenheim.'

'I don't want to see Pappenheim.'

'You do if you did but know it. He's got news for you.' Percival pointed his nose accusingly at Daniel's forehead. 'So I don't want any ingratitude or coyness. Just come along with your uncle Leonard and everything will be all right.'

So saying, Percival linked his right arm with Daniel's left and propelled him gently but very firmly in the direction from which he had come.

'My car's in the Goetheallee,' he explained. 'I wonder why they don't name one after Beddoes.'

Ten minutes later they were driving through the main gate

of the barracks. A soldier standing outside the guard room gave them a shifty look, and Percival stopped the car.

'Come here and salute,' he hissed.

'Sorry, sir. Didn't recognize you in civies.'

'So you were going to let a stranger drive straight in?'

The soldier gave a hopeless shrug. Rather surprisingly, Percival ignored this and said quietly:

'Put the barrier down, Fusilier, and only raise it when you have recognized the people arriving. Low morale,' he said to Daniel as they drove on. 'They don't like being in an empty barracks.'

And indeed a feeling of desertion crept off the ground like a mist. The windows of the barrack-blocks were as blind as vacant eye-sockets. Already, one would have thought, there were weeds pushing up through the asphalt of the parade grounds. The two women and children, who were trailing away with their bathing towels as Percival drew up in front of the Mess, only made the emptiness more eerie: it was as though they were the last human beings who would be allowed to leave before the whole scene were petrified for ever.

'Pappenheim is upstairs,' Percival said. 'The Mess staff is much reduced but I don't manage too badly. I take it you could do with some dinner?'

Remembering the food he had last eaten here, Daniel shuddered violently, a reaction which Percival misunderstood.

'No silly jokes this time,' he said, and led the way to the ante-room, where Pappenheim was morosely drinking beer in a far corner. He did not get up to greet them but flapped a limp hand and contrived to wrinkle the bald skin on his scalp, as if smiling with that instead of with his face.

'We dine alone,' said Percival.

In the dining-room the great table was blank except for three places laid at the bottom end, which was lit by a single casuarina candelabrum. A trolley by the wall carried bottles of wine and a burner, over which Percival now busied himself with a chafing dish.

'My uncle taught me,' he explained: 'a man of many gifts.

I shall be about ten minutes, so perhaps, Herr Pappenheim, you would like to entertain our friend.'

Pappenheim swallowed hard and emitted a guttural noise as of getting into his bottom gear.

'I like so much the English understatement,' he said. 'Entertain. Ho, ho.'

Another grinding from his throat, and now he was moving in second.

'You have had a disagreeable visitor,' he announced to Daniel.

'Why should I discuss it with you?'

Pappenheim was not at all perturbed by the hostility in Daniel's voice.

'Because I can help you. Let me tell you,' he said, 'that when the new German Army shall be fully existing I shall be an important person in what you call its Intelligence.'

Daniel received this in sulky silence.

'This means that I am already privileged to have much information. I can tell you of some matters which you are needing to know.'

'The only thing I need is to be left in peace. By all of you.'

'You'd better listen,' said Percival from the trolley: 'you really had.'

'And where do you come in?'

'The Oberleutnant and I,' said Pappenheim, 'have discovered, since the night of the feast here, that we are of mutual assistance.'

'What's that supposed to mean?'

'Let's say,' said Percival, 'that we have interests in common. Now sit quiet like a good boy and listen to what the kind German gentleman is telling you.'

'Ja,' said Pappenheim. 'You have no doubt been told that when Professor Dortmund died the Nazi authorities were assured that no one could understand his work and that it had in any case no scientific application."

'Nor has it.'

'You will know more than I do about that. Nevertheless, in

1944 a rumour started in some scientific circles that Dortmund's theories, if properly worked upon, might indeed have surprising practical results. So there come some high-ranking visitors to the University here; but once again the Professors said that there was nothing to be done with the Dortmund papers, and they repeated that Dortmund had been at the end very sick. And since this was 1944 and there were more urgent things to give worry, the matter was again put by.'

'On what possible ground,' said Daniel, 'was it supposed that Dortmund's theories might lead to "practical results"?'

'That I cannot tell you. The fact remains that it was believed, and believed strongly enough for the rumour to stay alive, in some quarters, until this very day.'

'Nobody reputable has ever suggested—'

'—I did not say the quarters were reputable. Quite the reverse. It was the Nazis who listened to the rumour in 1944, and the rumour is part of their legacy.'

Pappenheim wrinkled his scalp into an expression of disapproval and sorrow.

'A legacy,' he said, 'which not everyone has renounced as thoroughly as we like the world to think.'

Percival came over with the chafing dish and helped all three of them to slices of veal cooked in cream and mushrooms..

'You see,' he said wistfully to Daniel, 'why you are so sought after?'

He fetched two bottles of wine and started to pour.

'Eat it while it's hot,' he said. 'Otherwise it's apt to congeal.'

It was so hot that it burned Daniel's tongue.

'Von Bremke?' he spluttered.

'Drink some wine . . . Not as far as we are aware. Von Bremke has always been a neutral figure – wouldn't you say, Herr Pappenheim?'

'The Herr Doktor was among those who urged, in 1944, that nothing was to be gained from further enquiry into the papers.'

'He's been urging that lately,' said Daniel. 'Though when I first came he was more encouraging.'

'Perhaps he was. But perhaps he now has some notion

about the . . . outside interest . . . you have aroused, and is try-ing, in his discreet and neutral way, to give you warning.'

'Against what, for Christ's sake?'

'Inquisitive men,' said Percival, 'who are liable to turn nasty if they don't get their way.'

'But it's all so childish,' Daniel whined. 'There is nothing to turn nasty about. My results – if ever I'm left alone to get them – will be about as practical as Clarabelle Cow.'

'Who is this Fraulein Cow?'

Percival said something in German.

'Ho, ho. Your English humour. But,' said Pappenheim fiercely to Daniel, 'it is not so funny after all. Listen. Because of some things which have happened in the war, I am not en-tirely trusted. Pappenheim, they say, he could be one of those who does not wish to forget. And so, to show them they are wrong, I am giving all my time, for five years now, to finding out about those people . . . who do not wish to forget. Who want back the Germany of 1939. Now, to want such a thing is to want, as you say, the moon, and to want the moon you must have faith. Crazy faith. Once you have that you will believe anything you wish to believe, and these people wish to be-lieve that there is a secret in the Dortmund papers which can help to make them powerful once again. If you tell them there is no such secret, they will not listen. They will tear you into pieces to find it. I know these people. You must believe me, Herr Mond; you must trust me.'

But Daniel saw a long line of cattle trucks rolling through the night to Erfurt, and Pappenheim, ten years younger, yap-ping orders through the door of a first class compartment to a faceless group with knee boots and sub-machine guns. He might or might not believe him; he would never trust him.

'You are thinking,' said Pappenheim, 'the same as all you English. "He was one of them." Yes, Herr Mond, I was one of them. I did not complain. I joined no conspiracies against them. I did whatever they told me because I was afraid of being shot dead. And so now that they are defeated and gone I do not want them back. I am just as sincere in my way, you see, as you are.'

Daniel shook his head and pursed his mouth.

'These ... recidivists,' he said. 'Who are they? Where are they?'

'They are Germans and they are everywhere in Germany. There are not yet many of them but they are widespread and determined. And if there is encouragement, others will join them. If they should make some success ... if they should have something – like this secret – which would enable them to deal with our Government, with other Governments ...'

'I've told you: there is no secret. Not in the way they mean.'

'And I have told you: they will not choose to believe this.'

Percival collected their plates and set down a dish of interesting cheeses.

'The truth is, Mond,' he said, 'that either way you're up the creek.'

'But this is ludicrous. You can't tell me that this country, to say nothing of the occupying powers, is incapable of disciplining its lunatic fringes.'

'Disciplining?' said Percival. 'What naughty words you left-wingers use when you're upset.'

'I'm not upset.'

'Good. Because there's more to come. You see, a lot of people ... Americans, for example ... who have invested heavily in Europe and its recovery, are rather uneasy just now. About Communism and so forth.'

'Reactionary elements.'

'Let's just say worried. Even the dear old British Labour Party makes them nervous. So like all greedy capitalists they are keeping a careful eye on their investments ... which is harmless and conventional enough. But within the large organization necessary for this purpose there are bound to be shades of opinion, variations of policy and method; and since operations are secret, operators not always strictly accountable, it is not easy to control these.'

'People can be disci— Dismissed.'

'Not,' said Percival, 'if they have made themselves indispensable. Let us take a case in point. A highly skilled American director of agents, who has an impressive war-time record and an unrivalled knowledge of this country, who since 1945 has continued to do invaluable work ... but who holds (alas) to rather embarrassing political theories. One of these has to do with what used to be called the Balance of Power: you know, if there's a giant strutting around in seven-league boots, then when no one's looking you lend the dwarf a banana skin. To cripple the giant and make him more appreciative of your investment.' He flashed his glasses at Daniel. 'Have some more brie.'

'You're saying ... that the American secret service here in West Germany is supporting neo-Fascism? To impede democratic progress?'

'That would be grossly overstating it. All I'm saying is that from time to time, illicitly but very discreetly, the resources of one American director and his branch are being used to equip malignant political dwarves with banana skins. And sometimes even with landmines. Herr Pappenheim is very anxious that you shouldn't tread on one.'

'Earle Restarick?'

'Exactly so,' said Pappenheim with a smug purr.

'The whole thing should be publicly exposed.'

Both Percival and Pappenheim sighed deeply.

'First of all you'd have to prove it exists. You might as well try to net the old man of the sea.'

'You almost seem,' said Daniel, 'to approve of it.'

'Naturally one admires professional expertise. But we've told you where we stand. We want to help you – and you don't appear very grateful.'

'Because I can't take it seriously. For the sake of argument, I'll grant what you say about these Nazi survivals and even about this American group which helps them sometimes. But why should the Americans interest themselves in anything so preposterous as this mythical secret? Why should they help these Fascists to pester me?'

'The director is a romantic, so perhaps he believes in the old rumour. He is also rather eccentric: he doesn't like Jews.'

Daniel lowered his head. This at least he was ready to believe.

'So consider,' said Percival. 'On the one hand some fanatical Germans, supported, however unofficially, by American money and resources. On the other hand . . . you. Don't you think you should accept Herr Pappenheim's offer?'

'What is his offer?'

'The same,' said Pappenheim, 'as I would have made to you the other night – if you had been more patient. Protection. My department does not yet exist officially, but I can promise you that.'

'Does nothing have official existence in your world?'

'That is its charm,' Percival observed. 'It's something the British are very bad at understanding – which is incidentally the reason why I myself can't offer you what Pappenheim can. British Intelligence over here is all on an official basis and therefore woefully clumsy. Men in bowler hats and policemen's boots. The Labour Administration dug up our wartime network. They said it was immoral.'

'Good for them. And just who and what are you?'

'A junior officer serving in a battalion of infantry. What could be more official and above-board than that?' Percival wagged his chin. 'Now I think – don't you? – that you should say thank you to Herr Pappenheim for being so kind.'

'Herr Pappenheim,' said Daniel slowly, 'says he will protect me. This also means, I take it, that he would help me if I wanted to leave Germany and . . . the others . . . tried to stop me?'

'Very much what we had in mind. On one condition, of course.'

Pappenheim gave Percival a warning look, but he shook his head.

'No, Herr Pappenheim. When Englishmen make an agreement, they like to get all the clauses straight from the start. It saves ill feeling or disappointment later on. On one condition,' he said to Daniel: 'that before you leave you tell us what you don't want to tell them.'

Daniel jerked to his feet.

'*You* believe it too,' he shouted; '*you* think there's something you can use.'

He walked away along the black table.

'I might have known. Why else should you offer your help?'
Percival lifted the candelabrum from the table and followed Daniel.

'The lights are all out,' he said; 'if you'll allow me to show you the way . . .'

As they came to the top end of the table, the candles lit the crossed colours on the wall. Tonight they were furled and sheathed in tubes of black leather which were tipped with brass. Underneath them the infant Prince Charles played with his woolly ball.

'If you change your mind,' Percival said, 'you know where to find me.'

But Daniel did not hear him. He was standing absolutely still, while the cold sweat started down his thighs from his crutch, and looking at the photograph of Prince Charles, at the ball with its strands of wool. Knitted, woven, somehow intermingled to form a central core and then to protrude, singly but very close together, at the surface; with the result that the surface looked continuous, until inspection revealed that it was made up of thousands of little woollen dots. The sweat poured down his calves to his ankles. Christ. Jesus Christ.

'Do you want to sit down again? Or shall I ring for a taxi? You don't look at all well.'

'That's because I've got a lot on my mind,' said Daniel, the buttocks quivering beneath him: 'I think I'd like to walk.'

Part Four

THE OO-WOO STUBE

To celebrate their return from Exercise Broomstick, Giles Glastonbury decided to give his officers a party, to which he also bade Daniel and Doctor Motley, at the Oo-Woo Stube. This interesting establishment was in Hannover, and Giles accordingly booked rooms for the night in a large hotel near Hannover station, so that his guests might recuperate in comfort and return to Göttingen at their leisure.

At first Daniel was not at all keen to go. In so far as he could make sense of his situation and the new elements of which Percival and Pappenheim had (truthfully or untruthfully?) apprised him, it now seemed more than ever desirable that he should finish up and get out. There was no time for larking about in Hannover and limping home with a crapula. Besides, it could hardly be his kind of evening, since the staples of the Oo-Woo's entertainment (he understood) were tarts and gambling. But his affection for the friends whom he had hardly seen in ten days, his pride in being invited by their leader to their private celebration, overcame his objections: and after all, as Julian James pointed out, this would be the last 'significant spree' for some time; for now that Broomstick was done, there must be intensive preparations, in the light of what they had learned or failed to learn from it, for Apocalypse, which was only just over three weeks away.

So late in the afternoon of September the first, Daniel found himself waiting on Göttingen station for Fielding Gray. Julian was driving the other two subalterns to Hannover in his Citroen, Giles was taking Mick Motley in his Bentley. Although either car would have had ample room for Daniel and Fielding, it was apparently assumed that after the separation imposed by Broomstick they would sooner have the journey to themselves.

'He's had to stay behind at Divisional Headquarters,' Giles had said, half apologetic and half conspiratorial, 'but he'll meet you at the station here at 5.15. These German trains are really quite comfortable and you've probably got things to talk about.'

Which was true enough, Daniel now reflected, as he watched Fielding march down the platform towards him in an arrogant brown felt hat. *But how much can I tell him? How much do I want to tell him?* Although Fielding, unlike Jacquiz Helmut, would not automatically incline to scepticism or scorn, Daniel had an unpleasant feeling that, should he seem to be asking for help, Fielding would quietly duck out. Where difficulties were theoretical, or where only advice was sought, Fielding was a shrewd counsellor; but if it came to action, inconvenience, commitment . . .? Sadly, Daniel remembered Jacquiz's remarks about the Dragoon officers who had returned home in mid-campaign rather than tolerate discomfort.

'Broomstick,' said Fielding briskly, 'was a fiasco.'

'Oh? Giles seemed content when I saw him.'

'The Squadron did all right. But the Fusiliers just farted about.'

'I thought they were so reliable.'

'At doing things by numbers. But when a little flexibility, a little imagination is required . . . They spend the whole time saluting each other and forming themselves into three ranks.'

'Suppose it had been real,' Daniel said diffidently, 'then the familiar discipline might have helped to keep them sane.'

Fielding gave him a sharp look. The train came in.

'First class.'

'I've taken a second class ticket,' Daniel said.

'Then you can pay the difference.'

'You seem rather prickly this afternoon.'

Fielding flushed with annoyance.

'I'm *not* prickly. Just fed up with exhibitions of incompetence. Fusiliers who can't read their maps. People who buy the wrong tickets.'

The train pulled out. The phallus-tipped tower in Daniel's street seemed to quiver for a moment, as if it were going to stretch out over the intervening roofs and yank him back to his duty. Remembering that Fielding had had a large part in preparing Exercise Broomstick, Daniel decided to forgive his ill temper and sit it out in silence.

'They haven't realized,' Fielding grumbled, 'that modern war is going to be a matter of small groups which must move very fast and act independently. That any man's got to be ready to set off on his own at a moment's notice. I asked one of their platoon commanders to send an N.C.O. and three men to set up a check point two miles away. The N.C.O., a senior corporal mark you, was scared out of his wits. The platoon commander took me on one side, said his men wouldn't be able to find their way there by themselves. All right, I said, Trooper Lamb would take them in the Land Rover. But, said the platoon commander, they won't be able to find their way back: the platoon will have moved by then. All right, Lamb could bring them back too. But, he said, my men will be unhappy away from their mates. As though they could all spend the entire exercise huddled together like sheep.'

'What happened?'

'In the end I had to detail some of my own men, who were badly needed for something else, and tell the Fusiliers to get on with the only thing they *can* do – digging bunkers. We didn't want the bunkers but they had to do something, and they were all happy as field-mice. Then their C.O. came along and said, "Glad of some good men to do the spade work, eh? Can't see any of your chaps helping." I could have shot him.'

Daniel imagined the Fusilier Colonel's lugubrious head popping like a balloon in a shooting gallery and went into a cascade of giggles. This cheered Fielding up.

'Sorry I was bloody,' he said. 'How have you got on, Danny? You look rather tired.'

'I've had several surprises. Disagreeable ones.'

'Dortmund was off the rails after all?'

'No. It might have been better if he had been. It's more as though he'd suddenly switched on to an utterly unexpected branch line . . . which led away into a fairie country. You know that poem of Browning's about Childe Roland riding to the Dark Tower? You get a feeling that he's passed into a region which isn't shown on any map, that he'll never be able to return.'

Fielding looked at him carefully.

'All you mean,' he said, 'is that things are not working out quite the way you thought.'

'That's certainly true. But they're working out. Oh yes, they're working out.' Daniel gave an awkward little laugh. 'You see, the other night I had a kind of . . . revelation. There was a picture I was looking at, and all at once I knew, *knew*, what Dortmund was after, as though he himself had suddenly appeared with a diagram. Since then everything's fitted as closely as a jigsaw puzzle. It's only a matter of a few days now, checking and confirming and tying a loose end or two, and the whole thing should be finished.'

'Then you ought to be very pleased.'

'That's just it. It's all so very different from what I thought. Everything's changed, Fielding.'

'Might one ask how?'

'It's not the material, it's the way of looking at it. If you set a particle in motion, it makes a definite path, a thread through space. At a given instant you can *either* say, as we usually do and as I have been doing, that we have such and such particles in such and such positions; *or* you can think of it in terms of these threads having reached certain points in the course of their elongation.'

'Like a plate of spaghetti?'

'Yes, except that each strand is growing all the time, and the truth at any given moment is not the entire mass of the spaghetti – that represents the past – but only the positions occupied by the end of each strand and the pattern which these points make up.'

'Where will all this get you? Effectively you've still only got a set of particles in certain positions.'

'You remember,' said Daniel, 'that Dortmund is concerned with very small quantities?'

' "Zeta" you called it. Something which is as small as it can be without disappearing altogether.'

'More or less. Well, I thought this "zeta" was to express

the entities he wanted to deal with. That wasn't quite right. "Zeta" applied to these strands: it is the smallest possible amount by which a strand can be lengthened. It expresses the development of a strand from one instant to the next.'

'A different way of looking at things, as you said. You'll forgive me, Daniel, but I don't see anything so very mysterious in all this.'

Daniel swallowed hard.

'Suppose ... suppose you followed a strand of spaghetti backwards. Retraced its path with your eye. For a time you'd be able to follow it all right, but then you'd lose it in the labyrinthine muddle made by the rest of the spaghetti. But if you retraced this path in the smallest possible segments – zeta by zeta, so to speak – you could never lose it. You could trace it right back to its origin.'

'And so?'

'And so, Fielding, if I take a certain kind of space – any kind of space – and a particle which is moving in it, that particle has a previous path which I can explore back, zeta by zeta, as far as I wish. I can never lose it. And unlike a strand of spaghetti, that path won't just end somewhere on the bottom of a plate.'

'Rather sinister, put like that . . .'

'There could be metaphysical implications. Dortmund never got round to these, or I don't think so. Neither have I. Yet.'

'Don't look so depressed about it. Anyone would think you expected to find the Devil at the end of the thread.'

'There's a sense in which somebody might. The kind of person who isn't interested in metaphysics.'

'Daniel? I don't—'

'—Ten days to finish off,' said Daniel, tense and abrupt, suddenly conscious that the comfort of companionship had beguiled him into going too far. 'Two weeks at most. Then I shall go. The sooner the better.'

Fielding's face flushed with pain.

'Just like that? You sound ... *glad* to be rid of us.'

The train stopped in Hannover station. They walked in silence along the platform and down into a tunnel-way crammed with summer flesh, brown and ripe beneath brief liederhosen. Zigarren. Dortmunder. Bieren. Reisebüro. Stadtplan. Into the open. Ernst August on his horse, pale green in the evening sun, father of his folk.

'The Central-Hotel, Giles said. Look half-left from the equestrian statue, he said, and you can't miss it.'

'There's something you haven't told me, Daniel. I always knew you'd be glad to get back to Cambridge, but now . . . you . . . sound . . . different. Feverish. There's more changed than you've said.'

'Much more. There it is. Just over the street.'

'Then tell me.'

Fielding's voice was peevish, as it had been on Göttingen station.

'Funny thing,' said Daniel, remembering this; 'there was no inspector on the train to check the tickets. Unusual in Germany.'

'Don't you trust me?'

'Yes. But I don't want to tell you. I'm sorry if I've roused your curiosity, but it's for your good not to know. I wish to God I didn't.'

Fielding flushed again and bit his lip.

'You're quite sure it's as . . . serious . . . as you think?'

'Quite.'

They crossed the tram-lines to the Central-Hotel.

The Oo-Woo Stube was something of a surprise. Daniel had been led to believe that it boasted a bar for the sale of drink and women and an inner room in which, roulette being forbidden in Hannover, some variant of Boule was played; and he had wondered why Giles Glastonbury, who took an educated interest in his pleasures, should have thought such a place worth a special visit. He now found out. Beyond the gambling room was another bar, champagne only, and a tiny theatre, in which one could watch, at intervals of half an hour and for a charge of fifty marks a time, a selection of ingenious and obscene cabaret acts. Giles, the perfect host, had paid a lump sum and arranged that members of his party should be admitted to the theatre as and when they chose throughout the evening.

'It's a hangover,' Giles explained to Daniel, 'from the gay days just after the war. They'll stop it any time now. Any minute, I wouldn't wonder. I hope it's still going when Detterling passes through.'

'Detterling?'

'Didn't anyone tell you? Captain Detterling the M.P., late of our regiment. You'll like him. He's stopping off for a night or two next week on his way to Baden Baden.'

Music struck up and the curtains parted. There was a whinnying noise from the champagne-only bar, where Messrs. Lamprey and Bungay were comfortably settled with three magnums.

'I want,' said Giles, 'to get into the front row. Just to see that nothing's faked. Coming?'

'I'm all right here, thanks.'

Julian James and Fielding Gray had disappeared. Not wishing to hurt his host's feelings, Daniel waited until the spectacle on the stage (a Roman Senator being pleasured by four female slaves) was well under way, and then slipped through to the gambling room, where Mick Motley was sitting with a huge pile of counters in front of him.

'Wretched poor game this, but it's been going for me. I'll give it a rest and buy us a drink.'

Daniel started reluctantly back towards the theatre.

'Not, if you don't mind, in there,' Mick Motley said.

They walked into the ordinary bar.

'You may think I'm old-fashioned,' Motley went on, 'but I don't approve of that sort of thing. Besides, I hate champagne.'

He ordered two brandies. When a woman sidled towards them he jerked Daniel away to a far corner where there was an empty table with only two chairs.

'It's funny,' he said. 'When these cavalry chaps got here they just about saved my life. Do you know, the Fusiliers were too snooty to talk to me. Me and my Liverpool accent. Then along came these Dragoons, who were too grand to talk to the Fusiliers but seemed to have all the time in the world for me. How do you explain that?'

'A kindred spirit. Racing, gambling . . .'

'But that's just it. That's *all* we share. In other ways I can't follow them at all. You know where Julian and Fielding have gone?'

'No.'

'To a sort of club where there are boys. I heard them talking about it at dinner.'

'Only curiosity, I expect.'

'Even so, it's disgusting. And that business through there. It's abuse of God's gift.'

Earle Restarick came in, ordered a drink at the bar, drank it down in one, waved gaily to Daniel, and went out.

'Who's that?'

'One of my fellow students from Göttingen.'

'Doesn't look your type to me. Too cocky.'

'He's American.'

'Ah . . . Where was I?'

'Abuse,' said Daniel, 'of God's gift.'

'Yes. Well, you see it's not that I'm a prude. But I believe in doing things the natural way and doing them privately. A man can have all the fun he needs like that.'

'And do you, Mick?'

'The Fusilier wives,' said Motley with a hot look. 'When they meet me in public, they're as snooty as their husbands. Worse. But they're always ringing up in the afternoon . . . "Doctor, I've got such a terrible headache." So along I pop with my little black bag, and there they are, all alone and hardly able to keep their hands out of my fly for ten seconds.' Motley giggled. 'And the other rank wives are just the same. But one has to be more careful there, of course.'

'But this,' said Daniel, 'is adultery. Surely an abuse of God's gift?'

'Mortal sin, yes, but not *too* bad as long as you don't try to avoid the consequences. By doing unnatural things or using contraceptives.'

'Now you *have* surprised me.'

'I know. And it would surprise Giles and the rest of them too. That's why I can't think what they see in me.'

'It could be,' said Daniel, 'that they simply find you likeable.'

'Oh,' said Motley: 'do you think so?'

'Or,' said Daniel, annoyed by this disingenuousness, 'perhaps they think it prudent, what with the lives they lead, to have a physician dancing attendance.'

Motley considered this without taking offence. Julian and Fielding came in.

'Nothing but tram-conductors and middle-aged waiters,' Julian said, while Fielding glanced spitefully at Daniel. 'I shall stick to Giles's hospitality from now on. Do you suppose he'll stand me one of these women?'

'You can perfectly well afford one yourself,' said Fielding.

'That's not the point. It's Giles's party.'

Giles came in.

'Quite good, that first turn,' he said. 'And the next will be even better. Two niggers in a girls' school, the man promised. I *do* hope they don't close down before Detterling comes.'

'A Member of Parliament watching that filth?' snorted Motley. 'Unthinkable.'

Everyone laughed at such naïveté.

'The trouble is,' said Giles, 'that we'll all be so busy in barracks by the time Detterling arrives. Perhaps you can bring him, Daniel?'

Daniel shrugged non-committally. Bungay and Lamprey came in.

'Very lust-making,' they said.

'That reminds me,' said Julian to Giles. 'Does one have to pay for one's own women, or are you treating?'

But this question was never to be answered. Two tall, blond men, having moved silently from the bar, were now confronting the group round Daniel and Motley. One of the men inclined himself toward Daniel.

'Disgusting Jew,' the man said softly.

Giles Glastonbury shivered and his face went mottled.

'You're talking to my guest.'

'Who is nevertheless a disgusting Jew. But if you think him worth the trouble, you know what you can do about it.' He clicked his heels. 'Von Augsburg. My friend here will make the arrangements.'

Von Augsburg went out. It had all happened so quickly that it was only when the second German began to speak that any of them realized what was in train.

'In the bombed area along the Limmerstrasse,' said the second man in a calm, reasonable tone, 'there is a place which we often use. It was once a stable, but now—'

'—Stop this nonsense,' said Fielding, who was the first really to grasp what was being said. 'Either apologize for your friend or get out. But stop this childish talk.'

'It doesn't matter,' said Daniel. 'For God's sake don't let's have any trouble.'

'It is,' said the tall blond, 'for this gentleman to say.'

He looked straight at Giles, who said nothing.

'I am waiting, sir.'

'Five-thirty tomorrow morning,' Giles said. 'Send a man—'

'—Giles, for Christ's sake—'

'—Send a man to meet us outside the Central-Hotel, or we shan't find the way.'

The blond bowed.

'Good. The weapon, sir, to be the sabre.'

'Suits me. And no padding.'

'Giles, please be sensible. Be your age.'

'Excuse me, sir, but for many years in these affairs—'

'—If we're going to do this,' said Giles, 'we'll do it properly. Your man picked a fight and now he's got it. No neck guards and no padding. Bare buff. That's how we used to do it where I come from.'

Daniel felt a ridiculous and tearful urge to cheer which he at once suppressed.

'Please, Giles,' he said. 'I really don't mind. Stop all this before it's too late.'

'You may not mind,' said Giles Glastonbury, 'but by God, I do.' And to the blond, 'Five-thirty then.'

'Very good, sir. We shall try to arrange a doctor.'

'No need,' said Mick Motley. 'I'm one.'

'You keep clear of this, Mick,' said Giles. 'It could land you in trouble.'

'I wouldn't miss it for the world,' Mick Motley said.

Shuffle, shuffle; beat. Beat . . . beat, and shuffle.

On three sides they were enclosed by damaged yet still substantial walls. On the fourth they were screened by two large piles of rubble, a gap between which revealed an apparently interminable prospect of desolation. Somewhere, only a few hundred yards from them, a city was waking to a new day; yet the intervening no man's land of broken bricks had insulated them totally. They might have been the last men on the last morning of the world.

Beat . . . beat, shuffle, beat. Shuffle, shuffle: beat.

At one end of the wrecked enclosure were Mick Motley, Fielding Gray, and Daniel; Giles had forbidden his subalterns to be present. At the other end, a sheaf of sabres under his arm, stood the German who had negotiated with them the previous evening and a tubby little man who had guided them here from the Central-Hotel. In between, stripped to the waist, the swordsmen danced.

Beat, shuffle; beat, shuffle; beat.

It was not the dance that Daniel expected. He had fatuously imagined the rapid thrust and parry, the nimble circling movements, of a Fairbanks Jnr. encounter on the screen, and was surprised, rather disappointed, at the cumbrous exercise which he was now watching. For several seconds at a time the heavy sabres would stay crossed and still, except for a slight quiver which gave them an appearance of prying antennae. Then, as though some piece of essential intelligence had passed back down his blade and into his arm, one or other of the fencers would disengage and execute, almost in slow motion, it seemed, a ponderous lunge or cut; upon which his opponent, also in slow motion, would move his weapon to parry with an ugly clack, retiring his back foot and then his front over perhaps twelve inches of the gritty floor. They kept,

Daniel noticed, always in the same axis: something (convention, honour, a mere limitation of technique?) disqualified lateral movements whether for evasion or attack.

Beat ... beat ... beat. Shuffle, shuffle: beat.

He had come, Daniel supposed, because he was the ultimate cause of what was doing. He was not responsible, he had tried to stop it, but he was the cause, and rightly or wrongly he felt that he should be present to see what passed and bear his champion what aid he might. Secretly and guiltily he was excited and flattered; nor had he properly considered, even yet, what nuisance or scandal such an affair might bring about. And what a story to tell Jacquiz! *'In the end, of course, it was all very childish and they stopped as soon as one of them was scratched. Still, Jacquiz, it's not every day that one is the subject of a duel.' 'I must say, Daniel ... a privilege. The Glastonburys have always been noted as duellists – one of them called out Cumberland but Prinny put his foot down. And of course Giles fenced for the Army, so you had an exhibition of real style.'*

Shuffle ... shuffle ... beat.

Who had told him that Giles fenced for the Army? Fielding, of course, as they were coming downstairs in the hotel. 'So with any luck it'll be all right,' Fielding had said. 'He can play about with the German, then slice a millimetre off his hide and call it a day.' Well, all Daniel could say was that if this was top-level fencing he didn't think much of it. It was beginning to be a bore; let Giles slice off his millimetre so that they could all go home to breakfast.

Shuffle. Beat.

The only trouble was, as even Daniel now began to notice, that Giles's movements were becoming slower, sweatier and clumsier with every exchange, whereas the German remained as cool and as deft – in so far as one could be deft with these clanking great weapons – as he had been at the start. Von Augsburg was beginning to tease Giles, and Giles was losing his bate. A particularly loutish cut at the German's ribs was easily parried, and Giles was all but caught by a vicious riposte. Von Augsburg grinned; Giles, mottled and furious, dragged himself back two steps. The German pursued; Giles

grunted and swept wildly at his head, leaving his whole body
exposed; and although, once again, he was just in time to
parry the riposte aimed at his stomach, the two further steps
he now retreated were made with a shambling feebleness which
showed that he was at the end of his strength. His knees were
trembling, his sword-arm drooping, his chest heaving, his
mouth dribbling. With a broad smile of anticipation, his tongue
protruding slightly through his teeth, von Augsburg surveyed
the plump, slimy torso before him, like a butcher's favoured
customer at leisure to choose his cut. Giles made one last
desperate thrust straight for the German's navel; and von
Augsburg, with casual grace, rolled his wrist down for a
simple parry – only to find Giles's blade, which had swerved
up over his guard, sawing along the tendons of his neck.

'Oldest trick in the book,' said Fielding to Daniel: 'let them
think you're beaten and wait for 'em to get careless.'

But Mick Motley had seen more than Fielding had.

'Get an ambulance and fucking quick,' he shouted as he
ran for the staggering German.

Fielding moved off between the two piles of rubble. Motley
busied himself with a small black bag which the tubby German
produced. Daniel confronted Giles.

'It's not serious really?' Daniel said.

Giles did not answer.

'You didn't mean it?' Daniel persisted.

'He shouldn't have smiled like that,' Giles Glastonbury
said.

Some thirty hours after these events, Daniel was visited at
his lodgings in Göttingen by a very large Englishman with a
very small head.

'Tuck,' announced the large Englishman: 'Control Commission. Liaison Branch.'

He produced an elaborate identity card to support this
claim.

'My job,' he explained importantly, 'is to regulate the relations between British Military personnel and German civilians.'

'I'm neither.'

'You're involved with both. This business in Hannover.'

'What about it?'

'You'll hear what in a moment,' said Tuck in a bullying way, 'but let me first advise you to change your tone. You may think, like a lot of people, that the Control Commission's finished with—'

'—It's nothing to me either way.'

Tuck's shoulders heaved until his head almost disappeared between them.

'I have authority,' he boomed, 'equivalent to that of a lieutenant-colonel, and I am acting, in this instance, in concert with the consular service. Now then. There is a young German in a hospital at Hannover, and it's quite possible that he'll die there. Whether he does or not, grave embarrassment has been caused. It is thought that you are possessed of information which has bearing on the matter.'

'I was there, if that's what you mean.'

'Then you are to hold yourself in readiness to give evidence before a properly constituted board of enquiry.'

'When?'

'That,' said Tuck, 'nobody knows.' This pronouncement gave him a satisfaction which considerably softened his manner. 'You see, five years ago, even with a German civilian involved, it would certainly have been a matter for Court Martial. Five years hence, God help us, we shall probably have to kow-tow to the German judiciary. But just now,' he said, with profound relish for the type of confusion which, throughout history, had brought him and his kind a fat living, 'just now things are *transitional*. So an enquiry is to be held at which there will be German legal representatives, British legal and military representatives, diplomatic representatives, liaison representatives, welfare representatives, representatives, in short, of every conceivable interest involved. They will establish what happened and the forensic implications thereof, decide what sort of trial there is to be, and where. *When*, that is, we manage to get them all together.'

'As far as I'm concerned they'd better be quick. I'm off in a week or so.'

'Oh no, you're not,' said Tuck, reverting to the bully. 'It is essential that we show the Germans that we are acting in good faith. So we have guaranteed that all British witnesses will remain in Germany until the enquiry is convened.'

'And if I just go?'

'You'll be detained at your port of egress by the German police, and no British authority will interfere on your behalf. All that's already arranged.'

'I see,' said Daniel, who suddenly felt a hundred and seventy years old.

Tuck smiled. That is to say, a horizontal incision appeared in his wizened little head.

'But of course,' he said, 'if you wish to claim that there are special circumstances . . . of a compassionate nature, perhaps . . .'

'I'm just anxious to be gone.'

'Important business or professional commitments? I am empowered to recognize those. Are they so important, I wonder, that you'd be prepared to . . . er . . . deposit five hundred pounds with me as security?'

'I haven't got five hundred pounds.'

'I thought not,' said Tuck with a snap; 'so you'd better stay put, hadn't you? And a tiny word in your ear. If you do try anything on, we'll not only back the German police but we'll impound your passport for the next five years. We've got important work to do,' he said, blowing out his chest, 'and we're not going to tolerate any nonsense from the likes, Mr. Daniel bloody Mond, of you.'

About half an hour after Tuck's departure, Earle Restarick arrived.

'You see?' he said. 'I told you we wouldn't let you leave.'

'You mean—?'

'—I mean that we fixed the whole thing. We planted those two Germans in the Oo-Woo Stube. Of course, there was no guarantee that your chum would rise to it. But there was nothing to lose if he didn't, and once he did . . . Well, you've seen for yourself.'

'You reckoned on a duel?'

'Or something similar. A big enough row – with you in the middle of it – to call for official action. My employers remembered what I'd always told them, that the British feel mightily obligated to their guests. Not that I'll have any credit.'

'At least,' said Daniel maliciously, 'your man got more than he bargained for.'

'More than he bargained for, perhaps, but not more than my employers did. They wanted quite a splash, you see. They knew Major Glastonbury was a fighter and they selected von Augsburg as just the man to bring him out at his fiercest.'

'Funny,' mused Daniel. 'I should never have thought Giles had it in him. He always seemed so mild.'

'He had a bad streak. They often do in those old families of yours, and anyway it was on the record. He shot one of his own men during the war. Found him asleep while he was meant to be on guard, and shot him just like that.'

'I'm sure there was excellent military precedent for such a proceeding.'

This blasé comment was not an affectation; the events of the last two days had so numbed Daniel, for the time, that he was beyond being shocked by anything.

'In extreme situations, yes. Which is why he's still serving. But you'll agree that it takes an unusual temperament to shoot a comrade while he sleeps.'

'To say nothing of arranging for a comrade to be sliced up with a sabre. Ingenious, I grant you.' Daniel's temporary numbness had brought not only moral atrophy but also freedom from fear. 'But I don't suppose,' he went on, 'that you've come here to discuss the niceties of your profession. What is it you want?'

'Just to remind you that my employers have been as good as their word. They said they'd stop you leaving and they have. So hadn't you better tell them what they want to know?'

'I've nothing to tell.'

'That's not what that nice Curator in the library thinks.'

'Those librarians spend far too much time gossiping about

things they don't understand. Between them,' said Daniel gaily, 'they've apparently been broadcasting daily statements about my progress round half the Electorate of Hannover. But they only know what documents I ask for. Supposing I couldn't make head or tail of them?'

'Then my employers,' said Earle, 'will be very disappointed. So disappointed that I really couldn't answer for their actions. On the other hand, Daniel, they're not unreasonable. They quite see that you must have a proper opportunity to check back over your work and write it all up in a fair round hand. So they'll be happy to wait until this enquiry convenes. As that man Tuck doubtless told you – he's quite genuine, by the way – this will probably be some time, so you can't say you're being hurried. But don't abuse my employers' patience, Danny. You know how – what was your word? – *ingenious* they can be when they try.'

By the next day Daniel's blithe indifference had worn off, like the effect of a dentist's injection, and the nerves were starting to ache.

When Earle had left him, he had still regarded the Hannover episode as too unreal to have any consequences; even Tuck's official pronouncement on the subject had failed to convince him that it was more than a dream. It had happened in another country; or in a bubble of time, as it were, that had floated for an instant over the rubble, then burst and for ever ceased to exist. But the reality behind the dream started to make itself felt when Trooper Lamb arrived in the Land Rover with a note which excused Fielding from dinner that evening. He was now in charge of the Squadron, Fielding wrote, and up to his neck in work; Giles was in close arrest and relieved of his command indefinitely; they were all (he understood) to be brought before a board of enquiry; and he, Fielding, though for the time being he enjoyed the benefit of the doubt, might have some awkward questions to answer about his own role, which amounted to that of second and could be held to make him a guilty party.

At first this communication summoned up an almost laughable picture of Giles in a bare room contemplating a whisky bottle and a revolver; but when Daniel re-read it, he found that the use of phrases such as 'close arrest', 'indefinitely', 'guilty party', was less dramatic than functional; a disagreeable situation was being soberly described. In so far as he still refused to believe in this situation, he was sharply set right the next morning, when a uniformed despatch rider presented him, in return for his signature, with an imposing document which amounted to a subpoena given under the authority of the British Occupation with the full recognition and consent of the German civilian power. Or *vice versa*. Either way, the word of Tuck was upheld and Daniel Mond was trapped.

When this was fully borne in on him, Daniel attempted, in mounting misery, to cut away all accretions of fantasy and emotion and to calculate exactly where he now stood. He had found the answer to the Dortmund papers; it was not the answer which he had expected and which would have had only abstract significance, but something which, he did not doubt, could open up whole new areas of scientific discovery and exploitation. The method which Dortmund had invented could be used to seek out . . . what? He was still not absolutely certain, but after what had already been done either he himself or another, if made privy to his work, could find out in a matter of hours. It was, then, too late to turn back. Destroy everything he had written? It was written on his mind. Refuse to tell of it? But he was not strong enough, he knew, to endure pain, and pain, in one form or another, was what . . . 'they' . . . held in store for him. So tell them false? They would not be deceived for very long.

Well then. Pappenheim and Percival had promised help. But on their terms. Presumably they represented what passed for decency, the Western Alliance, 'our side', and certainly it were better the secret should go to them than to the others. Better, but still very bad; for if once it were known, by anyone, it could be used. No. If it was as momentous as he had reason to think, then he must never speak it. Never? They've got you where they want you, Danny boy: you're good and stuck.

Why was it that the low, the trivial, the greedy always

turned out to be right? For years such people had scented something here to their purpose. For years himself and those like him had replied that there was nothing, that it was simply an unsolved problem of interest only to the mind. He had believed this, sincerely and passionately he had believed it, and he had set himself to find the solution with the dedication of a scholar who unravels a tongue long dead and unknown, that thereby knowledge may be increased and celebrated for its own sweet sake. But now the lovingly deciphered tablets had yielded a hideous rune to raise the powers of the deep; the scholar must creep away in shame, and the low men, the grinning and the greasy and the cunning, had come, once more, into their own. Was there nothing they could not turn to their ends? Only silence, and they had long since found instruments and acids to slice and burn their way through that.

'. . . And so, Herr Doktor, I want your help.'

'What can *I* do, Herr Dominus?'

'Let me bring Restarick to you when he next comes. Then tell him that there's nothing here for those who've sent him, that there never has been, that there *can't* be.'

'I have told others that before, Herr Dominus. They did not believe me, it seems.'

'On your authority as one of the leading mathematicians in Germany . . .'

'If that authority – such as it ever was – was not accepted before, why should it be now? The only thing you can do is to convince them that you have failed. Presumably they have a mathematician of their own whom they will trust. You must take this man through your work and show him where and how you have failed.'

'Of course . . .'

'Listen to me, Earle. You must believe that I've got nowhere with all this. I didn't do too badly at the start, but since then I've got nowhere at all. Tell these . . . employers of yours . . . to send a competent mathematician along with you, and I'll show him. I'll show him just what went wrong.'

'Too easy, Danny boy. You could show him a thousand ways of getting it wrong as easy as spelling your name. We want to know what went right.'

'I'll show him that too. I'll show him everything that went right early on, all the stuff I've sent to Dirange in Cambridge, and then *he must believe me* when I explain how after that I simply lost the track.'

'You ever heard of Pascal's wager, Danny boy? You believe in God, see, and you go on believing, because you've nothing to lose if He isn't there and everything to gain if He is. Well, that's the way my employers feel about this secret . . .'

He must know the worst. He must at least find out precisely what power it was that he now had under his hand. After all, it might, it just might, be comparatively harmless. He had checked the Dortmund method through and through, he knew exactly how to use it. Set a moving particle in space, any kind of space . . . But this time it was going to be different. Take a real particle in real space; there is the thread, made by its path; follow it forward a little to determine this and that; then turn and retrace the way you have come, back to the point at which you started, and then beyond, back and back and back . . .

'. . . Officers' Mess? I want to speak to Lieutenant Percival . . . . Leonard. You know what's happened?'

'If you mean the case of the *beau sabreur*, the whole barracks is heaving with it.'

'I mean the enquiry. I'm not allowed to leave.'

'Tough titty.'

'You said . . . Could you and Pappenheim still get me out?'

'Yes. In return for what we asked.'

'I'll give you all the stuff I've given Dirange. I'll show you how well it all went up till there, and then I'll show you when and how I stuck.'

'We're not interested in failure, Mond.'

'But failure's all there is.'

'Then you tell that politely to Restarick, and perhaps they'll let you off the hook.'

'That's just it. They refuse to believe me. Christ, Leonard, I must have help.'

'Why not try your cavalry chum, Captain Gray?'

'What could he do?'

'Sweep you up into his saddle and carry you into the sunset.'

The telephone went dead.

'. . . Officers' Mess .... Fielding. When shall I see you?'

'Sorry, Daniel. All this work for Apocalypse. And I've been politely told that though I'm not under arrest like Giles, it would be tactful of me to stay in barracks.'

'But I *must* talk to you.'

'That's another thing. I think they think that we might cook something up between us to fox this enquiry.'

'Not about Giles. Something else. Can I come up and see you?'

'No, Daniel. They wouldn't like it.'

'But Fielding—'

'—*No*, for Christ's sake. Things are quite bad enough.'

'FIELDING . . .'

But again the telephone went dead.

Daniel was in the forest near the Warlocks' Grotto, looking for Julian James. Since he couldn't see Fielding, he would find Julian instead, and Julian, he knew, was in the Grotto with Trooper Lamb. If only he could find his way through all these trees. But of course! He needn't go forward, he could turn back, trace his path back, become a thread through space, threading back to where he last saw Fielding, so that he could speak to him again. Daniel was a particle in space, and Daniel was also outside it, tracing its path back. Back and back and back. There were no trees now (yet surely they had stretched to world's end?), only emptiness and, very far away, a dull red sun. In the sun was Fielding, but he would never reach him now, because the particle that was Daniel had gone as far back as it could go. There was a blinding flash which had once, aeons before, been its birth, and then Daniel, the Daniel who was watching, was alone in no-space, before the universe and before time.

'Oh God,' moaned Daniel as he woke, 'what have you let me do?'

And then, the next morning, Trooper Lamb drove down the street in the Land Rover and out stepped a cool, confident customer (the word seemed appropriate) with an air that was two parts military to one part lackadaisical.

'Detterling,' said the customer as soon as he was through Daniel's door.

'Captain Detterling? Er . . . M.P.?'

'The very same.'

'You've been expected. Giles Glastonbury was worrying in case they closed the Oo-Woo Stube before you got here.'

'I shan't have time for the Oo-Woo Stube, thank you all the same. I'm on my way to Baden Baden, and I was intending to spend two nights here visiting a unit of my old regiment. But what do I find? One of my oldest friends under house arrest, another friend confined to barracks like a common trooper, and a whole lot of gratified Fusiliers goggling and giggling like schoolboys at a public birching. A very nasty spot of trouble. Which is why I've come to see you. To get your account of the matter, and then explain to you the mildly modified version which I want you to give for the future.'

'At the enquiry?'

'If necessary.'

'Shan't I be on oath?'

'Please,' said Captain Detterling, 'do not make trivial difficulties. It is important that we get your story in line with the one the rest of them will tell. First of all, will you kindly tell me what you think happened?'

Daniel told him.

'Thank you,' said Detterling. 'Now this, in case anyone

asks you, is what *really* happened. The business in the Oo-Woo Stube remains unchanged, except that the two Huns were far more aggressive and insulting. Von Augsburg, for example, called you a filthy, Jewish, homosexual pig.'

'Rather overdoing it?'

'Courts of enquiry like everything in black and white ... Even then, Giles did not take up the challenge, until the second German called him a shit-swallowing coward in a voice that was heard all over the room. Later that night, Giles explained to you all that his sole intention in fighting this duel would be to make von Augsburg look ridiculous. He was hardly going to scratch him. Even so, he insisted that this Army doctor – what's his name?—'

'—Mick Motley—'

'—Motley should be on hand just in case, as the Germans had made no mention of medical assistance. As to the duel itself, it was quite obvious to you from the beginning that Giles was just playing with his man and waiting for the chance to inflict some quiet humiliation. It was most unfortunate that his front foot slipped on a patch of damp and turned a harmless feint into a full-bodied lunge.'

'I see,' said Daniel. 'I don't think I need object to any of that. What about Fielding and the doctor?'

'Fielding will do whatever I tell him. The doctor is grateful to you all for what he calls "a barrel-load of laughs" over the past few weeks. Being a Catholic, he can translate our motto, *Res Unius, Res Omnium,* and he is commendably clear as to its present application.'

'So now we just sit and wait for the enquiry?' Daniel said.

'No. This will be my first visit to Baden Baden since 1936,' said Detterling reproachfully, 'but I am going to give up the first three days of it while I fly back to London *via* Berlin. In both cities I shall tell certain people the unsolicited story which you have just told me. That the duel was viciously provoked, its outcome quite accidental. I think they can be got to believe this and will agree with me that it would be a waste of time and money to bother with further enquiry. But there may have to be concessions to save Teutonic face, and people may come knocking on your door for a statement. So you're quite sure you've been telling me the truth? Particularly about that most unfortunate patch of damp?'

'Quite sure,' said Daniel gleefully. '*Res Unius, Res Omnium,* as you say.'

Part Five

VENERY

FIVE days after Captain Detterling's visit, Major Giles Glastonbury was released from arrest and posted instanter to staff duties in Hong Kong; Captain Fielding Gray was confirmed in command of the 10th Sabre Squadron (until such time as it should rejoin its parent regiment), and Daniel Mond was notified, by special despatch, that he might consider the injunction against his leaving Germany 'indefinitely suspended'. Which being so, he thought, let's go while the going is good.

For all the work which he could do on the Dortmund papers and their possible application was now done. He knew what he knew. What, if anything, he was going to do with his knowledge, he must decide later. Meanwhile, there was comfort in the thought that no one else could share it, not without his personal assistance every step of the way. Even if his enemies stole or photographed the hundreds of pages which he had written over the months and which were now packed away in his suitcase, they could make nothing of them without his aid; for all of this work was in the form of rough notes, untidy and often illegible, pitted with gaps and omissions, too compressed, even at their most lucid, for the most expert mathematician to unravel. He had deliberately avoided making a formal summary or any kind of fair copy. His secret would leave Germany with him. In his head. Tomorrow. Only pain could prise it from him; and now he was free to leave the country where pain was threatened. Tomorrow. 'You know how ingenious they can be when they try.' Tonight.

Tonight? But before he went he must say good-bye to his friends on the hill. He had been much in their company; there was no knowing when they would meet again; he must do the proper thing, he must bid them to dinner and drink their health. Unwise to linger? Let it be that very evening, then,

and after dinner he would catch the night train to Hamburg
and the early morning flight on from there.

He telephoned Fielding Gray's office in the barracks, was
told by his Sergeant-Major that Fielding was out, and tried
Lieutenant Motley's Medical Inspection Centre. Yes, Mick
would be delighted to 'beat up the boys' for Daniel's farewell
dinner, sad it was so sudden, what would they do without him,
just one thing, old dear, this evening wouldn't be any good
because there was a night training scheme. Daniel hesitated.
Tomorrow then? Yes, Mick couldn't see any reason why not,
he'd tell the boys at lunch time, he'd ring back if there was a
hitch. Eight o'clock at the Alte Krone? Prima, prima, and
now here was a lance-corporal cook with a rupture and advanced impetigo.

A day lost. But did it really matter? He was free – legally
free – to leave Göttingen when he chose. The devilish thing
about his previous detention had been that 'they' had contrived to make use of official sanctions. Now he was officially
released, and if there should be the slightest reason, during
the next thirty-six hours, to anticipate being molested, he
would seek official protection. Besides, if he went off too
quickly, Earle and his colleagues would think that he was
panicking because he had something to hide; but it he hung
about a bit, he would be behaving consonantly with the attitude which he had always tried to maintain, that he had
nothing to tell and therefore nothing to fear. So he would
spend this afternoon and this evening tidying up his room
in the University building and saying good-bye to von Bremke,
tomorrow he would take a long last walk in the country for
old times' sake, and after that he would dine his friends and
catch the midnight train. A good way of ringing down the
curtain. This settled, he left his lodgings, stopped at a travel
agency to book his seat on the flight from Hamburg (as he had
supposed, there was nothing at a suitable time from Hannover),
stopped at the Alte Krone to book a table for six at eight p.m.
the next day, and went on to a friendly Gasthaus for a lunch
of assorted sausage and beer.

'. . . And so you're leaving us, Herr Dominus?'

'Yes, Herr Doktor. Tomorrow night.'

Von Bremke produced a clean handkerchief, pursed his lips, and wiped them carefully.

'You would be free to dine with me at my home before you go? This evening?'

'As it happens, yes. But—'

'—Very well, then. Here is my address.'

He handed Daniel a card.

'But, Herr Doktor. Your wife. You said—'

'—My wife is dead, Herr Dominus. You will be doing a lonely man a kindness. My hour is seven.'

When he left von Bremke, Daniel went to his own room. There was little enough to do there. The filing cabinet was empty save for a few discarded and useless notes. He went through the drawers of his desk and found nothing of interest except a forgotten request from Robert Constable, which had been addressed to him c/o the University, to give an approximate date for his return. This he could now answer in person quite soon enough. There was nothing to keep him. He stood up and waved farewell to Archimedes. Earle Restarick came in.

'Well?' Earle Restarick said.

'I'm off . . . in a day or so.'

'Nothing to tell us?'

'There never was anything. And now I'm free to go . . .'

'I suppose so. Care to have dinner? For old times' sake. Tonight?'

'I'm engaged.'

'Tomorrow?'

'Engaged.'

'The next night?'

'I shan't be here.'

'I suppose not,' Earle Restarick said. 'Well, remember this, Danny. I *did* like you when you thought I did. Those weeks in the spring . . .' He went towards the door. 'You coming now? We could take a little walk.'

'Sorry,' Daniel lied, with an easiness which, even a few

weeks before, would have appalled him: 'I've got some more
stuff to clear up in here.'

Ten minutes later, while Daniel was looking at Archimedes
to pass the time until Restarick should be well off the premises,
Leonard Percival came in. Apart from their brief conversation on the telephone, this was the first Daniel had seen or
heard of him since the dinner with Pappenheim in the deserted
mess.

'Long time no see,' Percival said. 'So you're off?'

'Tomorrow night.'

'And you weren't even going to say good-bye?'

'Our brief acquaintance hardly required it.'

'Perhaps not. Who,' said Percival pointing at Archimedes,
'is your friend?'

Daniel told him.

'I remember. Displacement of liquids. Killed by soldiers
while working out a problem in the sand. Which reminds me.
You can't really imagine,' said Percival sadly, 'that they're
going to let you disappear just like that?'

'They've no way of keeping me.'

'I grant you they've had a spot of bad luck. No one could
have known that Captain Fix-it, M.P., would come along.
But after all, they're bound to have a few more nasty little
tricks ready to try.'

'What makes you think so?'

'Word gets around in my profession. And after a time you
get to know the other fellow's style. This last stunt was typical.
Typical of clever but retarded minds with strong romantic
impulses aggravated by schizoid tendencies. All fascists
suffer from a basic fantasy. They see themselves as knights of
the round table. Swords and armour. They have ludicrous
ceremonies and they swear blood-curdling oaths. They're like
a gang of children . . . but you know how *persistent* children
can be.'

'You all seem like children to me. And now that Nanny's
restored order, I'm going to leave the nursery and return to
adult company.'

'You're making a silly mistake, Mond. You may find it difficult to take Pappenheim very seriously, but he understands the issues, he doesn't wallow about in fantasy, and by and large he wants what is right.'

'In your opinion. But just whom do you represent?' Daniel said. 'And how did you get into this anyway?'

'Have I told you about my uncle Rupert? An interesting man with influence in the most peculiar places. He got me into this, but just what he got me into I'm not at liberty to say. All you need to know, Mond, is that Pappenheim and I are (a) "goodies" and (b) sane. The other lot are (a) "baddies" and (b) as mad as dervishes, and they'll stop at nothing to get what they want out of you. So I'm giving you a last chance: tell us what you've discovered here and then let us get you out of Germany. Because you won't get out on your own.'

'There you are, you see. You're as mad as they are: you keep insisting that I've got something to tell.'

'I _know_ you have. It's not just what those librarians have told us— Yes, yes, yes,' he said as Daniel opened his mouth, 'we've used exactly the same sources as the other side. It's a recognized licence in the profession, one which we often adopt, by common consent, to save time. But I'm not going on what those librarians say. They can't know much. I'm going by _the look on your face_. On the few occasions I've met you, Mond, I've looked very carefully, through my very powerful glasses' – he tilted them so that they flashed straight into Daniel's eyes – 'into your moody, sensitive, intellectual face. And now I'd stake ten years' pay that there's something behind that face, something that's given you a most unpleasant shock and which Pappenheim and myself and the very sane interests we represent want to hear about with no more ado.'

'I don't give a damn,' said Daniel, 'for you or Pappenheim or the sane interests you represent or the psychopaths with whom you compete. I'm a free man with a British Passport, I'm leaving for England tomorrow night, and if anyone lifts a finger to stop me, I shall yell for the police.'

Leonard Percival sighed.

'All right,' he said. 'I wish you and your British passport the best of British luck.'

'. . . So you see,' von Bremke said, 'I was so much looking forward to your arrival in Göttingen. I had hoped to know you well, to be of help perhaps. To talk, from time to time, of England, of which I have good memories. But just before you came my wife's illness was found to be other than we had hoped, and I was much preoccupied. And now it is too late.'

They were sitting in von Bremke's modest but pleasant garden just outside the town, in a summer-house, to which an elderly and uniformed maid, who had served the indifferent dinner, now brought coffee, a candle and three kinds of liqueur on a big brass tray. Von Bremke thanked and dismissed her very formally, then started to pour the coffee.

'Now you are going,' he said, 'and it is too late.'

'I'm so sorry about your wife.'

Von Bremke shrugged.

'Kümmel, cointreau or aurum?'

'Aurum?'

'An Italian Liqueur made of orange. You should try it if you have never done so. It has a most beautiful colour. That is why it is here. My wife loved the colour.'

He poured. Daniel examined the colour in the light of the candle, sniffed, sipped and nodded politely. It looked and tasted like an inferior curaçao.

'My wife,' said von Bremke, 'died of the same disease as Professor Dortmund. It is to talk of him that I have asked you here tonight.'

God, thought Daniel, shall I never hear the last of him? Then, be patient, he told himself: be kind to this sad old man. Only another twenty-four hours or so, and you'll be on your way. Listen to von Bremke and part friends.

'The Dortmund papers,' von Bremke was saying, 'were my first failure. Until then I had enjoyed every success and might have looked for the highest esteem of all. But when I set my hands to the Dortmund papers, I found that they were in a class which I could never enter. I was . . . second-rate.'

'Just unlucky?'

'Second-rate. But of course I refused to realize this at the time. I insisted for many years that because the papers meant nothing to me they could mean nothing to anyone. Before the war, and again in 1944 when they sent people here to enquire, I insisted that the papers were the product of a disordered mind. I even said this to you some weeks ago.'

'I remember.'

'That was because I was jealous,' said von Bremke sedately. 'You had solved part of the problem, and I was jealous, and so I told you that the rest would just be madness distilled from pain. Yet even as I told you, I knew that this was not true. For as I watched my wife die, there was no madness. She remained very clear. And anyhow I knew, I had always really known, that Dortmund's illness had not affected his work. Rather, it was the other way. His work, what he found, had hastened his illness.'

Von Bremke lit a small cheroot and poured himself the last of the aurum.

'And so now I ask myself,' he went on, 'what is it that you have found? I am no longer jealous, I am simply curious. Would you care to gratify a lonely and curious old man, Herr Dominus? After all, I too have worked at this, so that we are partners, in a way. I should think it a great kindness if you would tell me what I failed to find.'

'There is . . . nothing,' said Daniel miserably.

'I cannot believe you. Whenever I have seen you lately, you have had an . . . excitement . . . about you, such as does not belong to men who find nothing.'

'Anxiety, that's all.'

'Yes, but also fulfilment. Oh, I quite understand, Herr Dominus, that you would not wish to tell me the details of your work. But it would give me great pleasure to know, very roughly, what you found at the end of it.'

Just for a moment, Daniel wavered. Be kind, he said to himself: part friends. What harm can it do if I give him a very broad idea? He could never learn how to *use* the method; even if I told him what it was for, he could never work through the

intricate steps by which I came at it. He does not even know
how to read Dortmund's notation. And yet, Daniel thought,
there is something not quite right here. Von Bremke is playing
on my sympathies, exploiting his own loneliness and bereave-
ment, in a way that I should not have expected and which
degrades his dignity. If he can bring himself to do that ... And
besides, if once he was told the conclusion, he might, just might,
be able to work back from it, piece the method together,
solve the notation. Better not risk it; better fob him (politely)
off.

'There are great uncertainties,' Daniel said. 'When I get
back to Cambridge, when I've had time to check and confirm,
then I will write to you.'

'I see,' said von Bremke coolly. 'You are leaving Göttingen,
leaving the papers, before your work is properly confirmed.
Unwise, Herr Dominus; unsound.'

Daniel stiffened. He had laid himself open to this imputa-
tion, he knew, but it was still an affront to his professional
pride. He was on the point of justifying himself, then pulled
back; vanity was the oldest trap of all.

'There is no more, Herr Doktor, to be said.'

'Yes, there is. One thing. Please do not be angry with me,
and please do not think I am angry with you, for withholding
confidence.'

Good. They would part friends after all.

'But do one favour for me instead,' von Bremke was saying.
'Professor Dortmund was buried, by his request, in the mountains. But it is not far, and before you leave you should, I think,
visit his grave. A gesture of respect. And besides,' he said to
the puzzled Daniel, 'you will find something to interest you.'

'An inscription? A statue perhaps?'

'Something to interest you. You will go?'

'If you ask it.'

Why not? Part friends, humour the old man's whim, give
an aim and end to tomorrow's expedition.

'The grave-ground in question is not so easy to find,' von
Bremke said, 'but I have made a little map.'

'Thank you ... And now, Herr Doktor, if you'll excuse

T—E

me. Tomorrow will be a long day. My very best thanks for all you have done.'

'You have not finished your aurum.'

Daniel drained the sticky liquid. When von Bremke was satisfied that the last drop was gone, he led his guest, in complete silence, to a door in the garden wall and bowed him into the suburban road outside.

Von Bremke's map had some instructions at the bottom. According to these, Daniel's best plan was to take a coach into the mountains as far as Goslar and thence a local bus to a hamlet called Erding. Prominent in Erding was the Gasthof Frühlingsgarten; here he must turn to the right and follow a road which after half a mile formed a T-junction with another and rather more important road. If Daniel turned left at the T-junction and walked for something under a mile, he would find the 'grave-ground' which he sought lying at the end of a footpath which branched off the road to the right.

Since he had the whole day before him and since it was a delicious September morning, he decided to walk the five odd miles from Goslar to Erding. Though he still regarded von Bremke's request as somewhat peculiar, he was exceedingly glad he had come. It would be nice, he thought, to look back on a last day of tranquillity among the mountain forests. Although there would be other good things to recall about his sojourn in Germany, they were not very many, most of them having been cancelled out, as it were, by disagreeable events which had in some way stemmed from them. The splendid days he had spent with Earle in the spring – how could he remember these with pleasure when all the time Earle had been concealing such treacherous intent? Even the hours he had passed with Fielding and the Dragoons were tarnished by the memory, which had become more sickening as the occurrence receded and so could be seen in a proper perspective, of von Augsburg as he staggered to the ground, the blood bubbling through the fingers with which he clasped at his mangled throat. Von Augsburg (who would now, they said, recover) had probably deserved everything he got; but the welling blood,

Fielding's knowing remark, the look of satisfaction on Glastonbury's face ... these were associations which must leave
an ugly blot on all memories of those concerned. All in all,
Daniel thought to himself, this day in the mountains is perhaps the first and only day I have spent in Germany which
has not been somehow contaminated.

And after all, was von Bremke's request so very odd? Was
it not appropriate that he should pay his respects at the tomb
of the man whose secret he had been probing all these months,
whose secret he (and he alone) now shared? There was a bond
here, however distasteful, which must be acknowledged. Besides, there was ... 'something to interest you'. It might even
be something spectacular; for von Bremke had not indicated
the position of Dortmund's grave in respect to the rest, and it
was therefore reasonable to suppose that it possessed some
immediately visible, some unmistakable distinction.

But whatever this might be, it could wait a little. Daniel
was hungry and thirsty after his walk; he decided to have an
early lunch at the Frühlinsgarten before he completed his
journey. After he had eaten, he spent some time enquiring, in
his phrase-book German, what time he could get buses back to
Goslar. At last it seemed tolerably plain that a bus left
Erding at half past three and would arrive at Goslar in good
time for him to catch another back to Göttingen at four o'clock.
He could be back in his lodgings by seven at the latest, with
ample leisure to bath and finish off his packing before he met
Fielding and the rest at eight. Having thus established his
line of retreat (a phrase and a conception which he owed to
Fielding), he walked slowly through the high afternoon to
the T-junction. It was now just before two: an hour, say,
for the walk to the graveyard and back, half an hour, more than
long enough, to admire the Dortmund monument and indulge
in suitable reflections.

When he had turned left, in obedience to von Bremke's
instructions, at the T-junction, he found that the road on
which he now was led along the bottom of a valley, the two
sides of which were rapidly closing in. By the time he had
walked half a mile further, the fir-crowded slopes were so

near on either side that as soon as one set a foot off the road, one must start to ascend. Presumably the footpath he was looking for led up to a cemetery set in a clearing on the right-hand slope – a clearing, then, which must surely be visible at any minute now. But as he walked on down the road he scanned the slope ahead in vain. Another quarter of a mile: still nothing. Another furlong. Of course, the trees were very thick . . . and here at last, on the right, was his footpath; it must be, though track would have been a better description. There was something familiar about it, and as he climbed he remembered: he had come this way before but much quicker, which explained why he hadn't spotted it sooner. When the slope grew suddenly steeper, he was certain. In a minute at most he would breast a little ridge and be looking down from a sandy bank, down into the 'Warlocks' Grotto'.

So this was it. This was what von Bremke, who had never used the word cemetery, had meant when he spoke of Dortmund's 'grave-ground'. A grave-ground with one grave: the slab of stone in the centre. Well, and why not? If Dortmund wanted to be buried up here, and if the authorities had allowed it, who was Daniel to complain? He walked down to the centre of the bowl and stood over the stone. Somewhere away in the woods a dog barked and others answered it. 'Something to interest you.' Just the setting? Or the eccentricity of Dortmund's choice? Or was there something inscribed here, some lapidary pronouncement on human vanity which von Bremke had thought would be to Daniel's taste? But there was nothing. Nothing to be seen on the rough surface of the stone, either on top or along the sides. More barking, nearer now. The Germans, he had heard, were keen huntsmen, with elaborate codes and ceremonials. What did one hunt in September? Wild boar? Daniel thought not. Hare, things like that? What was it to him? He would sit here, on the soft pine-needles by Dortmund's tomb, for ten minutes, and then walk back for his bus. But was it Dortmund's tomb? or just a joke of von Bremke's? The joke would have no point; but if it was a grave there must be *some* mark. He looked again. Nothing on top. Or on either of the longer sides . . . but *here,*

at the further end from the entrance to the grotto, just above
the carpet of pine-needles, a tiny Maltese cross; and
underneath – scrape away the pine-needles, how mournful that
barking was – carved in small, very plain letters, *Dormiat
Dortmundus:* Let Dortmund Sleep.

Appropriate and even dignified (despite the pun), but
hardly worth a long expedition. Not that he was sorry he had
come. How interested Trooper Lamb would be to know what
was in the grotto he had named. Those dogs couldn't be more
than a few hundred yards away. But he wouldn't be seeing
Lamb again, he supposed, so he must remember to ask Fielding to tell him. Funny, the barking (baying?) seemed to be
coming from all round. Trees made for very odd acoustics.
Why a Maltese cross? Hadn't someone once told him they were
unlucky? Something to do with the Knights Hospitaller and
their practice of black magic? But wasn't that the Templars?
Witchcraft and sodomy. Something in Spencer about it:
'There whilom wont the Templar Knights to bide, Till they
decayed through pride.' He had better get up and go before he
fell asleep. Like Dortmund. Dormiat Danielus. Let Daniel sleep.

His head nodded, he dozed, snored loudly and woke himself up. This really wouldn't do. Slowly he rose to his feet,
shook his head, brushed some pine-needles off his trousers,
started towards the entrance to the grotto. A man standing
there, a man dressed in green, with a dog. A tree. Then another man, another dog, another . . . He turned his head to
look round the grotto. Filling every gap in the trees was a man
in green, green jacket and kind of green plus-fours, and with
every man a dog, the man standing, the dog sitting, tongue out,
panting, otherwise silent, looking at Daniel. Hunting wild
boar? No: hunting filthy, Jewish, homosexual pig.

'A reminder, Daniel,' said one of the green men in the
voice of Earle Restarick. 'A reminder that you can't get away
from us. If you try to leave Göttingen tonight, we shall stop
you. We shall hunt you down. For the rest, we're giving you
another week. Seven days from today I shall come to you and
it will be time for you to tell us what you know. Now, come up
here beside me.'

Daniel climbed the bank to Restarick's side. The green man at the entrance to the grotto (grave-ground) opened a satchel and produced something furry, which he set on the down-slope of the bank. It scampered down to Dortmund's stone and sat there, sniffing, scratching, whimpering, giving an occasional furtive glance from side to side. Trapped. There was a high whistle. The dogs bounded down the bank; the hare hopped up on to the stone slab, sat there, for perhaps a third of a second, in a begging posture, and was then engulfed.

'They're very hungry,' Earle explained with a seraphic smile, 'but very well disciplined.'

There was another whistle in a slightly lower key. Each dog scrambled back to its master. On Dortmund's grave the half-eaten hare, still just alive, twitched its legless rump and screamed. Earle Restarick turned, and within ten seconds every man and every dog had vanished into the trees.

Part Six

INTERLUDE

'DANIEL, what on earth . . . ?'

The diners stared at him as he shambled across the floor of the Alte Krone.

'There was an animal in pain. I didn't know how to kill it, I could hardly bear to touch it, so at first I just sat there . . . trying to comfort it. I thought it would never die. So eventually I picked it up and . . . smashed . . . its . . . head on Dortmund's grave.'

Daniel's guests exchanged glances.

'You were so late,' said Fielding soothingly, 'that we started without you.'

'That's all right. I . . . I . . .'

'Hadn't you better go and wash before you eat,' Fielding said. 'There's rather a lot of blood.'

But Daniel sat down in the empty chair at the end of the table and started to cry. Fielding nodded at the three subalterns (his subalterns now), and they rose to go. Mick Motley also rose.

'Please don't go. I'm so sorry about this. I . . . You must help me,' he blubbered. 'I'm not strong. Fielding . . . Julian . . . I'm not strong.'

Fielding nodded again. The three subalterns, with very odd looks on their faces, trooped out of the restaurant.

'I'll be in the bar upstairs if needed,' Mick Motley said. 'Drink a little wine, Daniel. At once. Then eat.'

After Daniel had drunk two glasses of hock, which reduced his outbursts to a quiet snivel, Fielding ordered him some soup and his favourite dish of sole, and then said:

'If you're to leave tonight you'll have to eat up and get going. Done all your packing?'

'I'm not going.'

'Oh?'

'I can't go. They ... showed me what they'd do if I tried. Until today I thought, this is a civilized country, with laws and policemen, nothing can keep me here now. God, how silly I was. Naïve. If I so much as set foot on Göttingen station, they'll ... they'll ...'

'Daniel. Drink that soup and then try to explain.'

Daniel did so. By the time he had finished his sole, he had given Fielding an adequate if disordered account of his situation, and had once again implored his help.

'I must say,' Fielding said, 'this business of Leonard Percival is as odd as any of it. I always thought he was rather interesting for a Fusilier, but *this* . . . You're sure he's not having you on?'

'I can't be sure of anything ever again. But he seems to know so much. He always knows what's happened, he always finds me when he wants me.'

'I wonder whether he knows about this afternoon. Has it struck you,' Fielding said, 'that Percival and this other fellow, Restarick, have never – well – never clashed? It's almost as though they'd agreed between them that when one of them was doing his stuff the other should stay well clear.'

Daniel shook his head stupidly.

'But that,' said Fielding, 'is by the way. The immediate point is this. If you think Percival's on the level, why not hand yourself over to him and Pappenheim and do what they ask?'

'No.'

'They'd get you out. Your secret would be in good hands.'

'No, Fielding. I can't trust them with it. Even if they're all they say they are, I can't trust them.'

'Convince me, Daniel. Convince me that what you've found is so terrible that no one else must know it. Come on,' said Fielding in a hard voice: 'convince me.'

'How can I?'

'By telling me.'

'But then—'

'—If you want my help, Daniel, you'll have to convince

me that there's no other way. Percival and Pappenheim, you say, have offered to lay everything on for you. But no, that's not good enough for you, you've come to me instead. It's going to be very difficult for me, Daniel; but I'll do what I can – if, and only if, you first convince me that it's necessary. And the quickest way of doing that is to tell me what you know.'

'How can I be sure you won't pass it on? After all, you're in the Army, you support that kind of people, you—'

'—For Christ's sake. The rest of them, Daniel, are asking you to hand all your stuff over and tell them mathematical chapter and verse. I'm not asking that. I couldn't understand it, for a start. I only want a rough idea of what's so terrible about it all. That couldn't help anyone much even if I did pass it on.'

The same old argument, Daniel thought, as von Bremke had produced.

'It might,' he said wearily. 'They might be able to work back.'

'Very well, Daniel. I swear to you,' said Fielding in a strained voice, 'on my honour as an officer and a gentleman, that nothing you tell me will go any further.'

An oath. But what did it mean? Captain Detterling, when the question of perjury was raised, had brushed it aside as a 'trivial difficulty'. He had further remarked that in this regard Fielding Gray would do and say exactly what he was told. If this was the attitude which held, among Dragoons, of an oath to be given before a court, why should Daniel believe in the oath which Fielding had given him now? Between them all they had destroyed any basis for truth or trust. Something of this he now faltered out to Fielding.

'You are failing,' Fielding said, 'to draw an important distinction. To me an oath sworn on the bible, itself a pack of lies, means little or nothing, particularly if it conflicts with the interests of a friend. But the oath I have just sworn to you was sworn on what I live by. The honour of an officer, I dare say, is an outmoded notion, the honour of a gentleman even more so, and I can hardly expect you to take them very seriously. But they are what I live by, *all* that I *can* live by. Will you accept that?'

'What does it mean, this honour? In what does it consist?' Fielding thought for some seconds.

'It means,' he said at length, 'that I can never betray someone if once I have undertaken care of him. As an officer, I am bound to undertake care of the soldiers entrusted to me. As a gentleman, I am bound to undertake care of those who have a just claim on me. But first I am entitled to make sure that the claim *is* just. That is why you must tell me what you know.'

'Very well,' said Daniel: 'I'll tell you.'

'Good. Now pay the bill for dinner and take me to where you live.'

As soon as they reached Daniel's lodgings, Fielding said: 'How much luggage have you?'

'Two large suitcases.'

'You must manage with one.'

'My notes take up most of it.'

'You must still manage with one. The rest of your stuff stays behind, as if you were just away for an odd night. So pack what you can into one suitcase, Daniel, and while you do so, pay me your journey money.'

Daniel jammed a comb into a hair-brush, wrapped them in newspaper, and started, rather jerkily, to put things into a sponge-bag.

'You remember,' he said, as if talking of a past almost infinitely remote, 'what I was telling you on that train to Hanover? A particle makes a strand on its journey through space. We follow this strand back, little by little zeta by zeta, so that we never lose it. Where do we finally arrive?'

'At the . . . origin . . . of the particle?'

'Theoretically, yes. At the origin of the particle, and so at the origin of matter. But this would take us too long. One cannot go nosing back through all eternity. But, Fielding, we can come at other secret places. We can come at the crisis points of the particle's existence. Have you heard of the electronic leap?'

'When an electron changes orbit inside an atom?'

'Yes. It happens suddenly and without warning, so that it is impossible to make accurate observations. But suppose we knew that it had happened recently. We could tag on, so to speak, to this electron and follow it *back* to the precise moment of the leap. Such a leap is completed almost instantaneously – during a zeta of the strand/particle's development. With this new method of Dormund's we could analyse the particular zeta. The crisis point. We could find out exactly what happened and how.'

Daniel picked up a bedroom slipper.

'Now do you understand?' he said.

Fielding's face showed a sense of anti-climax.

'No. Clearly it would be very interesting. Terrible ... no.'

'Fielding ... A crisis point in a particle's existence often indicates a crisis point in the atom to which that particle belongs. It can mean a structural change in the atom itself. And the atom's structure, remember, is normally bound together by the most tremendous forces.'

'You mean,' said Fielding, in a bored way, 'that vast amounts of energy are involved? That here we have the means of making bigger and better atomic explosions? I always rather thought it would add up to that.'

'Well, it doesn't,' said Daniel crossly. If he was to tell what he knew, he wished to be heard with suitable respect and interest. 'The technique for producing atomic explosions is comparatively crude. Let me remind you once more: by using the Dortmund method we shall be able to examine – what no one has been able to examine before – the precise behaviour of particles at the exact instant of fundamental change.'

'What you're saying,' said Fielding slowly, 'is that the method which you've discovered—'

'—Which Dortmund discovered—'

'—That this method gives you a new insight into the forces which bind matter together.'

'Bind the whole universe together. It's an absolutely basic concept. These are the forces which regulate the bahaviour of matter, which see to it that everything holds together and proceeds according to the rules. If once you start tampering with these forces, you are tampering with the foundation of existence. What does the expression "chain reaction" mean to you?'

'That a single atomic explosion might set off others, and these in turn—'

'—Exactly. As things are now, this could never happen, because the elementary explosions which we're capable of producing, and these only from a very special kind of atom, do not affect the stability of other atoms. But if once we understood the inner forces which maintain this stability, if once there were exact examination of the way these operate, then sooner or later someone would discover how to undermine or divert them, and then to start off a chain reaction would no longer be impossible. Don't you see, Fielding? Nature's stability could be infiltrated, its basic and binding principle corrupted. There would *not* be bigger and better explosions, as you put it: there would be . . . dissolution.'

Daniel folded his pyjamas, put them on top of his dressing-gown, tried in vain to close his suitcase, and sat despairingly down on his bed.

'Let me.' Fielding removed the dressing-gown and threw it on to the floor. There were two sharp clicks, and Daniel's packing was finished. 'You really believe it could go as far as that?'

'People are mad enough for anything.'

'I don't question that. I mean, do you really think that this knowledge could produce – well – this result?'

'In time, yes. Up till now scientists have been pottering about on the outer edge, but Dortmund's method could take them right to the heart of it all. It's a kind of magnifying glass, which would enable them to see, down to the last little detail all those vital things which so far they're only guessing about. What really happens, for example, when the electron "jumps". And from these they could learn the first and last secrets of all, Fielding – what is substance, what is the fundamental essence from which God—'

Fielding held up his hand as if to close the subject.

'When you asked me for help,' he said, 'what did you suppose I could do?'

'I don't know. I thought you might get hold of Captain Detterling. He's a friend of yours he'd listen to you. And somehow I'd feel safe with him.'

'You have a point. But it wouldn't do to draw attention to him. If we were to summon him here, they'd guess what we were up to before he was half an hour out of Baden Baden, and by the time he was here, you wouldn't be. Better, don't you think, to deliver you safely to him?'

'I don't follow.'

'Ah, my dear, but you do. From now on you follow all the time.'

'I don't—'

'—I'm now going to ring up for a taxi. In case anyone's listening, I shall tell the driver to take us to the station, but in fact we shall go straight to the barracks. In my room is a camp bed, all ready for use on Apocalypse (which, you may remember, starts in three days' time) and very handy for you to spend the night on. In the morning there will have to be adjustments. They will not be entirely to your taste—'

'—I can't under—'

'—But they will guarantee your safety, which at the moment is a more urgent problem than your comfort. And in three days' time—'

'—Fielding. Do please try to make sense.'

'I'm making the best of sense. Where's the telephone?'

'This is Squadron Sergeant-Major Bunce,' Fielding said.
'How do you do?'

'Sir.'

'And this is Squadron Corporal-Major Chead. He's our equivalent of a Colour Sergeant.'

'What's a Colour Sergeant?' Daniel said.

'Stores, sir – all that. Pleased to meet you.'

'And Trooper Lamb you already know.'

They were all in Fielding's office: the Sergeant-Major, who was tall and very thin; the Corporal-Major, who was tall and very fat; Trooper Lamb, whose acne was redder than ever; Daniel, still rather bemused after a rough night on Fielding's camp bed; and Fielding himself, who seemed to be enjoying some deeply satisfactory private joke.

'Sit down, please, gentlemen ... Now,' Fielding said, in the placid but slightly arch voice of one who is telling a child a bed-time story, 'my friend, Mr. Mond, has to be got out of Germany. For the next two days we must look after him here in the barracks. Then we shall take him with us on Apocalypse, and either hand him over to Captain Detterling at Baden Baden – if we get near enough – or else make such other arrangements as circumstance may suggest.'

There was a puzzled silence.

'So Captain Detterling's in on this?' said the Corporal-Major eventually, in a tone half of affection and half of apprehension. 'You never served under him, did you, Basil?' – this to Sergeant-Major Bunce.

'I've heard a bit about him,' said Bunce gloomily.

Daniel had a feeling that Detterling's name in these circles, like that of Jupiter among the ancients, had weight rather than respectability.

'Captain Detterling,' said Fielding firmly, 'is not immediately in question.'

'I can see that, Captain Fielding,' said Bunce more gloomily than ever; 'what I don't quite see is in what capacity your friend here is to accompany us.'

Interesting, thought Daniel: he has very sensibly asked how but no one has thought to ask why.

'Mr. Mond will travel in the Land Rover with Lamb and myself – acting as my servant.'

'Time for a change, eh?' said the Corporal-Major, and laughed with unnecessary loudness.

'That will do, Tom,' said Bunce. 'What about your man Lewis, sir? Soldier-servant is all he's good for. There's nowhere else I can fit him in.'

'Trooper Lewis,' explained Fielding, 'will be excused the manoeuvre by courtesy of the M.O. He is at this minute in the M.I. Room, where Dr. Motley is diagnosing a mild case of shingles. Lewis will stay in barracks with the rear-guard. Mr. Mond will take his place on Apocalypse – and take it to the extent of possessing his identity card. I've already given Lewis a certificate saying that this has been withdrawn from him for an administrative check, and here it is.'

He placed a folded and filthy piece of paper on his desk.

'Does he look like me?' asked Daniel. 'I mean the photograph?'

'The description fits quite well. That's all that matters.'

'A private soldier's identity card,' explained Corporal-Major Chead to Daniel, 'does not have a photograph. They'll get round to it one day, but just now only sergeants and above have faces.'

'The important thing at the moment,' said the Sergeant-Major bossily, 'is that Mr. Mond will have an official identity if questioned. And questioned he may very well be, if left alone for ten seconds, seeing as how there is a certain delicacy in his appearance which is not consistent with his role.'

'I rely on the three of you to see to that,' Fielding said. 'I want Mr. Mond kept out of the Fusiliers' way – and that means he'll have to be moved out of the Officers' Mess – I want him accepted without comment by the squadron, and I want him turned out as a passable Light Dragoon – and a passable soldier-servant – by early Friday morning when we leave for Apocalypse. Until then I don't want to see him at all – I'm sorry, Daniel, but if you think you'll understand why. Can you cope? Mr. Bunce?'

'Whatever you say, sir,' said the Sergeant-Major, with a kind of constrained gaiety, as of a governess at the family picnic.

'Corporal-Major?'

'At least he ain't got shingles,' said Chead, and wheezed with laughter.

'Trooper Lamb?'

'I can teach him to cook up the field rations and keep your kit straight, sir. He'd better bunk-up with me in the spare parts shed.'

'Good idea.'

Fielding rose from his desk. All except Daniel immediately rose too.

'Lesson one, Mr. Mond, sir,' said the Sergeant-Major, and heaved Daniel gently but firmly to his feet.

'Right,' said the Corporal-Major in the squadron stores, 'Lamb here can nip down to the mess for your luggage, and we'll start dressing you up to a credit to the squadron. Mugger?'

A long, yellow face peered round a pile of unappetising blankets.

'Denim trousers, demin blouse, field-smock, gaiters, boots, ammunition, and beret with badge.'

There was a brief noise as of a burrowing dog, and Mugger was standing by Daniel with the items ordered.

'Who's this then?' Mugger said.

'Trooper Lewis.'

'Don't look like Lewis to me.'

'What's in a name?' said the Corporal-Major.

'Stoppages. That's what's in a name,' said Mugger didactically. 'If I put this lot down to Lewis, they'll stop him three quid, four and a tanner.'

'Put it down to the Captain.'

'Who's going to sign?'

'I am,' said the Corporal-Major, and forged Fielding's signature immaculately on to Mugger's ledger. 'Saves the Captain being bothered,' he explained to Daniel. 'Like to try this lot on?'

'I had rather hoped . . . cherry trousers?'

'Walking out only. And from what I 'eard there's no walking out in store for you.'

'That is certainly true,' Daniel said.

'Make the best of these then. Don't be shy. Mugger and me, we're married men. What about some char, Mugger?'

Mugger went behind a counter and came back ten seconds later with three enamel mugs, villainously chipped, full of a hot, sweet, oddly invigorating liquid.

'Tea-bags,' Mugger said, 'and nicely laced with issue rum. Made it off the Fusiliers on the night exercise. Swapped our empty jar for their full one. Their C.O. never lets 'em have a rum-ration, see,' he said to Daniel, 'in case they all lose what little sense they got. So they won't ever find out. Not until some long-nosed fucker from Brigade comes round with a dip-stick at the annual inspection. They'll find out then all right.'

'You rotten sod, Mugger,' said Tom Chead easily. And to Daniel, 'Them boots all right?'

'A bit . . . unfriendly.'

'Just have to wear them in, that's all. Let's see you in that beret.'

'It does something for 'im,' said Mugger, after they had explained that the badge should be worn over the left eye rather than the right.

'Yuss . . . Do you know,' said Corporal-Major Chead to Daniel, 'when we're fitting out a new recruit, when we put the old skull and coronet up on his bonce for the first time, do you know what we say? "You can polish all you want, friend, but that skull will keep on grinning." That's what we say.'

Later on, Lamb took Daniel to have his hair cut by the squadron barber, who was a chirrupy and middle-aged little man called Geddes.

'Who's your friend, dear?' Geddes said to Lamb.

'New man for Squadron H.Q.'

'Well, it's a real pleasure to have some hair to work on for a change. You see, dear,' he said to Daniel as he settled him in the chair, 'one takes a pride in one's work, but it's not very easy when there's no material, which in the Army there usually isn't. Not with Sergeant-Major Basil Bunce about – he sends the boys along for a chop if there's so much as a teeny-weeny whisker within three inches of anyone's lughole. But with you there's a lovely lot to come off.'

Already the thick, black chunks were raining on to the floor.

'Might one ask, dear,' said Geddes, 'what your name is? I like to know the names of my clients.'

'Trooper Lewis,' said Lamb.

Going to be rather *confusing*, isn't it, in Squadron H.Q.? I mean, this one having the same name as Captain Gray's batman?'

'Lewis the batman's gone sick. Shingles.'

'Over-excitement, I wouldn't wonder. Fancy being batman to heavenly Captain Gray. Tidying his *things* and that . . . Get a look at yourself in the mirror, dear,' Geddes said to Daniel. 'Lovely job, though I say it myself.'

Though disconcerted to find that his neck was now naked as far up as the tops of his ears, Daniel was pleased to see that he looked much younger. More than this, he now looked pathetic and defenceless to a degree which, although he had always cultivated a meek demeanour, astonished even him. No one who now came across this shorn and shabby little figure in the ill-fitting denims would give it any attention beyond a glance of pity or contempt.

'If you've done admiring yourself,' said Lamb, 'we'll go and get some dinner.'

Midday dinner in the Dragoons' section of the other ranks' cookhouse was a social event. Gossip was exchanged, plans for the evening mooted or confirmed, wagers struck. Everyone was there and everyone was in something of a hustle; it was therefore, as Daniel realized, an ideal opportunity for Lamb to perform an important part of his mission, which was to introduce Daniel into the Squadron at large without at the same time arousing curiosity.

'We'll sit over there,' Lamb said. 'Not right in the middle and not in a corner. When they see you with me, they'll take you for granted. Those that are near enough will ask a question or so, but no one'll come over specially.'

'Then why not the corner? The fewer questions the better.'

'We mustn't seem to be avoiding the blokes. They don't like a new man to push himself forward, but they don't like him to be stand-offish either. They expect him just to be there, like everybody else.'

The event proved Lamb to be right. The two or three men who were already at the table at which they sat down nodded with friendly indifference. One said,

'Just in time for the Apocalypse lark, eh, mate?'

'Yes,' said Daniel shyly.

'Where've you come from then?'

'Transferred from Regimental H.Q.,' said Daniel, in accordance with Lamb's earlier instructions.

This provoked neither surprise nor comment. Daniel looked at the mess of Shepherd's Pie on his tin plate and resolutely began to eat.

'Sounds like one of them failed officer candidates,' he heard someone whisper further along the table.

'Runty little bloke. Like a worried rat.'

'Don't you worry about them,' said Lamb softly, 'but try to finish your grub. You're used to it by now, remember.'

Since the grub was not as nasty as it looked, and since the morning's activities had given him quite an appetite, Daniel cleaned his plate off creditably enough.

'Good,' said Lamb as they left the cookhouse. 'Word'll go round that there's a new lad arrived who's got an officer voice but failed for a commission. There's plenty of those about these days and you look the part – all brain and no muscle. Now then. At fourteen-fifteen hours we're due with the Sergeant-Major . . .'

'Come to attention, Mr. Mond,' the Sergeant-Major said, 'when you enter my office. Heels together, stomach in, chin up. That's it. Now sit down please. From now on, sir, I shall address you as Trooper or Dragoon, since we may as well begin in the way we mean to go on.

'Well then, Trooper Lewis. The act of coming to attention before your superior implies formal recognition of his right to give orders and your readiness to obey them. Once you understand that, we shall agree very well. Indeed, once you understand what the formality signifies, the formality itself is dispensable. With intelligent men this is usually the case: only fools need to be constantly reminded of their subordinate status, because only fools forget it. It follows that discipline is often soundest where it is apparently laxest, as in this Squadron. So do not be misled by our laxity, Dragoon Lewis. It is only permitted because each one of us has an exact understanding of his place, or perhaps I should say his *area*: each one, that is, knows exactly how far he can go in any given direction. Within this limit we are allowed great freedom of manners and procedure. But once that limit is passed, Trooper Lewis, once a man forgets his place or his area, then our whole structure is threatened and we get very firm. Much firmer than regiments which employ a stricter discipline in the normal course. I believe you've met Major Glastonbury, lately our Officer Commanding?'

'Yes.'

' "Yes, sir," or "Yes, Sergeant-Major." A courtesy, Trooper Lewis. Courtesy is always desirable if formality is not. The distinction is important ... Well then. Major Glastonbury is famous among us for shooting a sentry who was asleep on active service. Few regiments these days would forgive such a proceeding. We accept if we hardly welcome it. *That sentry had finally forgotten his place,* and we realize, since we are allowed such freedom within our places, just how unforgivable that is.'

'But this freedom is an illusion, Sergeant-Major. In return for minor privileges you've sacrificed the most important liberty of all – liberty of choice.'

'If liberty of choice means a sentry is free to go to sleep and endanger his comrades, Trooper Lewis, then we're well rid of it.'

'I mean that in all essential matters you are bound to defer.'

'No. In all *military* matters we are bound, ultimately, to defer. How else would you run an Army?'

'Military matters like haircuts? I hear you're very keen on those.'

'Tiresome but necessary. If senior officers from outside see long hair, they get suspicious, and then they come poking and prying and interfering. If you want to be left in peace in the Army, you must conform in the small things, Trooper Lewis. Just like if you're having it off regular with another man's wife, you keep your fly buttoned as long as he's still in the house.'

'All right. But my complaint is that you leave no area of moral choice.'

'In private affairs we leave morals pretty much to the soldier concerned.'

'But if a moral conviction conflicts with a military decision?'

'A political attitude, Mr. M———Dragoon Lewis, if I may say so. If you're sitting in an armchair sticking flags in a map of campaign, you can afford moral convictions. If you're lying in a ditch dodging bullets, you cannot. Because bullets, Trooper Lewis, don't share your moral delicacy . . . even supposing you have it, which most of us don't.'

'You're evading the issue, Sergeant-Major.'

'I don't need you to tell me that, Trooper Lewis, but I'm too busy just now to say any more. Now then. Captain Fielding says we get you out. I don't ask why, because that would be beyond my place. It's either private or it's hush-hush, and so to know about it is beyond my place. What I do, Trooper Lewis, is help to get you out. While you are being got out, your place is that of a soldier-servant. You wait on the Captain, as you will be shown how by Trooper Lamb, you address all your military superiors – which in your case means every living soldier, Trooper Lewis – with courtesy, and you do just what they ask of you, though it'll be mostly me and the Corporal-Major that does the asking. That's your place, Trooper Lewis, and if you stay inside it you will receive nothing but kindness and respect. Move out of it, and God help you.'

Later that afternoon Lamb introduced Daniel to the accommodation which they would share for the next two nights in the 'spare parts shed'. This was a large shack at the back of a hangar in the Motor Transport Lines. Since these latter were at the extreme upper limit of the barracks, the shack afforded its occupants, as Lamb remarked, a degree of privacy rare at his level in the military scale. It also afforded little enough space, being crammed with shelves and crates which contained anything from tiny screws by the thousand to large and jagged sections of armoured car; but Lamb had cleared a pleasant alcove for himself under a window with a view of the fields to the south-west, and he now found room to erect a camp bed for Daniel alongside his own. Other attractions, tucked away behind a kind of wardrobe in which hung a comprehensive selection of pistons and Lamb's dress uniform, were a basin with running cold water and a gas-ring. The former did for what Lamb called 'ablutions and a pisser', the latter for the occasional 'cuppa and fry-up'. No need to go out for anything short of a shit. Lamb was very proud of being so self-contained.

'How come they let you live up here?' Daniel asked.

'Security of classified equipment. All this stuff's worth a packet, so someone's meant to watch it during after-duty hours.'

'But surely you don't stay in every evening?'

'Well, it's all rather a fiddle really. That security business – the Corporal-Major thought it up. We're friendly, you see . . . Anyway,' he went on quickly, 'it's cosy living here and I'm sorry we're not staying for the winter. There's a smashing stove the other side of those machine-gun brackets.'

Winter-quarters, thought Daniel dreamily, remembering a word from the grammar books. Snow piled outside the window, Lamb and the Corporal-Major drinking tea over the stove, one or other occasionally leaving the warm circle for a piss in the pisser and hurrying back . . . Yes, it would be cosy to be a Trooper with no worries, living among spare parts.

'Time for a few lessons,' Lamb said, 'before tea. I'm going to take that camp bed down again and show you how to put it up. Then I'll show you how to take care of the Captain's webbing and the rest. I stood in as batman when Lewis was last on leave, so I know all his little fads . . .'

That evening the Corporal-Major visited them in the shack, bringing a bottle of whisky.

'Came to see how you'd settled in,' he said. 'Get us a pot of char, Lambkin, and we'll spike it with a spot of this.'

'Get the tea, Danny,' said Lamb, 'and show him how well you're learning.'

To the accompaniment of muttering and giggling on the other side of the wardrobe, Daniel made the tea.

'Not bad, Dan. What do you say, corpy?'

'Not bad at all ... So we're calling the Captain's friend by his Christian name, are we?'

'I'm just the batman,' said Daniel. 'The Sergeant-Major made that very plain. So what else should he call me?'

'Aye.' Chead looked hard at Daniel. 'Bit of a rum do, eh?'

'Very rum, Corporal-Major. I'm afraid I can't tell you.'

'No more I should have asked. If we were meant to know, we'd have been told.'

'You accept that? You're happy for information to be given or withheld as someone else sees fit?'

'Suits your book just now, don't it?'

'Yes. But I'm surprised you take it so easily.'

'Well now,' said Tom Chead meditatively. 'You remember we were talking about Captain Detterling this morning, and I said as how I'd served under him?'

'I remember.'

'Well, Captain Detterling had a word he often used – Necessity. It was an old Greek idea, he used to say. Necessity was what was there and couldn't be changed, see, or not by the like of us. It was a kind of framework for things, like Standing Orders. So the best way to go on, Captain Detterling used to say, was to accept these orders, this Necessity, without kicking up a fuss, and then wait and see what happened next. He was quite right, you know. Never a dull moment, so long as you can wonder what will happen next; and the less you know about it first, the more fun it is when it happens.'

'But you surely miss a lot of ... fun ... by not knowing why?'

' "Why" is something for officers to know, Danny boy,' the

Corporal-Major said. 'It gives 'em ulcers and breakdowns and Field Marshals' batons. I'll settle for my stripes and a good laugh, now and again, at other people's expense. And now I'll be getting home' – he glanced regretfully at Lamb and then at Daniel – 'to my old woman. She's a bit of Necessity if ever there was.'

The next afternoon it was decided that Daniel was ready to undergo a test. He was to go along to the Guard Room by the main gate, report to the Fusilier Guard Commander that the spare parts shed would be unoccupied during Apocalypse, request him to make a note of this for the information of the officer commanding the rear-guard, and then return to Lamb in the M.T. Lines.

'But,' said Daniel, 'Fielding – Captain Gray said I was to keep away from the Fusiliers.'

'Yes. But the Sergeant-Major says we've got to make sure you can cope with 'em if you need to. Now don't forget: anything with badges on its shoulders – salute it like I've shown you.'

As Daniel walked down to the Guard Room, he considered the problem of the only Fusilier who really concerned him, Lieutenant Leonard Percival. So far there had been no sign of him; but then so far Daniel had been kept very close. Once given the conditions which would prevail during Apocalypse, the constant liaison and interaction which their role surely required between Fusiliers and Dragoons, it seemed unlikely that he could avoid Percival's notice all the way from Göttingen to Baden Baden. And if Percival spotted him, what would he do? Expose him as a fraud? Threaten such exposure unless Daniel agreed to accept his protection and his terms? And for that matter, where did Percival, to say nothing of Earle Restarick, think he had got to now? They must both have been trying to track him down since his disappearance from his lodgings. In the barracks, he was probably safe from Restarick, even if the latter knew he was there; but he was not safe from Percival, who was officially qualified, who had an official duty, to denounce him. Futhermore, once on the march he would be safe from neither. An unexpected break-down perhaps (he imagined a remote cross-road with a little shrine), or a rendezvous at night, Michael Lamb and himself waiting hour after hour for Fielding, and then at last the baying of the hounds through the forest . . . But surely Fielding would have given thought to all this. No point in anticipating difficulties. Wait and see, like the Corporal-Major said: it was more 'fun' that way.

He paused in the doorway of the Guard Room, came creditably to attention, concentrated on the protocol which, Lamb had instructed him, was required in dealing with Fusiliers.

'Leave to fall in, Sergeant, please.'

'Yes please, Dragoon.'

'With your permission, I have a message to deliver.'

'Please state your message.'

Daniel did so.

'Thank you, Dragoon. Fall out, please.'

Daniel turned smartly to the right and marched out.

'Come here,' bellowed a voice: 'that Dragoon.'

Dimly, Daniel was conscious that a car had passed him and gone out through the gate.

'Failing to salute the commanding officer in his car,' howled the voice.

A wrist with the royal arms on it brandished what looked like an enormous pair of wooden scissors under Daniel's nose.

'Sergeant of the Guard,' roared the voice.

'SIR.'

'Escort at the double to put this idle Dragoon in a cell.'

'Excuse me, Regimental Sergeant-Major Holeworthy,' said Basil Bunce's voice from somewhere over to the right, while Daniel, remembering Lamb's instructions for emergencies, stood stock still and stared straight ahead.

'*Well*, Squadron Sergeant-Major Bunce?'

'I witnessed the incident, Mr. Holeworthy. The colonel's car had almost passed the Guard Room as this man stepped out of the door. He couldn't possibly have seen it in time.'

'Is that what you saw, Mr. Bunce?'

'It is, Mr. Holeworthy.'

'Well, I saw something different, Mr. Bunce. I saw this sloppy idle soldier wandering out of the Guard Room like a mental deficient in the family way. *I* saw—'

'—I'll request you not to insult my men, Mr. Holeworthy.'

'This thing isn't a man, Mr. Bunce. It's a heap. Look at its dress. Those denims would be a disgrace to a Jewish Armenian nigger boy digging shit-holes in the Corps of Pioneers.'

The Sergeant of the Guard and two men with rifles formed up facing Daniel.

'Escort . . . Two paces forward . . . *March.*'

'If you insist, Mr. Holeworthy—'

'—I do insist, Mr. Bunce—'

'—Escort . . . A-bout . . . *Turn*—'

'—Then I think you should know, Mr. Holeworthy—'

'—Prisoner and escort . . . double . . . *march*—'

'—That this man is certainly a Jew, though not, I think, Armenian or Negroid.'

'Prisoner-and-escort-halt,' rapped the R.S.M. 'A Jew, are you?'

'SIR,' bellowed Daniel.

'Then I don't suppose you could know any better. Escort-fall-out-and double-awayeee. Now, you from the Dragoons. Repeat after me. Next-time-I-see-the-Commanding-Officer-in-his-car . . .'

'Next-time-I-see-the-Commanding-officer-in-his-car . . .'

'I'll-salute-so-smartly-that-I-rupture-myself.'

'I'll-salute-so-smartly-that-I-rupture-myself.'

'Rupture-myself what?'

'Rupture-myself SIR.'

'That's better. Good afternoon, Mr. Bunce, and thank you for tending your explanation.'

'Good afternoon, Mr. Holeworthy, and thank you for respecting it. You come along with me,' said Bunce to Daniel; 'we don't want any more trouble.'

They marched away at a stiffish pace, Daniel finding the same embarrassment in keeping step as he did when he walked with Jacquiz Helmut.

'I'm sorry to have been a nuisance,' he said.

'Not your fault, just bad luck. I was afraid something like that might happen, so I followed you in case.'

'Thank you.'

'We shouldn't really have risked it,' the Sergeant-Major went on, 'but we had to give you some practice in taking care of yourself. I thought you came through it very well.'

'It's just a matter of knowing the idiom.'

'Like I've told you before,' said Basil Bunce, 'it's the small things that count. Saluting and saying "sir" – if you only do that at the right time you can plot a mutiny and no one the wiser. Etiquette, that's what you've got to watch. And that's why he let you off – he'd gone further than etiquette allowed, and he knew it, and he let you off.'

'Just how far, Sergeant-Major, does etiquette allow him to go?'

'As far as he likes short of personal malice. And he's not a malicious man. Just stupid.'

'What would have happened,' said Daniel, 'if I'd been put in a cell?'

'If they hadn't rumbled there was something wrong about you, you'd have been kept there for two hours, then released under open arrest, with a charge laid against you for neglect to the prejudice of good order and military discipline. Later on, you'd have been brought up in front of Captain Gray. Since the Fusilier R.S.M. would have been witness against you, etiquette would have required Captain Gray to punish you severely. Seven days confined to barracks, I'd expect.'

'How can one be confined to barracks on Apocalypse?'

'Your punishment would have been postponed until you got back.'

'I'm not coming back, Sergeant-Major.'

'No more you are,' said Bunce; 'I almost forgot.'

That evening Michael Lamb took Daniel to the NAAFI. They drank very thin beer and listened to a jangling piano on which someone was playing, over and over again, the theme tune from The Third Man. When Daniel went to buy his round of beers, the manageress, a young and beautiful German, told him that she could not accept Deutschmarks.

You had to pay in something called, apparently, 'Baffs'.

'British Army Field Vouchers,' Lamb explained, 'what they pay us with. Sort of joke money, like you have for Monopoly. No use except in Army canteens.'

'Can't you get paid in marks?'

'We can, but they don't like it, so they make us give two weeks' notice. It's policy, see? They want us to spend our money in barracks, not down in the town.'

'I'm afraid I can't get you a drink.'

'I'll get us all the drink we want, Danny. Your turn when we're out on Apocalypse. Okay?'

'Okay.'

So Michael Lamb bought more thin beer, and the piano jangled (Porgy and Bess now), and the air became vile with cheap cigarettes and sweaty denims. And Daniel remembered reading somewhere that a soldier's real home always remained his regiment (even long after he had grown old and left it), and he thought to himself that he was beginning to understand why. There was peace of mind here, that was what it amounted to. Even the foul-mouthed R.S.M. Holeworthy, so far from destroying it, somehow guaranteed it. He might shout you into the ground, he might put you in a cell or even in irons, but in the last resort he was there to protect you. No stranger would come through the barrack gate without R.S.M. Holeworthy knew his business; no one would come knocking on your door at night without *his* say-so first. Such a man (not malicious, just stupid) and others like him meant safety here.

Safety here. (Home, home on the range, the soldiers sang.) But tomorrow it would be different. Tomorrow they would leave the NAAFI and the spare parts shed and head out into the open. Would the soldiers carry their peace of mind, their sense of home, with them wherever they went? Would Holeworthy and Bunce continue to guard them, and Daniel with them, against the world? Or would they all, once out of the barrack gate, be raw and vulnerable, at the mercy of the intruder in the dark? Nothing the like of him could do about it, as Corporal-Major Chead might have said: wait and see.

Part Seven

APOCALYPSE

AT a steady twenty-five miles an hour the column of Dragoons made its way down lanes and side-roads, proceeding west from Göttingen towards the spa-town of Bad Salzuflen.

'It's ten miles odd from Bielefeld,' Fielding had explained to the assembled Troop Commanders before they left, 'Bielefeld being the centre of the Assembly Area. We shall be sitting just outside Bad Salzuflen for about twenty-four hours, while they make the final preparations before ordering the advance.

The Land Rover which contained Fielding, Lamb and Daniel was followed by a large truck which contained the Corporal-Major in the front and Mugger with miscellaneous stores in the back. Much of these consisted of emergency field rations, since the Dragoons would sometimes be well in advance of the Fusiliers on whom they were theoretically dependent for supplies of food. Behind the truck came twelve armoured cars (three Troops of four), and behind these another truck which carried a technical Sergeant and a selection of tools and spare parts. Followed yet another armoured car – the one in which Fielding would ride when actually leading his Squadron in battle. Last of all came a second Land Rover in which were Sergeant-Major Bunce, his driver and also Trooper Geddes the barber, the latter's function in current proceedings being, to Daniel at least, obscure. To this Land Rover was attached a large trailer which contained 'administrative stores' in the form, preponderantly, of drink.

'As you all know,' Fielding had said to the 'O' Group, 'this is different from our usual order of battle, but it's what they think best for us in the courier role. I've no real complaint, except about one defect which has become more and more obvious in exercises over the last month. They refuse to allow us our own decontamination unit. This means, among other things, that we must draw our anti-radiation suits from the Fusiliers, which could cause serious muddle and delay.'

He says it as earnestly as if it were real, Daniel had thought as he stood listening with Lamb beside the Land Rover. He's enjoying the make-believe of death and devastation; part of him, just a small part, wishes that it *were* real. Perhaps a small part in all of us does. Chaos, anarchy, an end of responsibility and law ... A new kind of freedom when the old kinds have grown so stale.

'Still, it's too late to bother about that. I've told them but they wouldn't listen. The upshot is that we shall be issued with our anti-radiation gear by the Fusiliers when, and only when, we have received orders to proceed to a contaminated area.'

'Can't they dish the stuff out while we're waiting in Bad Salzuflen?' Julian James had said.

'No. It's still very much on the secret list and they don't want it paraded round one moment longer than is strictly necessary for training purposes ... By the way, the Fusilier officer in charge of issuing it is Leonard Percival.' For a split second Fielding's eye had caught Daniel's. 'Try to be nice to him and then perhaps he won't keep us hanging about ... Trooper Lewis.'

'Yes, Fie— Sir?'

'Please go over and ask the Corporal-Major if he's happy about the emergency rations. If he's ready I think we all are. Any questions, gentlemen?'

And now, at eight o'clock on a blue morning which carried a light bright chill of autumn, the column was winding through the woods and fields *en route* for its parody of war. Fielding, who had not seen Daniel for two days, had at first addressed him only with sparse and official briskness, possibly to hide embarrassment; but now that they were well under way, he was beginning to relax.

'What's Michael managed to teach you, Danny?' he asked.

'Most of the things which I shall need to know. But I'm still not too sure of myself with that field cooker. It has a malignant disposition.'

'Not to worry. Whenever we can we shall eat in German pubs or restaurants.'

'With official blessing?'

'Very much not. We're meant to imagine war-time conditions and live down to them. But as far as I'm concerned, since the whole thing's imaginary, the discomfort may as well be too.'

'A sound philosophy of training?'

'A matter of personal taste. We're prepared to risk our necks but not to live like pigs.'

'Funny,' said Daniel. 'When you were talking to them about decontamination units, you seemed to be treating it all quite solemnly. Yet now you're laughing at it.'

'I was talking about a problem of logistics,' Fielding said, 'and I was taking it more or less solemnly because I'm interested in such problems. I am not interested in sleeping in a slit trench or eating hard-tack.'

'But surely,' Daniel insisted, 'you're meant to be training yourself to do just that?'

'I find this ascetic strain in your character rather out of keeping, Daniel.'

'You're evading the question.'

'Pass me that map-case, would you? We shall not be popular if we get on the wrong route and tangle with other units.'

The same technique, Daniel thought, as the Sergeant-Major had used the other day – pleading urgent official duties as a refuge when faced with disagreeable truths. To Lamb he said,

'I forgot to tell you, Michael. That Warlocks' Grotto of yours – there's a man buried there under the stone.'

It was a measure of his confidence in his escape that he was now able to think of the Grotto without distress.

'I always knew that,' said Lamb unexpectedly. 'I saw the little cross.'

'Oh?' said Fielding, looking up from his map. 'You never mentioned it.'

'I liked the place,' said Lamb, 'and I thought it might put you off going there.'

'Why, Michael?'

'You don't like the dead, sir. I've seen the way you screw up your face – when we pass a cemetery or stop for a funeral.'

'Now that,' said Daniel, 'is very interesting.'

Fielding turned his head from where he sat in the co-driver's seat and looked back at Daniel.

'I find you rather trying this morning,' he said. 'You'll oblige me, both of you, by keeping your mouths shut unless first addressed by me.'

By the time he had established his Squadron Headquarters in two adjoining suites of the Schwaghof, a commodious hotel four kilometres outside Bad Salzuflen, Fielding had recovered his good humour.

'Pity we're going to have such a short stay,' he said.

'Even so, won't it cost rather a lot?'

'No. These rooms have been "requisitioned". The bill goes in to Divisional H.Q.'

'Will they pay it?' Daniel asked.

'Normally not. But just now there's one of our chaps, Ivan Blessington, doing A.D.C. to the General. He'll see it's taken care of – he'll pop it in with the General's expenses.'

'So we're here by courtesy of the tax-payer?'

'Do stop grumbling, Daniel. If your conscience bothers you, you can put up a tent in the car park. Now, I'm going into Bielefeld to find Ivan Blessington and get some advance gen. about what's going on.'

Fielding went off with Michael Lamb. Julian James and Piers Bungay came in with the Sergeant-Major and started to pin an enormous map on the wall. There was a whistle from the car park underneath the window.

'Fusilier C.O. playing up on the wireless,' came Trooper Geddes' fluting tones. 'He wants to know our exact position, and he wants to talk to Captain Gray on the set.'

Sergeant-Major Bunce stuck his head out of the window and said,

'Give him the map reference, and tell him that Captain

Gray's been sent for by the General's A.D.C. Mr. Bungay, as 2 i/c, is coming to the set.'

'Must I, Sergeant-Major?'

'You must, sir.'

Piers Bungay went crossly out. Julian lifted a telephone and started, in a thoughtful voice, to order luncheon — 'a selection of cold delicacies for up to ten people' — and a case of hock. Daniel began to unpack Fielding's valise, this being what he was there for.

'I hope Piers won't say anything too silly on the set,' said Julian when he had finished telephoning. 'Where *are* we meant to be, by the way?'

'About a kilometre down the road, sir. Captain Fielding said that no one would notice the difference.'

'They'll spot it when they're given the map reference. It'll be about six figures out.'

'I think not, Mr. Julian. Trooper Geddes has clear instructions about where we really are as opposed to where we are really, if you take my meaning.'

'Jolly good, Sergeant-Major.'

Daniel laid out Fielding's blue silk pyjamas. Four waiters arrived bearing a table covered with Julian's cold delicacies, a fifth brought in a case of hock, and a sixth a tray of glasses. The manager came beaming up behind and said that payment could be made in any currency, including whisky and coffee. Julian took him on one side. The Corporal-Major came in and without a word to anyone heaped a plate with the most delicate of the delicacies; then he joined Julian and the manager in the corner where they were busy muttering words like 'cocoa', 'blankets' and paraffin'. Daniel, mystified, laid out Fielding's shaving things and helped himself to sour cream and red caviar. Piers Bungay returned from the wireless.

'Well, sir?' said the Sergeant-Major.

'He was really very awkward. First he said that if we were where we said we were, that is where we ought to be, then he should be able to see us from where he was, which he couldn't. So I said we'd taken great trouble with our camouflage, but somehow he didn't seem convinced. Then he dished out what he called Security Orders for Overnight Encampment. He said that no one was to have anything to drink; that Bad Salzuflen was out of bounds to all ranks and so were all German villages, hotels, restaurants and shops whatever; that there were to be no lights or fires after dusk, when everyone must go to bed anyway, except for a thirty per cent picket; and that everyone was to stand to in full equipment every two hours during the night. Do you think he could be going potty?'

'I don't think we need worry, sir. I doubt whether he'll have time to come bothering us.'

'I wouldn't be too sure of that. He sounded jolly officious to me. After all, you know, we are technically under his command. And that's another thing. He wanted to know why Captain Gray had gone off without getting his permission.'

'What did you say?'

'At that point I just gave up. I said he'd have to ask Captain Gray himself but that for the life of me I couldn't see it mattered.'

'Unwise, sir?'

'He certainly seemed a bit put out, I must admit . . . I say, some greedy pig has woughed all the smokers. Daniel, ring down for more smokers, there's a dear. One gets very hungry with this sort of rubbish going on.'

Daniel rang down for more smoked salmon. The Corporal-Major put down his empty plate and went conspiratorially out with the manager. Jack Lamprey came in and said:

'The Fusilier Colonel's down in the car park. He's looking rather batey.'

'I knew this would happen,' Piers said. 'Get rid of him, will you, Sergeant-Major? I really can't bear any more.'

The Sergeant-Major drank a bumper of hock and went out. Looking down from the window, Daniel watched Mugger carrying an enormous crate of something straight into the hotel under the fascinated gaze of R.S.M. Holeworthy and the Fusilier Colonel, both of whom were draped round with so many items of military equipment that they looked like a pair of Christmas trees. Sergeant-Major Bunce, who now emerged unarmed save for a riding switch, had, by contrast, a somewhat dilettante air. Having saluted smartly, he murmured something into the Colonel's ear, whereupon, to Daniel's astonishment, the Colonel beckoned to Holeworthy and positively slunk away to his jeep. Thirty seconds later Mugger slopped out of the hotel entrance buttoning a large wad of money into his breast pocket, exchanged a friendly word with Bunce, and walked over to the stores truck, which the Corporal-Major was zest-fully disembowelling.

'I hope,' said Jack Lamprey, who had now joined Daniel at the window, 'that they're not overdoing it. During Broom-stick they got careless and sold all my bedding. There are limits, as I had to remind them rather sharply.'

'We shan't see *him* again for a bit,' said the Sergeant-Major as he rejoined them.

'What did you tell him, Mr. Bunce?'

'The simple truth, Mr. Piers. The area which he allotted us in his orders is an open meadow with a mound in the middle of it. On top of the mound is a memorial notice saying that three hundred and thirty-nine political prisoners were shot and buried there on May 10th, 1944.'

'How on earth did you know that?'

'I always carry that notice around with us, sir. It comes in handy if we don't fancy going where we're told.'

After this, since there was plainly nothing to be done until Fielding got back from Bielefeld, the Sergeant-Major went to sleep while Daniel and the three subalterns made up a four at Bridge.

That evening, after Fielding had rung up to say that he was dining in Bielefeld and wouldn't be back till late, the Corporal-Major proposed to Daniel that they should run into Bad Salzuflen for a change of air and a bite of supper. Although Daniel was not sure how wise this would be in his predicament, his confidence had been so far restored in the last few days, and he was so heartily sick of the hotel and the three subal-terns, that he accepted the invitation. After all, he thought, not much harm could come to anyone who was accompanied by Corporal-Major Chead.

The Ratskeller in Bad Salzuflen, to which they were conveyed (Mugger driving) in the stores truck, was heaving with soldiers of apparently every regiment in the world, Dragoons, however, being predominant among them. There were even, despite their Colonel's edict, a number of Fusiliers, these latter of a seasoned if not criminal appearance. The Corporal-Major, after surveying the crowd with genial distaste, selected a quiet table in a corner and studied the menu with ceremony. After they had all three ordered Russian Eggs to be followed by Ox-tail stewed in red wine, with a pricey hock and beer for Mugger who preferred it, the discussion turned on money. Mugger deposed that the takings for the day's sale of stores to the hotel manager were DM.512 Pf.20.

'And very handsome,' said Tom Chead. 'All gash kit? There won't be no trouble with the books?'

' 'Cept with those self-heating tins of soup. They're experimental, see? They was meant to be issued only when an officer said, and a signed report sent in about them when we got back.'

'Mr. Bungay's acting as second in command, so he's the man to do that. In return we'll put another twenty marks on his cut – poor little bugger's always short. By the way,' said Chead, handing Daniel a ten mark note, 'here's yours.'

'What for?'

'You was there when it was fixed up. We like to keep everyone happy.'

'I shan't report you,' Daniel said huffily, 'if that's what you think.'

'It's the principle of the thing, Danny. If you give everyone a cut, you make for a cosy feeling of loyalty all round. Sodality, Mr. James calls it.'

'I'd much sooner not—'

'—Take it and hold your tongue,' said Mugger. 'Responsible people like me and the Corporal-Major, we've got enough to worry about without you airing your morals. Now then, corpy. Distribution. Forty marks to Mr. Julian James, who first got the manager talking—'

'—He won't want it. He's got plenty and he only does it for laughs.'

'Sodality,' said Daniel primly. 'Make him take it.'

'Quite right,' opined Mugger. 'Sixty marks to Mr. Bungay as 2 i/c – that's without the extra twenty for this report he's got to write. Forty for Mr. Lamprey, though he was no help, but we've got to keep him sweet after that balls-up with his bedding on Broomstick. Ten for Danny here, fifty for Basil Bunce, leaving two hundred and—'

'—Well, well,' said a wheezy voice, 'if it ain't my dear friend Mugger.'

A diminutive Lance-Corporal of Fusiliers, who had a face like an intelligent herring's, was standing behind Mugger with a hand on both his shoulders.

'You great long thieving streak of luke-warm yellow piss,' said the Lance-Corporal. 'Where's our fucking rum?'

'I don't know to what you allude,' Mugger said.

'That rum what you pinched on the night exercise. It took me over a year,' said the Lance-Corporal, blinking his eyes at Daniel, 'to make that jar of rum, being as how our mob are so close with it. And then up comes this bleeder on a dark night, talking as smooth as the serpent in the garden—'

'—I'll tell you what,' said Tom Chead, 'you're upsetting my digestive juices, that's what. We don't want none of your insolence, nor we don't want your rotten rum. So just move on, soldier, before I send for the management.'

'Pardon me, my lord.'

The Lance-Corporal gave a piercing whistle, and a row of Fusiliers appeared behind him, cutting off Daniel and his friends in their corner.

'Now then,' the Lance-Corporal said. 'No one puts it over us, not even Earl Hamilton's light-fingered, cherry-arsed Dragoons, nine-month bellies and all. We'll have that rum, or else.'

'Baaah,' went Mugger like a demented sheep; 'baaaaah.'

Four things then happened in quick succession. First, several

Fusiliers, howling, battered Mugger's head with empty beer bottles; whereat a line of Dragoons rose like a wave from the centre of the room and crashed down on to the Fusiliers from the rear; a few seconds after which, thundering down the wide stairs from the streets with a furicano of whistles, came a mixed squad of British Military and German Civilian Police; whereupon Fusiliers and Dragoons and all else present turned to make common cause against a common foe.

'Sweet Jesus Christ,' said the Corporal-Major.

He picked up the prostrate Mugger, slung him over his shoulder, seized Daniel with his spare hand, and made for the swing doors which led to the kitchen, emitting a high and wavering 'Ta-whit-ta-whoo' as he went. Several Dragoons instantly broke away from the centre mêlée and followed. In five seconds flat they were all through the kitchen and out in a little yard which opened on to a back street.

'How many of our boys left in there?' called the Corporal-Major.

'Least six, corpy.'

'They'll have to take their chance.' But even as he said it three more men dashed out into the yard, 'Form up into two ranks, the lot of you. You two, carry this poor bloody Mugger. Picket . . . Picket, *shun*. Right turn. Quick march.'

Led by the Corporal-Major and followed by Mugger's stumbling bearers, the two files marched sedately down the side-street and across the square, at the far side of which they were halted at the entrance to another side-street, where Mugger had parked the stores lorry. This was now being watched over by a Sergeant of Military Police and four attendant red-caps.

'Right,' said the Corporal-Major. 'On the word dismiss, the picket will take a smart run to the right and mount the rear of the three-tonner. Picket . . . dis-*miss*. Trooper Lewis, up front with me.'

'What's this then?' said the red-cap Sergeant out of a brutal and broken-veined face.

'Town Picket from the 10th Sabre Squadron, Earl Hamilton's Light Dragoons. Thank you for watching our truck, Sergeant. You may fall out.'

'Who are you telling to fall out?'

'I'm telling you to fall out.' Tom Chead pointed to the three stripes, surmounted by a crown, on his upper arm. 'Corporal-Major they call me. Equivalent of a Colour Sergeant or Staff Sergeant, which is one up on you, matey, so many thanks for your kind enquiries and good night.'

'Town Picket, you say,' said the Sergeant without moving; 'and what's that man being carried for?'

'Drunk. Which is what Town Pickets are for. Sweeping up drunks.'

'No one told us you were mounting a picket.'

'All aboard?' called Tom Chead, ignoring the Sergeant, and swung into the driver's seat.

'Just a minute,' said the Sergeant. 'Driving your own picket are you?'

'Usual driver of the vehicle indisposed.'

Tom Chead pulled the starter. The engine turned over several times but didn't catch. A second and longer attempt produced the same result.

'You can sit there pulling all night if you want,' the Sergeant said. 'I've removed the rotor-arm, a precaution which you should have taken yourself and neglect of which is a chargeable offence. Now then, Corporal-Major: your name and number if you please.'

The Sergeant of Military Police, with his men grouped behind him, was standing on the pavement; and since the three-tonner was parked on the left-hand side of the street, the conversation between him and Chead was now being conducted across Daniel, who, true to Michael Lamb's advice, was staring straight ahead. As he did so, a man crossed the street from the other side, paused on the pavement about ten yards from the Sergeant, and stared back at Daniel through the wind-screen. Although his appearance was not familiar, Daniel knew him, or rather, knew that he knew him. Just where he had met him or in what circumstances, he could not have said; but met him he had, if only once, however briefly ... Where?

When? The man, who was stocky, hatless, short-haired and wearing a smartly cut mackintosh, continued to stare quietly up at Daniel, without moving, without giving any sign of recognition.

'All right,' said Tom Chead, leaning across Daniel, 'two hundred marks for that rotor-arm back.'

'It is an offence to attempt to—'

'—Three hundred.'

'Make it four.'

'There's some of my blokes still caught back there in the Ratskeller,' said Chead. 'Get them out, and you can have four.'

'Five.'

'Done. C.O.D.'

The Sergeant took his men over the square at the double. The man in the mackintosh continued to gaze placidly into the cab of the three-tonner.

'Narrow thing,' said the Corporal-Major. 'All our profit gone. And all because of bloody Mugger and his baahing.'

'Why did that annoy them so much?'

'Old soldiers' tale. Wessex Fusiliers means country boys, see, and country boys means shepherds, and shepherds means fun and games with sheep. Just before the war they caught one of 'em at it – in the middle of a manoeuvre on the Salisbury Plain. So ever since then, when anyone wants a rise out of 'em . . .'

Where had he seen that man before? And why did he just stare like that? Daniel wiped the sweat from his forehead with the sleeve of his field-smock.

'. . . Same with the Cumberland Light Infantry,' Tom Chead was saying, 'only in their case it was a cow. In India too. You know what a fuss them Hindus make about cows, so when they found this squaddy on the job there was a perishing riot, so there was, and they had to call reserves in to squash it. Well, the only spare troops near enough was a Brigade just about to sail home from out of Bombay, so they got this Brigade off the troopship, and very nearly had a mutiny on their hands for good measure. You never saw such a pig's breakfast. And here's that bloody red-hat, and not before time . . . five hundred I said, matey, and five hundred it is.'

Chead passed the notes to Daniel, who passed them to the Sergeant, who licked his thumb before counting them. Four rather bedraggled Dragoons were then released and climbed into the back of the truck. The Sergeant did them the honour of replacing the rotor-arm with his own hands and waved them on their way like royalty. As they passed the short-haired man on the kerb he swivelled his head to follow them.

'Nothing they won't do for money, them red-caps,' said the Corporal-Major. 'You take the Italian campaign. They drew protection money out of every cat-house from Syracuse to San Remo. The Mafia wasn't in it . . . Anything the matter, Danny? You don't look so good.'

'I'm all right,' said Daniel desperately. 'What was that noise you made down in the Ratskeller? Like an owl.'

'Calling the boys off, that's all. We've always used that call in the Squadron. It means trouble coming, watch yourselves, pack it in. A look-out's call. "Ta-whit-ta-woooo . . ." And talking of look-outs, Danny boy, there was someone watching you in that street back there. I saw him and so did you, which is why you're looking like a land-mine went off under your crutch.'

'I . . . I don't know who it was.'

'Never mind. You're all right with us.'

Perhaps, thought Daniel; but when it came to the point, you all got out of the Ratskeller quick enough and left the Fusiliers to face the music. Neatly done, I grant you, and of course it would have been asking for trouble to stay; the fact remains that it was the Fusiliers ('Baaah') who stood their ground and who are now, doubtless, sitting in cells.

The three-tonner drew up in the car park of the Schwaghof.

'Two of you stay in there with Mugger,' the Corporal-Major shouted back; 'the rest of you go and get some kip. I'll have to take Mugger on to the M.O.,' he told Daniel: 'he was looking even worse than you do. Want to come?'

Daniel nodded. The idea of seeing Mick Motley gave him comfort. Motley, while his behaviour might be erratic, was a man who helped other people, as opposed to hitting, bribing or tricking them, and so in a small way served the cause of decency. Just now, Daniel thought, a little decency was what he needed.

They drove down the road for another mile, looking for the Fusilier encampment.

'That'll be it . . .'

Chead turned the three-tonner through a gate on the left. What seemed to be about fifty men sprang out of the ground with rifles trained on the driving cab. R.S.M. Holeworthy loomed out from among them.

'Turn those headlights off,' he yelled. 'Do you want the entire enemy air force to know where we are?'

The Corporal-Major sighed and doused his lights.

'With your permission, R.S.M. A sick man for the M.O.'

'Leave the truck and carry him.'

Led by a terrified Fusilier who clearly did not know the way, Chead and Daniel and the two Dragoons carrying Mugger stumbled down row after row of tents which were pitched with parade ground exactness. During the third time round Daniel tripped over a tent peg and went sailing into an enormous net which turned out to be camouflaging Mick Motley's ambulance. Inside the doctor was drinking whisky by candle-light with a morose Staff Sergeant.

'Guesties,' said Mick thickly. 'Drinkies?'

'No, thank you, sir. We haven't had any supper yet. On account of Mugger here what's fallen down and bust his napper.'

Mick looked sillily at Daniel.

'Seen a ghost, boy? Staff, get them all some soup, poor sods. Didn't you hear? They haven't had any supper.'

By this time Mugger was arranged on one of the bunks. Mick stood over him, staggered slightly, shook his head as if to clear it, and then bent down fairly steadily to make his examination.

'Fallen down nothing. He's been hit . . . hard.'

' 'Fraid so, sir. Bottles.'

'Then why lie about it? Hard enough to cure a man with-

out being told lies. But that's what it is in the Army. Lies,
lies, lies.'

The Staff Sergeant, who had been pouring soup into cups
from a saucepan, distributed it among the Dragoons. An acceptable kindness, Daniel thought. Everywhere else in the
Army you either got much more than you wanted or else
nothing at all, according to somebody's whim. But here in
Motley's ambulance ... Motley ... ambulance ... 'Get an
ambulance and fucking quick.' The rubble in Hannover. The
tubby man who had guided them from the hotel and had the
black bag ready. The man in the street in Bad Salzuflen. So.

'Jesus, Mary and Joseph,' Mick Motley said. 'They've
half killed the poor bastard. Who did this? There'll have to be
an enquiry. Which of you were there when it happened?'

Daniel looked at Motley, who looked at the Corporal-
Major, who looked back.

'No,' said Motley. 'No enquiry if we can help it. I'd say,
Corporal-Major, that he took a nasty toss in the stores lorry,
sustaining serious damage to the scalp as he fell, and probably
upsetting a box of tins, some of which fell on his head and
face and caused the minor injuries. But since he was alone in
the back while you were on the move ... ?'

'Alone,' confirmed Chead.

'. . . Then no one except himself can tell us.'

'Will he be all right?' said Daniel.

'I'm not certain. Not till I've had him X-rayed. You,
Staff, get these men to help you shift that camouflage net.
We've got to get him to B.M.H. in Bielefeld.'

'The R.S.M. won't like us driving through the lines at
night, sir. Enemy aeroplanes—'

'—Are you mad, Staff?' And then, very low, to Daniel,
'I'll cover up as best I can, but if he dies there'll have to be
an enquiry. So you'd better start thinking now ... Take your
men home when they've moved that net, Corporal-Major.
There's nothing more you can do.'

Five minutes later the Dragoons and Daniel stood by as
the Ambulance started. R.S.M. Holeworthy came screeching
through the night.

'Mr. Motley, sir, do you want every aeroplane in the enemy air force to hear you?'

'Emergency, R.S.M. For hospital in Bielefeld.'

'But there's no way out of camp, sir. You're bang in the middle of the tent lines.'

'You pitched tents round my ambulance?'

'I never knew you'd want to use it, sir. After all, this is only an exercise.'

'Well, unpitch them, do you hear? You must clear a path for me to get this ambulance out. NOW.'

'But the only way is through the officers' lines, sir. They're mostly asleep.'

'I think,' said the Corporal-Major, 'that our lot had better push off.'

As they climbed into the stores truck at the gate, Daniel heard noises of rapidly swelling turmoil from the centre of the Fusilier camp.

'Poor old Mugger,' said Corporal-Major Chead, 'how he'd have enjoyed it. I hope the poor bleeder don't die. There'll never be a storeman to match him. Crafty he was, to the very depths of his rotten old soul.'

Fielding returned from Bielefeld very late and told them that the next day they would be driving on to Kassel, which was to be the central point of the east-west Start Line from which their army would begin its advance. As he had expected, Ivan Blessington was possessed of information which he was not meant to pass on and which gave a pretty fair idea of how the manoeuvre would develop. They could be more or less sure, Fielding said, that from Kassel the army would advance due south, the division to which they themselves belonged being deployed on the extreme right-wing, nearest, that was, to the Belgian and French frontiers. Since the enemy was advancing from the east, their division would be the last to make contact; and it was most unlikely that the Fusilier/Dragoon 'Courier' services would be required until several days had passed. Although the exact route which they would be told to take from Kassel was uncertain, the probability was that they would proceed straight down the arterial road through Marburg, Bad Homburg and Frankfurt, and then on to Heidelburg.

When Fielding was told something of the row in the Ratskeller he was displeased with all concerned, and the more so when Basil Bunce observed, albeit with great tact of phrasing, that it was Fielding's own fault for leaving the Squadron leaderless for so long. A telephone call to the British Military Hospital in Bielefeld revealed that Mugger was on the danger list and made Fielding's temper less stable still; but the Corporal-Major pulled things round with an idiomatic account of the confusion in which they had left R.S.M. Holeworthy and the Fusilier encampment. After four brandies – large ones which he did not, Daniel noticed, drink slowly – Fielding was entirely restored to good humour. He listened sympathetically to Daniel's tale of the watcher in Bad Salzuflen, pointed out that this was a very good instance of just how safe Daniel was (for had not the stocky man been powerless to act?) and then dismissed his entourage to bed.

The next morning, very early, Fielding was summoned by the Fusilier Colonel to hear his official instructions for the drive to Kassel. They were to proceed by the direct route *via* Paderborn, Fielding told his 'O' Group on return, and to make their camp in a bombed area near the autobahn. The Colonel was most emphatic that this time he would not tolerate any variations on his orders: hotels were out. They would be in Kassel for between twelve hours and twenty-four.

After the drive had begun, Fielding told Michael Lamb and Daniel that he had rung the B.M.H. again before they left. Mugger, though still on the danger list, was doing well.

'And a good job,' Fielding said to Daniel. 'If Mugger's all right, they'll probably accept this tale the Doctor's thought up about how he fell down in the back of the stores truck. Certainly, those Fusiliers who hit him will keep quiet, and so will Mugger: honour among thieves. The only trouble is that the Fusilier C.O. wants to kick up a fuss. He's heard that some of our chaps were in the Ratskeller, and he wants to know why they weren't arrested by the M.P.'s as well as his own. I told him that Dragoons were clever at taking care of themselves in these situations, but that didn't help matters. He's not very keen on me at the moment. And if he did stir up the shit, it's always possible that you might be among those that fell into it. Which in the circumstances would be less than happy.'

'Surely, nothing much can happen while the manoeuvre's still going on?'

'No . . . Unless Mugger died and some busybody got hold of it. They'd have to cover themselves jolly quickly then.'

'Busybody?'

'We have them.'

'I'd got the impression there was nobody you couldn't fix.'

'Nobody important. The trouble comes from the very small busybodies – the self-righteous National Serviceman who writes to his mother who writes to her Member of Parliament. The latter we can probably cope with – but by that time it's also gone to the press. Meditate on this, Daniel: in our society the big rows are always started by small people – the ones who have nothing to lose and are glad of a little attention.'

'But in this case?'

'No one in the Squadron will say anything. That's all I can promise.'

'But you seem quite confident about it all.'

'What else? Do you expect me to go round crying?'

They were coming into Paderborn now. Daniel looked up at the crazy roof of the cathedral and remembered how he had been there (it seemed ten years ago) with Earle Restarick in the spring. Then he looked down at the main entrance and saw a group of men with red armlets, among them Pappenheim.

'Official observers,' said Fielding. 'There'll be a lot of press-men too.'

'German?'

'English. The lot. Liddell Hart & Co. This is the biggest thing in the military year.'

'I thought the generals were trying to keep it quiet.'

'Until it happened, yes. But they can't keep the journalists out of a show like this.'

'Pappenheim was there with the observers.'

'Why should you worry?'

'First that tubby man from Hannover, now Pappenheim.'

'He probably didn't even see you.'

'The tubby man did. He knows where I am.'

'What can he do about it?'

'They said they'd hunt me down. Anything, an accident, the sort of thing that happened to Mugger. Oh, Christ.'

'Stop it, Danny,' said Michael Lamb. 'We're here with you.' He gestured over his shoulder at the column behind. 'We're all here with you.'

But Daniel had changed the mood of the morning, and little more was said until, two hours later, they reached Kassel.

After they had been in Kassel three days, the Dragoons began to be jumpy. They had been warned to prepare for a stay of up to twenty-four hours, and twenty-four hours, amid the dismal ruins of the flattened slum to which they were allotted, would have been long enough. But first one day went by and then another; unit after unit rolled past them and away to the south; at last even the neighbouring Fusiliers departed; and still the armoured cars and their attendant crews stood idle and without orders among the rubble.

'I can't understand it,' Fielding kept saying. 'The theory is that we must be well up with the attacking forces so that we can do our stuff the moment someone lets off an atomic shell. And until then we're meant to stay close to the Fusiliers for liaison. They've been gone for over twelve hours now.'

The autumn weather, so brilliant when they left Göttingen, had turned grey and damp. A fire had been contrived from old packing cases and assorted debris; but fuel was now exhausted, and only a last poor ghost of warmth came from the black pile of ash.

'Send out a party to collect logs, sir?' said the Sergeant-Major. 'There's those woods the other side of the autobahn.'

'No,' snapped Fielding. 'We may be told to saddle up at any moment. We don't want to have to hang about for anybody.'

'They ought to be occupied, sir. Just sitting here's getting them down. Inter-troop football, sir, all against all, three matches. If we can clear a pitch out of this rubbish.'

'Just as you think best, Sergeant-Major ... I can't understand it at all,' Fielding said.

The Sergeant-Major moved off to organize a clearing party. There was a sceptical but good-humoured cheer, and then the work was quickly and keenly under way.

'How easy it is to keep them happy. As long as they have something, anything, to do. You know,' Fielding said, 'I drove round the town this morning to see if I could pick up any news from anyone. Even Div. H.Q. was packing up to move forward. The General and Ivan had already gone, otherwise I might have learnt something. As it is, I honestly believe we're the last unit left in Kassel. One wonders if they've simply forgotten us.'

'Didn't the Fusilier C.O. say anything before he left?'

'Just that we were to stay here until we received further orders.'

The sun broke through and immediately went in again. The remains of a rotting ceiling collapsed on to a jagged pile of bricks. Fielding and his three officers moved away from the dead fire and started giving desultory encouragement to the soldiers who were clearing the football pitch. Over the waste land came a small, round man wearing a duffle-coat, a haversack and an enormous trilby. Daniel shuddered, thinking that it was the tubby man of Hannover and Bad Salzuflen; but as the figure drew closer he saw a kind smile across an innocent and unknown face.

'Alfie Schroeder,' said the little fellow: 'of the Billingsgate Press.'

'You'd better speak to the Squadron Commander,' Daniel said.

'I'd much rather speak to someone like you.'

'I don't know anything about what's going on.'

'Neither do I,' said Alfie Schroeder. 'Our military correspondent's got the piles, so they sent me at the last minute.'

'You won't learn anything here. The war has passed us by, it seems.'

Alfie Schroeder gave Daniel an odd look, and said,

'I'm sticking to the human angle. I heard a little tale about one of your chaps being taken off half dead to the military hospital in Bielefeld. That's why your lot's still here – so's they can put a hand on anyone who might help with the enquiry. Care to tell me about it?'

'How is he? Mugger?'

'Neither better nor worse, they say.' He gazed solemnly at Daniel. 'I've seen your face before. In the paper.'

'Impossible. My sort don't get into the paper.'

'I've got a long memory for faces. Let's see ... Unofficial strike leader? No. Criminal offence? No. Pools winner? No, but warmer – I've got it, by God I have. Winner of the Spinoza Prize for Mathematics. April, 1951. "Daniel ... er ... er ... Mond, receiving the award from the Chancellor of Cambridge University in the Senate House." What are you doing here, boy? National Service?'

'What else?'

'They must be mad, wasting a chap like you as a private soldier. There's a story in this if you'll go along with it.'

'I'm not allowed to talk to the press.'

'Balls to that. A winner of the Spinoza Prize can talk to anyone he wants to.'

Michael Lamb came up.

'Who's this, Danny?'

Daniel introduced them.

'Mr. Shroeder's interested in Mugger.'

'In Mr. Mond,' said Alfie.

'He says,' Daniel went on desperately, 'that we're being kept here in case there's an enquiry about Mugger.'

'Bugger Mugger. People get hurt every day. It's not every day I find a Spinoza Prize winner arsing about as a common soldier.'

'Watch it,' said Lamb.

'No offence meant. I'm a Labour man myself. But you see what I mean.'

'No,' said Michael Lamb, 'I don't. This man's called Trooper Lewis and he's got an identity card to prove it.'

Daniel produced Lewis's filthy piece of paper.

'Lewis, Edward Paul. Which explains why your friend here calls you Danny, I suppose. There's more in this,' said Alfie buoyantly, 'than meets the eye.'

'Danny's just a nick-name.'

'Tell that to your Auntie Flo. I'm never wrong about a face once I've seen it.'

'You only saw a photograph,' said Daniel.

The Corporal-Major joined them.

'Bloody fire out? That's all we need. Who's this then?'

'Schroeder of the Billingsgate Press,' said Alfie. 'Perhaps you'd like to tell our readers what it's like to give orders to a ruddy genius.'

Tom Chead looked at Daniel and then at Alfie.

'Forget it, matey,' he said. 'Run along and forget it.'

'I've got my job to do.'

'And I've got mine. You leave my soldiers alone. You've no business poking your nose in.'

For answer Alfie opened his haversack and took out a box brownie which he trained on Daniel. There was a ponderous click.

'Pardon me,' Alfie said, 'but I've got a duty to my public. They'll be very interested to see a photo of Mr. Mond here all dolled up and collecting his Spinoza Prize, along with another one of him in his denims doing his National Service just like anybody else. It's the sort of thing which keeps them happy in a democratic age. Keeps my editor happy too. Though he may have some questions about why Mr. Mond says his name is Lewis. Anyone got any answers?'

'Yes,' said the Corporal-Major. He twisted Alfie's arm until the camera fell on the ground, and then stamped on it.

'My Brownie,' said Alfie softly. 'Years I've had it.'

'I told you. Leave my perishing soldiers alone. Busting in here, you and your camera, you might be anyone at all.'

Alfie bent down and picked up the crumpled camera.

'My Brownie . . .'

'Security,' blustered the Corporal-Major. 'How do I know you're what you say you are?'

Alfie held out a press card.

'You only had to ask.'

'Schroeder. What kind of name is that?'

'Good enough to stir up the Billingsgate Press when they see it at the end of a telegram. They're going to be very upset when they hear what you've done to me and my camera. And they're going to believe what I tell them, even without a photo. You should have let it go as it was. You haven't helped Mr. Mond, not one bit.'

Alfie turned and walked away across the waste land, holding the brownie in front of him with both hands. Daniel went after him.

'Mr. Schroeder, I'm so sorry . . .'

Alfie walked straight on.

'He didn't mean it. He's a kind man, really, but he's my friend, you see, and he thought— Mr. Schroeder. You've got to keep quiet about me. You must. *Please.*'

'That's better,' said Alfie, stopping and facing Daniel. 'Now. Why have I got to keep quiet?'

'If you tell anyone who I am, it'll be very bad for me . . . and for those who are helping me.'

'Why?'

'I'm on the run.'

'What have you done?'

'Nothing. Nothing wrong, that is.'

'If you told the Billingsgate Press about it, we could—'

'—No. I can't tell anyone about it. If I did, they might – well – find out a whole lot more. Or there might be new pressures on me. I can't explain.'

'Mr. Mond,' said Alfie, 'you're talking in riddles, but it's obvious there's something big here. If I tip off London, even the little I know, something big's going to come of it and they're going to be very pleased with Alfie Schroeder. I want them to be pleased, Mr. Mond; I need their pleasure.'

'I need your silence.'

'Then you'll have to show me that your need is the stronger.'

For some seconds Daniel cast about for ways of doing this; then he thought of Fielding Gray and what he had said during that last dinner at the Alte Krone.

'On my honour, . . .'

'What honour, Mr. Mond?'

'My honour . . . as a Jew.'

Alfie Schroeder removed his trilby, blew into it several times, and replaced it. Then he handed Daniel the broken brownie.

'So you take it,' he said. 'You'll find the film still inside. It would have been all right, because I'd wound it well on. It would have come out, that picture. Shalom, Daniel Mond.'

The little figure walked on over the waste land. Daniel returned to the Corporal-Major and Michael Lamb.

'He's gone, Danny? Good riddance.'

'He left me his camera. With the film in it. Undamaged.'

'Oh,' said the Corporal-Major and turned heavily away.

'But what's the good?' said Daniel. 'If we're just stuck here until they call us back for an enquiry, what's the good?'

Fifty yards away a football thudded against a wall and a roar went up from the spectators. A despatch rider bumped over the rubble from the direction in which Alfie Schroeder had disappeared.

'Captain Gray?'

'Fetch him, Danny.'

When Fielding opened the envelope, he said:

'At last. But it's not the route I thought. We're to go back to Paderborn and south-west to Bonn. And there's another thing. They think Mugger's going to die.'

At least, thought Daniel, they're not keeping us here, they're letting us advance.

'So they're sending a Special Branch man to Bonn to meet us,' Fielding went on— 'he'll want to interview anyone who knows anything about it.'

Since the order to start had been received late in the afternoon, it was nearly dark by the time the Squadron reached Paderborn, where they turned left down the main route for Dortmund.

Dormiat Dortmundus.

This time the Squadron Sergeant-Major was riding with them in Fielding's Land Rover, as Fielding wished to consult him over the *affaire* Mugger.

'We'll have to take our line from Dr. Motley, sir. From what Tom Chead tells me, the doctor's prepared to support this tale about Mugger falling over in the stores truck . . . unless Mugger dies.'

'What difference does that make?' said Fielding crossly. 'No need to make difficulties just because the poor chap's dead.'

'The doctor's a Catholic, sir. He probably thinks that murderers should be brought to book.'

'But that would mean Daniel here giving evidence. And then where should we all be?'

'I dare say the Corporal-Major's evidence would suffice, Captain Fielding. Again, it all depends on the doctor. If he refrains from mentioning that Daniel . . . Mr. Mond . . . Trooper Lewis was mixed up in it . . .'

'But where is the bloody doctor? How can we know what he's going to say?'

There was no answer to that. The doctor had last been seen retching from his ambulance window as the Fusilier convoy drew out of Kassel. Heaven alone knew where that lot had got to by now.

'Anyway,' said Fielding, 'the doctor himself won't know what he's going to say till he knows whether or not Mugger's really going to die. So if this Special Branch chappie catches up with him while it's still in doubt, what's he going to do then?'

'I really couldn't tell you, sir.'

'What was your impression, Danny? You were there – damn it.'

'Just what Mr. Bunce says. Mick knows we don't want an enquiry since I'm mixed up in it all, but if Mugger dies that won't count. Mick's very firm over some things.' Decency, he thought; he could destroy me with his decency.

Night was now down. A thin drizzle was slanting across the headlights. A huge German truck with trailer overtook them, the trailer lashing back within a yard of their bonnet as it passed and chucking mud all over their windscreen.

'Bastard,' said Michael Lamb. 'He must have overtaken the whole Squadron.'

'Not very hard, the pace we have to travel,' said Fielding. 'My God, how boring these treks are. Got that whisky there, Danny? In the small pack.'

Daniel passed the whisky forward. Fielding took a long swig and didn't pass it back. Sergeant-Major Bunce, next to Daniel, stiffened slightly in the darkness.

'First halt due, sir.'

'To hell with that.' Fielding took another long drink. 'We'll be lucky to make Bonn by midnight as it is.'

Bunce leant forward and quietly took the whisky bottle from Fielding's lap.

'You won't be wanting more of that, sir, not till we've halted for a brew-up. We didn't eat before we left Kassel, remember.'

'Quite right, Mr. Bunce. Sorry.'

'Nothing to be sorry about, sir. If I might suggest . . . There's a good wide margin of grass just here by the look of it.'

Lamb drew off the road on to the grass. Fielding jumped out with a torch and walked back, signalling the other vehicles into the side.

'Cook him something quickly,' Bunce hissed at Daniel, 'and don't let him have that bottle.'

Bunce went off down the column. Daniel opened some tins of stew and emptied them into a saucepan, while Lamb got the oil-burner going. The drizzle, thicker now, swirled all about them, although they were huddled in the lee of the Land Rover.

'The Captain's working up for one of his moods,' Lamb said.

Geddes the barber came out of the dark.

'Hello, cookie,' he said. 'Bas Bunce says to mix these up in the Captain's din-din.'

He passed six tablets of what looked like codeine across to Daniel.

'Crush them into the gravy, dear. Oh, and there's letters for you, Lambkin. Came in with the mail yesterday, but I clean forgot. By-ee for now.'

While Daniel served the stew into mess tins and crushed the codeine tablets into the portion intended for Fielding, Michael Lamb went round in front of the head-lamps to read his mail.

'Message for you, Danny,' he said in a puzzled voice. 'Just says, "Tell Daniel we hope he's enjoying his outing with his nice friends, and we look forward to seeing him when it's over. Earle." Who's he? What's he mean?'

Fielding and Bunce reappeared together. Daniel tried to pick up two mess tins for them, but his hands, shaking and wet with rain, slipped helplessly along the handles. Anyway, which was Fielding's?

'Come on, for Christ's sake. We haven't got all night.'

Calm now, calm.

'Here you are. I'm sorry.'

All four of them wolfed down their stew. Ten minutes later the convoy was on the move again.

'Fielding ... There's been a note from Restarick. They must be following.'

He repeated the message.

'There's nothing they can do. So long as you stick with us.'

'I don't like the sound of it.'

'Neither do I,' said Fielding savagely. 'One bloody mess after another. You're at the bottom of it all, and it's no good your whining. Pass up that whisky.'

'Sir?' said the Sergeant-Major.

'For God's sake don't be such an old woman, Bunce. I've eaten, haven't I?'

All of a sudden drowsiness overwhelmed Daniel. Those tablets, he thought; couldn't even get that right; one bloody mess after another.

'Whisky,' snarled Fielding from a thousand miles away.

Daniel just had strength to glance apologetically at the Sergeant-Major, and then sank down into the dark.

When Daniel awoke, stiff, cold, foul-mouthed, he and Lamb were alone in the stationary Land Rover.

'Where . . . ?'

'Bonn. They've gone to find out where we're meant to go to now.'

'What happened after I went to sleep?'

'Buncie threw the bottle out of the window, and told the Captain he was ashamed of him, being nasty to his friend and getting all worked up about nothing at all.'

'And then?'

'And then,' said Lamb reluctantly, 'the Captain started to shout. He was never appreciated, he said. He did all this for you and just had you grizzling at him for his trouble. He'd given up his university career to be in the Army (not quite true from what I've heard), and all the thanks he got was louts like Basil Bunce telling him his manners. Then he stopped as quickly as he started, said he was sorry about thirty times, and that was it. All over till the next time. It's always like that.'

'Often?'

'About once a month. Generally when things get niggling. Not really rough – he seems to like that – but niggling, like this business of Mugger. Untidiness, he calls it.'

Untidiness was now much in evidence. When Fielding and the Sergeant-Major returned to the Land Rover, they were both jittering with rage.

'Leave us without orders,' the Sergeant-Major said, 'all on our tod for days, and then bawl us out for being late.'

'And shunt us all round Bonn because they still don't know what to do with us . . . We'll leave the column here, Mr. Bunce, and go and find someone who makes sense.'

'Begging your pardon, sir, the Staff Captain said the column was cluttering up the street.'

'What does he want me to do? Dump the whole lot in the river? Daniel, go down the column and find Piers Bungay. Tell him I'm going to Div. H.Q. with the S.S.M. to get proper orders, and that he's to keep the Squadron right here till I get back.'

The Land Rover thundered off. Daniel wandered down the

line of vehicles, until eventually he found Piers Bungay and
Jack Lamprey, who were lolling against one of the armoured
cars and sharing a bottle of hock with the Corporal-Major.

'Hullo, Daniel. What's the news?'

Daniel told them and gratefully accepted a glass of
hock.

'I say,' came a young and haughty voice from the darkness,
'who commands here?'

A guardsman's hat with the circumference of a cart-wheel
and a peak which thrust down like a visor swam through the
murk towards them. It was supported on a column of battle-
dress just over five foot high, the whole having the effect of a
malignant toad-stool.

'Who commands here?' repeated the toad-stool.

'I suppose I do for the time being,' said Piers.

'Look here, then. I'm the Staff Captain, and I told your
Sergeant-Major, *myself*, to get all your infernal tank-things—'

'—Armoured cars—'

'—Armoured car-things out of this street. The B.M.'s livid.
This is Brigade Headquarters, he says, not the Odeon car
park.'

'But my Squadron Commander told us to stay put until he
got back. We don't know where to go, you see.'

'I can't help that,' said the toad-stool, petulant, 'you can't
stay here.'

Julian James lounged up.

'Hullo, Bagger, you old chiz,' he said to the toad-stool.
'What's the trouble?'

Bagger squealed with annoyance.

'Your bloody tank-things are blocking my street.'

'Your street, Bagger? He was always knocking off things
at school,' said Julian to the assembled audience, 'but we can't
let him get away with a whole street.'

Trooper Geddes arrived, waving a piece of paper.

'Mappy-reference just come over the wireless,' he announced. 'We've got to go there straight away.'

'Who sent it? Captain Gray?'

'No, sir. Divisional Intelligence.'

'I can't think what it's got to do with Intelligence.'

'What does that matter?' wailed Bagger. 'You've been told where to go by your wirelesss-thing, so for God's sake get out of my street.'

'But when the Squadron Commander comes back, he'll wonder—'

'—No, he won't. Someone else will have told him—'

'—Someone at Div. H.Q.—'

'—Supposing he doesn't find Div. H.Q.—'

'—Coming back here, expecting to find us—'

'—All alone in the dark—'

'—With nowhere to go—'

'—No one to talk to—'

'—I thought the S.S.M. was with him—'

'—Look, gentlemen all,' said the Corporal-Major. 'Mr. Bungay can take the Squadron on to this mappy-ref— map-reference. I'll wait here with the stores wagon for Captain Gray. That's if the Staff Captain here will kindly permit one vehicle to stay in his street.'

'I suppose so,' said Bagger ungenerously.

'Right,' said the Corporal-Major. 'Now let's just take a look and see whereabouts this map reference is.'

'Good idea,' said Bungay. 'Who's got a map-thing? . . . Ta. I can never remember: is it *up* first or across?'

'Allow me, sir . . .'

After a few moments the Corporal-Major said:

'I don't want to disappoint anyone, but that map-reference, it means this here street.'

'Bagger's street-thing? There you are, Bagger, we've been ordered to stay in your str—'

'—Not to stay here,' shrilled Geddes, 'but to come here, the wireless said.'

'Well, now you've come here and you can bloody well go. The B.M.—'

'—But no one's told us where to come next.'

'Just take this bloody circus away, that's all.'

A fierce, black-jawed little man, wearing a green beret and swishing a black cane with a silver knob, was suddenly inside the circle and revolving like a run-away light-house. Bagger saluted. No one else did.

'Now look here, whoever you are,' Jack Lamprey said, 'why not try to be a little more helpful?'

'I'm the Brigade Major, that's who I am.'

'Splendid,' said Piers. 'Perhaps you can tell us where to go. You see—'

'—Don't you address field officers as "sir" where you come from?'

'No. Now it seems that you and Division between you have made a perfectly ghastly cock-up about our—'

'—Captain Hennessy, I want this officer arrested for insolence.' And to Piers, 'You're arrested, do you hear me?'

'Yes. Now about our—'

'—I won't talk to someone who's been arrested.'

Fielding's Land Rover drew up. Fielding got out, took it all in, saluted the Brigade Major, and said:

'Mr. Bungay, Mr. Lamprey, Mr. James, Corporal-Major. The Squadron will move off in one minute flat. Main road south out of Bonn, right turning at 064279, thereafter halt on signal.'

'You can't take him,' screamed the Brigade Major pointing at Bungay. 'He's under arrest.'

'Galloping paranoia,' said Julian, loud enough for everyone to hear.

'Be quiet,' said Fielding very sharply. Then, grasping Piers by the collar, 'I'll take full responsibility for this officer. He will be available to face your charges at any time – if,' said Fielding looking meaningfully at the large audience of Dragoons around them, 'you can find any evidence to support them. Thirty seconds, gentlemen.'

He flung Piers away from him like a puppy dog in disgrace, mounted his Land Rover and drove on, leaving the Brigade Major frothing and Daniel unheeded.

'Come in the Sergeant-Major's Land Rover, dear,' said Geddes: 'the one down there at the back.'

Gratefully, Daniel accepted. As they left Bonn, he could just make out a river on their left and, on the right, a slope with

imposing houses; then he fell asleep. Some time later he
was jolted awake by a bump in the road and saw that the rear
lights of the column in front of him had formed a long red
path as of slowly twisting tracer which seemed to be working
like a corkscrew into the now unbroken blackness ahead. He
cried out at the beauty of it, thinking it must be a dream, and
slept once more.

When the dawn roused Daniel, he found that they were in
a little park which was dotted about with band-stands and
clumps of trees, and criss-crossed by streams that burbled
under willow-pattern bridges.

'Bad Neuenahr, dear,' said Geddes. 'Spa-town. But they
don't seem to have got round to patching it up yet.'

And indeed the band-stands were scabby with dead paint,
the paths overgrown with weeds, the grass scarred with nettles.
A royal garden, Daniel thought, in the last days of Byzantium.

'Brekker, dear? We've got a nice tin of skinless sausages.'

'No, thanks. I ought to get back to the Squadron Commander.'

'Suit yourself. He didn't seem too anxious for your company last night.'

Pondering this remark, Daniel walked slowly to Fielding's
Land Rover, which was a hundred yards away, beside a pond
and a miniature waterfall. Lamb was sitting on the back by
himself and singing, 'September in the rain.'

' 'Lo, Danny. We'd better get some breakfast ready for the
Captain. He's gone to talk to the Fusiliers.' Lamb gestured
down a long double avenue of trees. 'We're together again.'

They cooked up a pan of fatty bacon. Fielding came down
the avenue with Mick Motley.

'Give him some breakfast,' Fielding said. 'He has good
news.'

'Mugger's going to be all right,' said Mick. 'The Special
Branch man moved into the Kurhotel last night and had me
go over. Just as he was starting in, he had a phone-call from
Bielefeld. Mugger was sitting up and taking nourishment. So
off went the dick to get his story from source.'

Nevertheless, Mick seemed worried about something.

'Had you told him anything?'

'Luckily not. So now it's up to Mugger.'

'He'll think of something plausible and harmless,' said Fielding. 'We've heard the last of this.'

'How long have you been here?' Daniel asked Mick.

'Since yesterday. We've been half round the world since we saw you last. They couldn't decide where they wanted us. Or anyone else.'

'Ivan Blessington said something about that last night,' Fielding told them. 'There's some muddle about the Division which is impersonating the enemy. They changed direction when they weren't meant to, and no one's known what to do since.'

'In that respect at least,' said Mick sourly, 'the manoeuvre bears some relation to probable reality.'

'Si-irr,' came Geddes' voice, panting and fluting down the line of vehicles, 'green alert. Just came over the set.'

'Decision at last,' said Mick Motley. 'I shall be sorry to leave this ridiculous kurgarten.'

But that alone could not account for his evident uneasiness as he chucked away the remains of his bacon with a bad-tempered flick of the wrist and sloped off down the avenue which led back to the Fusiliers.

'He might have waited for a lift,' said Fielding, who soon after drove off with Lamb in the same direction. 'Don't forget,' he shouted back at Daniel: 'draw suits for me and Michael.'

Still too drowsy to be sure what this could mean, Daniel was hustled by the Corporal-Major into a crowd of soldiers, told to right turn, and marched off with the rest over the thick wet grass. After they had left the kurgarten and shuffled a short way down an elegant street, they were called to a halt by a large glass door, on which was blazoned SPIEL BANK. Through this they were fed by files into a thickly carpeted corridor and then up some stairs to where Leonard Percival was presiding over three roulette tables, all of them covered with what looked like diving suits made of fish scales. Leonard

Percival looked straight at Daniel and nodded affably. Then he flicked his fingers, and three Fusilier Sergeants, one to each table, began to distribute the diving equipment.

'I want three, please,' said Daniel when it was his turn.

'Three, laddie?'

Fusiliers, it seemed, were less formal on manoeuvres.

'That's right,' said Percival, who had come up behind the Sergeant. 'Trooper Lewis here is Captain Gray's batman. The third one's for the driver, I expect.'

He flashed his spectacles at Daniel.

'Sign here,' said the Sergeant; 'name and last three.'

'Last three?'

'Last three figures of your number,' prompted Percival kindly.

'I . . . er . . .'

'Nine-two-nine,' said Percival to the Sergeant, who looked surprised. 'Good morning, Trooper Lewis. See you later, I expect.'

Laden with the three suits, Daniel stumbled down the casino staircase to the corridor below, where people were trying the things on. Watching the others carefully, Daniel did the same. After some officious person had pulled a zip at his rear, he found that he was totally encased and looking out through a small window of perspex, feeling much as he had felt (stifled and humiliated) when he had first worn his gasmask as a child. In a matter of seconds the perspex filmed over and resisted all his efforts to wipe it clear. It then occurred to him that the film had of course been caused by his breath on the inside; but he could think of no way of dealing with it, other than by pressing the perspex on to his nose and waggling the latter like an internal windscreen wiper. Since this seemed foolish and was making him very short of breath, he tried instead, but without success, to find the rear zip that would release him. If only he could have air . . . AIR. Then some angel of mercy, who must have seen his struggles, unfastened the zip and helped him, from behind, to work the suit off his shoulders.

'Thank you,' panted Daniel, turning to his rescuer.

'Think nothing of it,' said Leonard Percival; 'but you might find it advisable, next time you put this on, to adjust the oxygen regulator' – he tapped Daniel's left breast – 'as an alternative to suffocation.'

With a gay wave Percival passed on down the passage. Daniel, feeling depressed, nervous, and much in need of his after-breakfast evacuation, gathered up his three suits and went through a door marked *Herren*. Just inside it sat an old woman who was wearing a long black dress and had a dish in her lap which held several silver pieces. Doesn't she know, thought Daniel, that the gamblers have all gone home?

He made to pass the old woman, but she thrust her saucer in his path. Daniel fumbled for his purse and found the only change he had was a five mark piece. Ludicrous; he couldn't give her nearly ten shillings. But he must get to one of the guarded cabinets. Now. He placed the five mark piece in the saucer and took up four silver pieces in exchange. One mark was quite enough. Evidently the old woman thought so too, for she rose, went into one of the cabinets, busied herself inside, then emerged and held the door open for Daniel. As he went in, she made to take the suits from him, but he shook his head, remembering what someone had said, that these were a new pattern, still very secret. Security, he thought, piling them on the floor. What a bloody nuisance they were; he would now have to lug them all the way back across the park.

'Danke,' he said when he came out of the cabinet.

But the old woman was gone. He passed through into the corridor, which was empty. They've gone and left me, he thought. The lights had been turned off and heavy curtains kept out the day. Left me in the dark with no one to talk to. He began to run down the corridor, the anti-radiation suits scratching at his face, twisting between his legs. As he ran, stumbling, sightless, sobbing, an arm came out to stop him.

' 'Ere we are at last,' Tom Chead said: 'Keeping the whole ruddy Squadron waiting.'

The leading elements of the enemy had penetrated as far as Worms, or so it appeared; whereupon Worms had had two 'tactical' atomic missiles pumped on to it and was now a devastated area, whither the Tenth Sabre Squadron, followed at some distance by the Fusiliers, was hastening to tidy up the mess. As they drove south the countryside became flatter and flatter, its hedges receding over the brown fields like enormous spokes which would all meet at some infinitely distant hub. Along the lonely little roads a house, even a lone tree, constituted definite events. An inn was a sensation, and near one such they halted at midday.

'Stand us a beer, Danny?'

'With pleasure.'

He pushed a coin over the bar to pay. The landlord shook his head and pushed it back. On the upper face, Daniel now saw, there was an unfamiliar design. And a date ... Quickly he scooped it up and paid with a note instead.

'Steady with that beer, Danny? What's the matter?

'Someone's passed a useless coin on me. That's all.'

Some hours later they made their base two miles outside Worms. Before they had been there long Mick Motley appeared in his ambulance and announced that he had come on ahead of the Fusiliers to set up a Rehabilitation Centre.

'So find me someone to rehabilitate,' he said.

But it seemed that neither Fielding nor anyone else had any very clear notion of what to do next. Exercise Broomstick, hitherto their most important experience of such matters, had been a carefully prepared affair in a quiet corner of the Harz; by means of prior briefing and appropriatetly planted notices some impression of a 'devastated area' had been created, and this had enabled definite tasks to be allotted which bore a discernible relationship to a theoretical situaton. Here in Worms there was no such situation. Undoubtedly one would have been contrived and imposed by the umpires, had not the enemy's irresponsible behaviour thrown the whole manoeuvre off balance and left the umpires marooned without information, about a hundred miles behind the invaders' front. They were still probably at least as far away as Stuttgart.

'And so,' Fielding was explaining to anyone who could be

got to listen, 'until the umpires turn up there's no basis for action at all.'

'What will these umpires do?' Daniel asked.

'They'll announce that such and such areas are considered impassable and tell us to arrange diversions. That so many people are littered about dead or half alive, and what are we going to do about it? That kind of thing.'

'I want someone to rehabilitate,' said Mick, who had been drinking rather a lot since he arrived.

'Oh God . . .'

'What's more,' said Mick, 'I'm going to take my ambulance into Worms and find someone to rehabilitate.'

Despite the tactful protests of the medical Staff Sergeant, the ambulance went roaring off.

'What we do know, sir,' said the Sergeant-Major, 'is that Worms has been destroyed by atomic shells. So oughtn't we to put on these here radiation suits?'

'And walk round looking like a load of farts with nothing at all to do?'

Daniel recognized the peevish tones he had heard on the road to Bonn.

'Well, sir, we can assume that so many thousand people are dead and look around for burial sites. We can—'

'—Look,' rasped Fielding. 'Just down that road is Worms, a prosperous centre of the wine trade and looking every inch of it. I'm going to assume nothing until someone comes and tells me to. It's not my job – or yours.'

'Imagination, sir? The city's a smoking ruin, the geiger counters are clacking away like castanets, the people – what's left of them – are wandering crazily round like damned souls. There's looting, rioting, rape, mayhem, parties of peasants with perambulators crowding all the roads—'

'—That will do, Mr. Bunce.'

Basil Bunce looked dejected. The ambulance came roaring back and Mick leered at them out of the driver's window.

'I've found someone to rehabilitate,' he said.

He tottered down from the cab, then climbed into the back and shut the doors with a crash.

'Whatever can he be up to?' said Piers Bungay.

'Well, if we're not going to do anything else, sir,' said the Sergeant-Major, 'we may as well brew-up.'

'Anything to keep you happy, Sergeant-Major.'

Bunce went away to organize the brew-up. Fielding lit a cigarette, puffed it, flicked at it impatiently and threw it away. Julian James, having set up a folding table and four camp stools, summoned Daniel, Bungay and Lamprey to Bridge. Just as they were picking up their hands, a large motor-coach drew up.

'Crikey, said Julian. 'The official observers.'

Led by a fat and cosy brigadier, official observers and journalists of every shape and complexion began to climb down from the coach. A Japanese gentleman was there, two Indians (quarrelling with each other), and several grinning Negroes; an obese Turk, palpably drunk, was there and also a tall Englishman whom Daniel recognized as a distinguished military historian; Pappenheim was there and so was Alfie Schroeder. Fielding saluted the Brigadier, who, though obviously a tolerant and amicable soul, was showing signs of displeasure.

'These gentlemen are all interested in observing the new Courier Team in action,' said the Brigadier, panting slightly as though from incipient indigestion.

'Well, we're the advance guard.'

'I know. We rather thought – well – perhaps you'd be wearing your radiation suits—'

'—I desire very much,' said the obese Turk, 'To see the fornication suits.'

'—And, well, sort of doing your job.' The Brigadier looked reproachfully at the Bridge four which, although now standing up to show respect for his seniority, was still bidding briskly.

'We're having our tea,' said Fielding, 'and awaiting instructions.'

'Four no trumps.'

'Is there nothing I can show these gentlemen?'

'Five hearts ... Perhaps,' opined Julian without being

asked, 'they would be amused by the Rehabilitation Centre.'

'He pointed to Mick Motley's ambulance.

'Rehabilitation Centre?' said Alfie, winking at Daniel. 'What's that?'

'It's where we take care of civilians and others badly affected by radiation.'

'That sounds interesting,' said the Brigadier doubtfully.

'Five no trumps. We are playing Blackwood, partner?'

'You. What is your duties?' said the Turk to Daniel.

'I'm the Squadron Commander's personal servant.'

The Turk kissed his fingers and started prancing obscenely about.

'Do you mind? There may be a slam on here.'

The Turk looked at Julian as though about to order him shot, then joined Alfie and the two Indians by the ambulance.

'Damned impertinence. Six hearts . . .'

There was a scream from inside the ambulance. Alfie, standing by the rear doors which he had just opened, was blushing violently. The two Indians were holding hands and tittering, while the Turk's face was swollen with prurience.

'The Rehabilitation is instructive?' whinnied the Japanese, and skipped over to have a look for himself.

'Of course, of course,' the military historian was saying: 'the old system of the field brothel under medical supervision. I'm delighted to find it restored – keeps the men clean and morale high. In an atomic war, you see, there'll be no bloody bishops to complain. They'll all be dead,' he concluded with relish.

'Six no trumps.'

'I like very much the rehabilitation.'

'I'm afraid,' said the Brigadier to Fielding, 'that I'll have to report all this.'

'That ambulance is nothing to do with me, Brigadier. It's on loan from the Medical Corps to the first battalion of the Wessex Fusiliers.'

'But I mean, all this slackness. Bridge and all that. What will all these frightful foreigners think?'

'Sir, oh sir,' came Geddes' deplorable falsetto, 'message

on the set. They've made a mistake. The atom shells haven't fallen here at all.'

'Where have they fallen?'

'They're trying to find out.'

'You see, Brigadier? If I'd committed my men in Worms, it'd have taken me hours to pack up again and start for the real trouble.'

'Of course, dear boy. Sorry I was cross. The fact is that this little party is rather a strain . . . Come along, gentlemen, please.'

The Turk lingered lustfully by the ambulance.

'Come along, Colonel Haq.'

The Turk still lingered.

'Colonel Haq, there's a bottle of whisky waiting in the coach. If you don't come now, those journalists will have drunk it all.'

The Brigadier made a clucking noise and the last of his charges boarded the bus. As it drove off, Pappenheim stared blankly back out of the window and Alfie Schroeder waved his enormous hat.

Fielding went over to the wireless set, where he spent several minutes. Then he said something to the Sergeant-Major, and the cry went ringing down the line:

'Prepare to mount in three minutes. South – for Baden Baden.'

'The trouble, of course, is the Americans,' Captain Detterling announced.

The sun was shining in Baden Baden, and Fielding, Daniel and Detterling were sitting in the garden of the Brenner's Park Hotel.

'I must be getting back,' said Fielding uneasily. 'I've a lot to do, and I'm not meant to be here at all. Officially the whole place is a radio-active inferno. Can I leave Daniel with you? His luggage is in the hall.'

'As I was saying,' Captain Detterling said, 'it is the new American clientele which is ruining everything. The reason is that Americans simply cannot understand servants. Their sickening affectations of equality, alternating with bouts of persecution mania, have destroyed discipline. One minute they are simpering over the chamber-maid as though she were their adopted daughter, the next they go into a fit of paranoia because they have realized that it is not their love which she wants but their money. All of which is very unsettling for the staff. This hotel has always been famous for its calm and elegance, but how can you have either when at any moment some rabid matriarch from the middle-west may start squealing that the barman has cheated her of sixpence?'

'Look,' said Fielding. 'I'm really in a terrible hurry to get back to the Squadron. I've brought Daniel here to deliver him into your safe keeping. Can I take it that you'll see him safely over the frontier?'

'And then,' said Detterling, 'they refuse to understand food. This hotel has only just reopened for the first time since the débacle. Herr Brenner has made heroic efforts to ensure that the cuisine should be what it always used to be – the most refined in Europe. So naturally it is very upsetting for him to discover that he now has to entertain a class which goes in either for footling vegetarian fads or else for enormous hunks of raw meat.'

'I'm due for a final briefing from the umpires in under an hour,' Fielding wailed. 'I must know what you're going to do about Daniel.'

'I am not a difficult man to please,' Detterling said, 'but I do like to receive what I'm paying for. Last night at dinner I was told I could not have a Bearnaisse sauce because there was no tarragon. Why was there no tarragon? Because some wretched American woman, the wife of a manufacturer of cheap brassières, had an allergy to it. If any came within a hundred yards of her, she was subject to uterine frenzy. So her husband had ordered that all tarragon be removed from the hotel, and he was obeyed because he had booked twenty-five suites for a four-day business conference next November. A business conference in Brenner's Park Hotel. It passes belief.'

'Will you take care of Daniel?'

'No,' said Detterling, 'I will not. I've already put up with enough inconvenience because of the follies of your damned Squadron. Think of all the time I sacrificed to sorting out Giles Glastonbury's nonsense. After a row like that, I should have thought you'd have more sense than to stick out your neck in this ridiculous way. Think of the trouble there'll be if someone finds out what you've done. Passing off a civilian as a Dragoon – it's an insult to the Regiment.'

'I've already explained the circumstances.'

'All Mond had to do was to hand himself over to Pappenheim and Percival. I've met Percival's uncle – a very sound man. If Mond will make stupid difficulties, why should I put myself out?'

'I don't know,' Daniel said. 'I just had a feeling I could rely on you, that's all.'

'Of course,' said Fielding, 'if you're afraid . . .'

'I am merely refusing to put up with unnecessary inconvenience. I came through my entire military career without a day's discomfort or annoyance, so you can hardly expect me to incur them now because of some silly scruple of Mond's.'

'His secret—'

'—Whatever his secret may be, it is his patriotic duty to hand it over to responsible people. I know something of these matters, and I know that Pappenheim and Percival are suitable recipients.'

'Come on, Daniel. We're wasting our time.'

Fielding and Daniel rose to go.

'Sit down,' said Detterling crossly, 'and listen. If you're determined to see this through, I suppose I must help you. *Res Unius,* et cetera, even if Mond is only a fake.'

Detterling lifted his left ankle with his right hand, placed it carefully on his knee, and then put his fingers together.

'I can't actually escort Mond myself,' he intoned, 'because I'm going to the races this afternoon with Max de Freville and I've got my cousin Canteloupe coming to dinner. But the answer's so simple I wonder you haven't seen it for yourself.'

'It isn't simple at all. Earle Restarick's people will be keeping a watch, both for Daniel Mond *and* Trooper Lewis, at every likely crossing place on the frontier. Now, we're going to be fully occupied here in Baden doing our courier stunt at last; and even if I could spare the whole Squadron to escort Daniel, there's no end to the dodges they might try to stop him getting across. That's why we were relying on you. There'll be a lot of good reasons why they won't want to tangle with a British Member of Parliament. If Daniel were once firmly under your protection, they'd probably call the hunt off.'

'I've already told you,' said Detterling, 'that I'm not at leisure for the task. Baden races only happen once a year, and one can't afford to miss anything. However, it is all, as I was saying when you interrupted me, exceedingly simple. Listen carefully, and I will tell you what you must do . . .'

When they left Detterling, Fielding and Daniel collected Daniel's luggage from the hall of the hotel and put it back in the Land Rover. Then they were driven by Lamb down a broad avenue, past the Kurhaus and the many-coloured terrace of the Trinkhalle, and up to the left on to the slopes which overlooked the town. All about them, as they went, leaves rustled and water glistened; while the hill which they must climb to reach the Squadron resembled nothing so much, with its little pavilions and carefully drilled trees, as a toy scene set down as a background for a child's model railway.

As they drove no one said anything at all until they had almost reached the camp at the top of the hill. Then Daniel murmured,

'I'm sorry you won't be there . . . at the end. After we've come so far.'

Fielding shrugged.

'You had to leave us sometime. We'll miss you, Daniel. But it's also rather a relief.'

At the Squadron camp the umpires were already waiting to brief Fielding. Daniel, in an end of holiday mood, went round saying his good-byes. But since the Sabre Squadron was at last about to go into action, no one had much time to spare for him.

'See you at Lancaster some day,' said Julian James; 'I must pay the old place a visit.'

'Don't forget,' said Basil Bunce gloomily, 'to send back Lewis's identity card.'

'Don't forget,' said Tom Chead, 'that you owe the Captain nearly four quid for that kit you're wearing.'

'Don't forget . . . don't forget us,' said Michael Lamb, and went back to checking his engine.

A little later an order was shouted down the lines and everyone started to put on his anti-radiation suit. Daniel put his on just by Mick Motley's ambulance, in which his suitcase was already stowed.

'Typical of the Dragoons,' Mick Motley was saying: 'they have all the bright ideas and leave others to do the dirty work . . . Anti-mist solution for the eye-piece – here.'

'I'm sorry to be a nuisance.'

'I don't mind, Danny. I'm glad to help. The fact remains that when the chips are down, so to speak, the Dragoons have always quietly disappeared. With the best of excuses, of course.'

'Detterling hadn't even a good excuse. Only that he was going with a friend to the races. He just said, "Motley's your man – and tell him I said so". He seemed to think he was doing you a favour.'

'They're clever at giving that impression . . . Don't forget to check your oxygen rate every fifteen minutes.'

'How long does the oxygen last?'

'About three hours. But you and I will be out of these things long before then.'

After that Mick's Staff Sergeant zipped up their suits and there was no further conversation.

The Sabre Squadron, with the ambulance in the middle of the column, wound down the hill, turned right along the wide avenue past the Trinkhalle and the Kurhaus, and then right again. Daniel peering through the porthole in one of the rear doors, saw a sign which said 'Schwarzwald'. The Squadron, he knew, would set up a base-headquarters somewhere on the edge of the Black Forest, and would then return to proceed with its task of purifying and disciplining a theoretically devastated Baden Baden. Meanwhile, Mick would stay at the base in the forest and set up his Rehabilitation Centre; and it was on the functions of this that Daniel's final escape would depend.

Slowly the column rumbled on. Daniel looked out of the porthole at the armoured car just behind. This, he knew, was the leading vehicle of Piers Bungay's Troop and contained, among other things, Bungay, to whom he had not had time to say good-bye. This was sad, as Bungay was not the sort of person he would meet again. Julian, yes. Fielding, yes, and even Captain Detterling. But not Piers Bungay, who was now locked away from him for ever inside his anti-radiation suit. Daniel hated to leave people for ever without saying good-bye; it was like forgetting to close an account which one meant never to use again. For year after year, he felt, his name would be set, on the first of every month, at the top of a new page in a ledger; but at the end of every month the page would still be blank, and the shop keeper would shake his head sadly, wondering what he had done to offend his client. Quite untrue of course. For most people in this world, whether shopkeepers or Bungays, did not sorrow over the empty page, they just put a line straight through the name at its head; but this too was sad, even sadder than reproachful remembrance. 'Don't forget us,' Michael Lamb had said; but how soon would Michael forget?

The ambulance came to a halt. Daniel, in accordance with his instructions, sat still in the back; until eventually a radiation suit opened the doors and beckoned him down. He could not even tell whether it was Mick or the Staff Sergeant. Whoever it was lumbered up into the ambulance and arranged some blankets on stretchers; then he opened a cupboard and dragged out what looked like a small deflated barrage balloon. With surprising deftness he tied a pair of cords round a fir-tree, tied two more round another fir-tree, and then gave the silver material a brisk shake, whereupon it unfolded itself and dropped a gleaming curtain to the ground, thus forming a small bell tent the apex of which was secured by the lines of cord stretched between tree and tree. Other such tents, sending out a susurration as of pliant tinfoil, were unfolding all round them; until the scene resembled an engineer's drawing which Daniel had once been shown of an envisaged settlement, crowned with domes, turrets and cupolas, on the moon. The figure in the suit took him by the arm, shook him out of his rapt contemplation of the miracle that was making around them, and guided him, through a complexity of overlapping flaps, into the tent. There he unzipped himself and Daniel, and worked his suit off his shoulders. It turned out to be Mick.

'Magic gadgets, these,' he said. 'This is where I live and examine my patients in ray-proof security.'

'Except that every one of them that comes in will bring contamination with him. To say nothing of what we've brought in ourselves.'

'They're experimenting with some kind of spray to deal with that. They're also planning lighter and more flexible suits in which it will be possible to work – even to perform surgery – so that one need never take them off.'

'Except to eat and defecate.'

'Stop making difficulties, Daniel. It's early days yet. Eating will be reduced to swallowing pills, and as for the other thing, they're planning a built-in chemical unit.'

'Charming.'

'Anyway, as things are we've got this tent, and you'd better make the best of it because there may be a long time to wait.'

'Can't we go out? It's such a beautiful day.'

'Not without wearing our radiation suits. The umpires would stop us. They're going to be swarming all round here – we're part of a very important experiment.'

'I do believe you're preening yourself, Mick.'

Outside there was a grinding of engines.

'That'll be the main body of the Squadron going back to Baden. They should be bringing in my first patients in about two hours.'

'Who will these patients be?'

'Spare soldiers from the umpiring units with tickets describing their supposed condition. I give them temporary treatment and then put the necessary admin. machinery in motion to deal with their cases. Which reminds me. We'd better make out a ticket for you.'

While Mick scribbled on a writing pad, Daniel looked out of a perspex panel in the wall of the tent. The observers' charabanc drew into his field of vision and emitted the observers. The Brigadier at their head was beaming and gesticulating; the obese Turk, just behind him and still plainly drunk, got stuck in the door and had to be pushed through by Alfie Schroeder.

'Here you are,' said Mick, handing Daniel a sheet of paper. 'Don't lose it.'

'What does it mean?'

'You'll see . . . Oh God. Not them again.'

The two Indian observers had come giggling into the tent.

'No nice lady today, doctor sahib?'

The Japanese scurried in behind them.

'Ah, the rehabilitation gentlemen. The rehabilitation is not so instructive this morning.'

Pappenheim came in, glowered at Daniel, and went out.

'Come along, gentlemen,' clucked the Brigadier outside: 'we shall be returning to the Rehabilitation Centre when it's in action later on.'

Noises of giggling, clucking, chirruping, panting and complaining faded away among the trees.

'I think,' said Mick Motley, 'that we'd better have some lunch and get a rest while we can. You're going to need all your strength, Daniel. Yes, indeed. All your strength.'

About two and a half hours later the first of Mick Motley's radio-active 'patients' began to come in. These were cases so badly affected that they could not walk and had been ferried to the base on improvised stretchers strapped to armoured cars. They were one and all prescribed 'deep sedation', after which they were laid in rows under the trees to die. They would be finally disposed of by working parties from the Fusiliers, who were expected to arrive that evening.

The official observers and journalists took considerable interest in this grisly charade, the journalists at least apparently feeling that some protest was called for. Although Mick Motley explained patiently that all those so far 'treated', being beyond hope, would in any case die in a few hours and painfully, this was not considered a good enough answer. The public conscience, it appeared, required radio-active humanity to live to the last gasp even if it would prefer not to.

'Look, gentlemen,' said Mick desperately: 'this is euthanasia, mercy killing.'

'Mercy killing,' said a hatchet-faced man in a tweed suit, 'is for animals. Surely medicine can do better than that.'

'Not yet it can't,' said Mick. 'The only hope left for that lot is God's grace.'

Alfie Schroeder, who was standing near Daniel, thought this so funny that he cackled with laughter; whereupon the Brigadier, who was looking rather distraught, led his charges away to their picnic tea.

'What's with you?' whispered Alfie to Daniel, lingering.

'The doctor's fixing something to get me out . . . How long is your lot staying here?'

'I don't know. Why?'

'It would be better if that German, Pappenheim, didn't see what happens.'

'What harm can he do you?'

'I'm not sure. But I think it would be better if he didn't know what's done with me.'

'I'll do my best.' Alfie grinned and produced a packet of laxative chocolate. 'Of course, if he doesn't like chocolate . . . One thing. If ever you can talk about all this, you'll talk to me first, won't you? You probably don't think much of the Billingsgate Press, but one good turn deserves another.'

'Agreed.'

Half an hour later, some less seriously afflicted patients arrived, straggling on foot in a long column which was guarded by two armoured cars. Daniel watched through the perspex panel as they were lined up outside the tent. A group of five men staged a breakaway; a machine gun chattered; an approving umpire made a note on his mill-board.

'Now then,' said Mick. 'I'm going to mix you in with that

lot. When you leave here you'll be a soldier from the first
battalion of the Cumberland Light Infantry, which is one of
the umpiring units, and you'll be impersonating an enemy
casualty captured in the ruins of Baden Baden. All right?'

'Surely one of the umpires will see that something's wrong?
They're watching every move.'

'No. The assumption is that enemy casualties, as opposed to
civilian ones, may have been wearing protective suits at the
time of the explosion.'

Mick pointed through the perspex. Several of the 'casualties' were indeed wearing anti-radiation suits.

'We're going to pass you off as one of them,' Mick said.
'Shock case.'

'My luggage?'

'Don't worry about that. Don't worry about anything. Remember, Daniel: no one ever interferes with an ambulance,
wherever it's going. Get the idea?'

'Restarick's people would interfere with a hearse, let alone
an ambulance.'

'Not unless they had reason to suppose you were in it. We're
going to take care of that now.'

Mick helped Daniel with his suit and then zipped him in.
He produced a pair of pliers and did something rather stren-
uous to the zip. After this he took the casualty ticket which he
had written out earlier for Daniel, added something at the top,
and handed it back.

'This is your passport,' he shouted into Daniel's ear. 'Don't
lose it. Now wait.'

The first casualty came into the tent. Mick examined his
ticket, said something which Daniel could not hear, endorsed
the ticket, and gestured the man out. The second casualty to
enter was one in a radiation suit. This time Mick took considerably longer reading the ticket. Then he showed the man a
corner of the tent, indicating that he was to wait there; after
which he looked slowly up at Daniel and nodded his head towards the way out.

Once outside, Daniel was approached by two men in radiation suits, who looked over his ticket and led him off towards

a group of ambulances which had accrued, Daniel supposed, during the course of the afternoon. They all seemed identical with Mick's. As he went, Daniel had a brief glimpse of Pappenheim, who was disappearing rapidly into a clump of bushes. Full marks to Alfie Schroeder of the Billingsgate Press ... though surely, Daniel thought, there could no longer be anything to fear from Pappenheim. From the others, yes; but there had been no sign of them since the note addressed to Lamb. Helped by his two escorts, he clambered into the back of an ambulance and was relieved to see his suitcase where he had left it. Presumably there was to be a convoy and Mick's ambulance was to make part of it. His guides raised their right hands in a kind of admonitory salute and stalked away.

A few minutes later he was joined by two more casualties, neither of them in radiation suits, who looked at him curiously but said nothing. Someone climbed into the cab in front; twice the engine failed to start, then the ambulance drew slowly away through the wood and bumped on to the road. So soon, Daniel thought; there could be no question of a convoy then. For the first time it occurred to him to look at the ticket which Mick had made for him. This, being written in a typical doctor's hand, was barely decipherable; but at the top Daniel could just make out the word 'encased' and the interrupted phrase 'suit only removable by'. Remembering Mick's business with the pliers, Daniel felt behind him with his gauntleted hands and failed to locate the thing of material which operated the runner on the zip. So that was it: no zip, probably other damage as well; so that no one could identify him or question him until he was cut out or otherwise released from his sheath of this new and secret material, which would doubtless require expert handling. 'Suit only removable by.' He had the best protection in the world: he was entombed.

And for all he knew betrayed. Who were these two men sitting with him? Who was driving? Where were they going? Hitherto he had assumed without question that Motley was on his side; that he had been told a certain amount by Fielding, had guessed as much more as he needed to know, and was therefore, out of his natural decency, lending assistance which only he could give. But why should this be so? Why should not Mick Motley have his own axe to grind? Almost everyone else seemed to have one. He could be sending Daniel anywhere – to Percival or to Restarick or to the Devil, for all Daniel knew, and not a thing he could do about it. He could move only with difficulty. He had forgotten to apply anti-mist solution to his perspex eye-piece before putting the suit on again (why hadn't Motley reminded him?) and by now he could hardly see. When his supply of oxygen ran out, as it would do in about three hours (according to the estimate Mick had given him) he would not be able to breathe. Suit only removable by . . . And if whatever or whoever was needed was not available? *Dormiat Danielus.*

Come, come. This was paranoia, this was panic. Unworthy of a Dragoon. Be calm. The ambulance, which was now going very fast, swung round a corner so sharply that all three of the rear passengers fell in a huddle on the floor. One of his unencumbered companions helped Daniel back to his seat and said something inaudible with an ugly twist of his lips. Daniel looked stupidly back and nodded inside his helmet. The ambulance, having picked up the speed it had lost on the turn, went faster than ever – apparently, thank God, down a straight road now. Daniel tried to peer out of one of the portholes, but his eye-piece was too misty for him to make out anything except an unwinding riband of grey. Calm. Of course Mick Motley was his friend. Then why did his two companions look so grim and threatening? Sheer fright, perhaps, at the speed. After all, one of them had helped him up very kindly; there was no reason to suppose they were his enemies. No reason at all. As for his oxygen, he had enough for about two hours and three-quarters. Of course someone would be available to release him long before then. Of course Mick knew what he was doing. Of course he was being taken to a safe place. Yes, but where? Well, it was his fault if he didn't know that, he should have asked Mick. Why hadn't he? Because he was bewildered, because he hadn't been thinking, because he had trusted Mick implicitly; and of course he was right to do so. Of course. Calm. Be calm.

After twenty minutes of driving dead straight and always at the same high speed, the ambulance made a long turn to the right, and then proceeded rather more slowly than before, taking occasional bends. After five minutes of this, Daniel was suddenly conscious of a noise like a telephone ringing in a distant room. The warning bell, he decided; they must be coming into a town. At this point the ambulance stopped. For ten minutes, twenty, nothing happened. 'No one ever interferes with an ambulance,' Mick had said. Thirty minutes, forty . . . For Christ's sake. Less than two hours of oxygen now, much less. The rear doors opened; a jaw with a cigarette clamped in it was thrust into the ambulance and two beady eyes looked at Daniel. The cigarette waggled, a yellow claw snatched his ticket, a forehead narrowed, a pair of shoulders shrugged in spiteful resignation, and the claw, having returned the ticket, was raised to a hat in mock salute. A round hat; French.

After a further wait of twenty minutes the ambulance drove on, sedately now, its bell ringing no more. Again it stopped, again the rear doors opened. Below them Daniel could see a blur of white. Two smaller blurs detached themselves, turned into orderlies as they came closer, took Daniel efficiently by either arm, helped him out of the ambulance, across some gravel, up some steps, down a corridor and into a room. Daniel thrust his ticket at them, gestured frantically at the back of his suit and then at the left breast where the oxygen control lay. One of them took the ticket, shrugged, gave it back, grinned at his colleague and followed him out of the door. Daniel rushed after them but the door was locked.

By his calculation (and if Mick had been telling the truth) he had just on an hour's supply of oxygen left. An *hour*? He hadn't allowed, he suddenly remembered, for the time during which he had worn the suit between leaving the camp above Baden and arriving at the forest base. That had been – oh God, God – at least forty minutes. He had perhaps a quarter of an hour left. He clawed behind him at the useless zip. He thumped on the locked door. He even yelled aloud inside his armour. Then he sank to his knees on the floor, weeping and praying to a God in whom he did not believe to send him succour; and at the end of his prayer the door duly opened to reveal Leonard Percival in battle dress and just behind him Earle Restarick.

For some moments both of them stood grinning down at Daniel. They've got me where they want me now, he thought. And then, why are they together? But what difference did that make to him? The deal which they would offer was already plain. They'd leave him inside the suit but set him up somehow with more oxygen – under constant threat of withdrawing supplies. Only when they knew what they wanted would they release him from his prison . . . or perhaps just leave him to die. But this was France, this must be a French hospital, surely . . . No. To judge from their triumphant smiles there could be no escape. It was all quite clear. Tell or suffocate: your knowledge or your life.

Daniel was still on his knees. He must get up or they would think he was imploring their mercy. With an immense effort (the oxygen must be very low now) he rose to his feet, staggered over to the wall and with his right gauntlet traced an enormous NO. Then he turned and faced them, standing very upright. For perhaps ten seconds he confronted their still smiling faces through the sweaty perspex; then the dark came up and swallowed him whole.

When Daniel recovered consciousness, he was in bed in a large and pleasant room the ample window of which framed a row of sunlit poplar trees. On either side of his bed sat Leonard Percival and Earle Restarick.

'You've no idea,' Percival said, 'the trouble they had cutting that suit off you. They jolly nearly had to use a blow-torch. You ought to be exceedingly grateful they got you out in time.'

'Gratitude's not my forte at the moment.'

'Come, come. Things might be a lot worse. Did you really think, Mond, that you could put an end to all your troubles just by leaving Germany? Didn't it occur to you that the sort of organization which Restarick here represented would have resources that transcended a simple frontier?'

'I was putting my trust in England. A man can be safe there. In England. In Cambridge.'

'Maybe,' said Earle Restarick, 'and maybe not. Anyhow, you're still a long way from England. In Strasbourg, to be more exact. How do you feel about putting your trust in the French?'

Daniel did not reply.

'Tell me,' said Earle, 'if you had got away ... to England ... what would you have done? When all the dons said, "Welcome home, Daniel Mond, and what have you brought back from Göttingen?", what would you have done?'

'I should have told them that I'd failed.'

'Even if it meant giving up your chance of a Fellowship and leaving Lancaster College?'

'Rather than tell anyone what I knew,' insisted Daniel, 'I should have told them that I'd failed with the Dortmund Papers.'

'Why?'

Daniel shrugged against the pillow.

'Do you think I might have something to eat? I don't know how long I've been asleep, but I'm damned hungry.'

'You were out for sixteen hours. They stuck a needle into you to make sure you had a nice long rest.'

'To get my strength back for whatever's coming next, I suppose.'

Earle twitched slightly and pressed a bell. A little while later a black nun came in with a tray of rolls and coffee.

'You know,' said Percival, 'we admire you. You've given us a lot of trouble, and you're just about as wrong-headed as you can be, but we really do admire you. So as a measure of our appreciation we're going to tell you a story. A story with a moral,' he said, flashing his spectacles. 'You'll like that, won't you?'

Earle looked away and Daniel went on eating.

'The story started,' said Percival, 'when certain inquisitive gentlemen in Whitehall heard that Dirange was sending someone out to have a go at the Dortmund Papers. Now as it happens, and although you didn't know it, quite a few people had a rough idea of what these were about; but since no one had ever been able to do the sums properly, it wasn't the faintest good. What was needed was someone to do a pukka job of working it all out, in the hope that this would confirm and add to what little had been surmised and, most important of all, enable the knowledge to be applied. And now here was wonder-boy Mond about to have a crack, and the betting was that he'd succeed.'

'Whose betting?'

'Let's just say the experts. These days, Mond, people like you go on record very early in your lives. In your case, when you won the Spinoza Prize. You'd already become a valuable national property, you see. So we knew all about your capacities – but we also knew you were a bit quirky. All this left-wingery and stuff. You being you, it was clear from the start that if the secret was the sort of thing we thought it was, then you'd do your damnedest to suppress it when you found it.'

'How right you were.'

'So we had to think up ways of bringing pressure to bear on you.'

'I wonder you didn't fit up a wheel and a rack.'

'We're not allowed to torture people,' said Percival, as though the suggestion had been entirely serious; 'not English people anyway. Not yet. It has to be psychological. So we consulted some of your friends at Lancaster—'

'—What friends?'

'It would hardly be fair to tell you. You'll just have to live with that.'

Jacquiz? Robert Constable? Was no one to be trusted any more?

'So we consulted some of your chums,' Percival was saying, 'and we found out that you had a very affectionate and dependent nature. If there was one thing which would really knock you flat, it was the withdrawal of love. So at this stage we made a very simple plan. Restarick here was to turn on his affection and then turn it off again; you were to be left in loneliness for some weeks; and then Restarick would come back, full of love after all, and you in your relief would tell him anything he asked you.'

'A good plan,' said Daniel bitterly; 'you don't know how good.'

'But,' said Earle, 'it went wrong. Just when you were nicely softened up, those Dragoons hit town. So no more loneliness. A new friend called Fielding Gray. Months of work wasted.'

'You knew so much,' said Daniel, 'didn't you realize the Dragoons were coming, and that Julian James had been at Lancaster, which made it at least possible that I'd get to know them?'

'Blind spot,' said Percival sadly. 'The very last thing anyone thought of was that you'd become pals with the military. So no one had checked on the Dragoons. An endearing example of British inefficiency . . . Anyway, there it was. Change of plan required. Love was out. The next best thing was fear.'

Percival rose and went to the window.

'There was nothing personal,' he said bleakly.

'I dare say not.'

'The same goes with me,' said Earle. 'I've told you before and it's true. I really was fond of you, Daniel.'

'But that didn't stop you later, did it?'

'Look,' said Percival, swinging in from the window, 'we're not going to apologize. Restarick and myself and the rest of us, we were acting on behalf of the free powers of Western Europe and of Great Britain among them. We needed what you knew.'

'And the way to get it,' said Daniel, 'was through my fear.'

'Right. So we started to frighten you. Up till then I'd just been keeping an eye on things. I sat upon that hill, a humble Lieutenant of Foot, receiving reports from Restarick and von Bremke—'

'—So he was in it too?'

'Holding the ring, you might say. Among other things, he was meant to keep an eye on your progress, and to play on your obstinancy by telling you the job couldn't be done, that

Dortmund was off his nut anyway — in the hope that you'd turn round and show him just how wrong he was. But that's all by the way ... As I was saying, there I sat in those barracks, and if things had gone right you'd never have known I existed. But when a new plan had to be hatched up, my help was needed. We had to convince you that you were in danger. We had to set up a myth of goodies and baddies and make you believe in it. So I took the first possible opportunity of introducing myself and Pappenheim as agents of the Saint George department, and we created a whopping great dragon: an entirely fictitious neo-Nazi conspiracy. With a bit of American aid thrown in because you, as an anti-capitalist, were sure to swallow that. Fear is like beauty, Mond; it lies in the eye of the beholder.'

Percival sat down on the foot of the bed.

'You won't need me to spell it all out from there. The technique was to have the dragon puff flame increasingly near your backside, and every time he did so renew St. George's offer to come to the rescue — on his terms of course. But then something else went wrong. Captain Detterling upset our little scheme whereby Restarick's "Neo-Nazis' were to have prevented you leaving Germany. Still, we were in high hopes. The dragon stepped up his puffing and your pants were getting hotter and hotter — till suddenly you vanished.'

'So that at least was genuine,' Daniel said. 'The Dragoons really were helping me?'

'For what use it was, yes.'

'It's important to me to know. Fielding Gray and the rest — they weren't just part of the pretence? They really did try to rescue me?'

'In their casual way.'

'At least their friendship was true.'

'Yes. But it didn't take us long to find out where you were — and we guessed what they hoped to do with you. Hand you over to Detterling, M.P., for him to do his fix-it act all over again. So we decided to let you get that far — indeed to make sure that you did. We persuaded the brass-hats to switch the atomic attack from Worms to Baden. It took some doing, and we were nearly refused, but at the last moment someone very important indeed weighed in on our side. The whole manoeuvre was switched, Mond, to get you unsuspecting to Baden Baden; you must have cost hundreds of thousands of pounds.'

'I'm flattered.'

'Meanwhile, someone had waited on Captain Detterling and told him, very firmly, what he was to do about you when you arrived. He didn't care about being told, but he's a responsible man, he has his country's interest at heart, and so, after a few things had been explained to him, he agreed to obey our orders. He would advise Captain Gray to hand you over to Dr. Motley for the last leg of your escape. And now I'm afraid you're going to be very disillusioned to hear that Mick Motley had his instructions too.'

'But you said . . . you said that the Dragoons were genuine, that they were what they seemed to be.'

'The Dragoons of the Sabre Squadron, but not Detterling, and not Dr. Motley. One of the things I sniffed out during my peaceful days in the barracks was that Motley, having made a corporal's wife pregnant, was reluctantly compelled to abort her. So it wasn't too hard to persuade Motley to come in on our side. I broke the sad news to him at Bad Neuenahr, while your lot were still in Kassel, and from then on he was running for our team. Don't think too harshly of him. He's got an old mother and about ten unmarried sisters to support.'

'And so . . . Motley imprisoned me in that suit and sent me on to you. You know, when I saw a Frenchman at the border, I really thought I was safe.'

There was a long pause.

'Listen to me, Danny,' said Earle. 'Someone's going to find out this secret of yours some day. Like Percival says, we already have some idea of what it's about. Why don't you just tell us and be done?'

'Decency,' said Daniel, gathering all his strength. 'Someone else may find out, as you say, and he may tell you, but it won't be me. To tell you would be to destroy what I live by.'

'A good answer, Mond,' said Percival austerely. 'But do you remember, when we started this explanation, I told you that the story had a moral? The story's not over yet.'

Percival smiled blandly, and assumed a didactic air.

'When you got here yesterday evening,' he said, 'our intention, as you seemed to realize, was to make you talk, by refusing you oxygen if you didn't. As I've told you, we're not allowed to torture people; but in this case we were covered, because it had all been rigged to look like an accident. Damaged suit, oxygen supplies exhausted, etc., etc. The French had agreed to co-operate, to make sure of their share of the secret; and in actual fact those radiation suits are the very devil to deal with. So we were going to torture you under the pretence of being unable to cut you free. Rather like the man in the iron mask. We'd have fixed up the oxygen and communicated with you by writing. As it happened, you passed out. But we could have fixed you up with oxygen just the same, left you in the suit, and then started our little game when you came round. But here you are – free. Haven't you wondered why?'

'Because I made it plain that I wouldn't surrender?'

'No. It was a good gesture, Mond, but you wouldn't have gone on writing NO for long, I promise you that.'

'Perhaps you are preparing some other kind of beastliness.'

'How many times do I have to tell you that we're not allowed to torture you? Our effort with the anti-radiation suit was our only chance in that line. Why, Mond, do you suppose that we've already abandoned it?'

'Look, Danny,' said Earle. 'Tell Percival what he wants to know. Tell him now, before it's too late. Otherwise he's going to tell *you* something – something which will really hurt. More than torture or anything else. Far more than the loss of your decency.'

Bluff, thought Daniel. They daren't go ahead with the oxygen treatment – probably someone higher up stopped them – so now they're trying to bluff.

'Believe me, Daniel. It will be better if you tell him.'

'As I understand the matter,' Daniel said, 'there was never

any real threat, even in Germany, and there certainly isn't now. I'm in a hospital in Strasbourg, and I'm free to leave for England any minute I choose. Of course, you can always turn childish – hide my passport, steal my money – but if you think that will help you, after all I've been through, you're even sillier than I thought. So kindly send for my luggage. I'm going to get up.'

'You haven't answered my question,' Percival said. 'We had you just where we wanted you in that radiation suit: why do you think we let you go?'

'I don't know and I don't care. I imagine that you or your superiors thought better of murdering me. Now please send for my luggage.'

'We let you go, Mond, because we thought of a better way. The oxygen game had its risks. The French doctor was nervous about keeping you in that suit. It might affect you mentally, he said. You might go into a claustrophobic frenzy and suffocate yourself. Or he might get the pressures wrong and kill you by mistake. And of course you're much too valuable to lose. Nevertheless we'd have gone ahead, Mond, had Restarick here not pointed out that, *you being you,* there was a very much simpler way, so simple that it hadn't occurred to me.'

Percival sniffed several times, then removed his spectacles and wiped his watering eyes with a handkerchief. He was, Daniel realized with horror, crying with amusement.

'Your friends in the Sabre Squadron, the only real friends you've had all along. I tested you about them just now, said they were casual and so on. But you insisted, and you were right, that in their way they were true. They helped you, and they didn't ask for anything back. Fielding Gray and his officers. Sergeant-Major Bunce, Corporal-Major Chead, Michael Lamb. Mugger, now happily convalescing in Bielefeld. Your friends.

'Now, if you don't tell us about the Dortmund Papers, Mond, your friends are all going to be ruined – just because they helped you. They aided you in impersonating a serving soldier, bad enough in itself. But what is far, far worse, they thereby made you privy to important official secrets: those suits, those special tents, the whole general method of a Courier Team's operation. *Not* things which you are entitled to know, Mond, but things which they enabled you to study, at close quarters, for over a week. Gray and the officers will be cashiered, Mond; Bunce and Chead will be reduced to the ranks and dishonourably dismissed. All of them, along with Lamb and Mugger, will go to prison. That's what will happen, Mond, unless you come across with what you know. Which brings me to the moral of this story: there's weakness in numbers. If you'd stayed on your own, Mond, you might have kept your secret. There was very little we could do to you – I've told you that. But when you asked other people for help, you were recruiting your own enemies. Every hand raised to help you, in the long run, was a hand raised to drag you down.'

For some minutes Daniel said nothing. Then,

'You'd better send for my suitcase. I shall need the notes which are in it. And who must I explain to? You or Earle could never understand.'

'There'll be someone here in an hour. Try to be ready by then.'

Earle and Percival went out. Five minutes later a black nun came in with Daniel's suitcase. Oh dear, he thought, oh dear, oh dear, oh dear. He got out of bed and looked through the window. A short drop on to the flower beds: no good that way. So he went to his suitcase, rummaged about for a time, and then found what he was looking for, tucked in a side-pocket with his supply of pencils. Oh dear, oh dear. 'They helped you,' Percival had said, 'and they didn't ask for anything back.' Fielding, Michael, Mugger. Basil Bunce and Tom Chead. My comrades of a week, my Dragoons, my Sabre Squadron. Yet even to save these he could not tell what he knew, for to do so would be indecent; it would be to murder the God in whom he did not believe; it would be to destroy his honour as a Jew. But perhaps there was a way (so simple that it hadn't even occurred to Leonard Percival) of keeping silence without also ruining his friends; for after all, Percival and his colleagues were interested in his secret, not in taking revenge. Or so he could only hope. And so he did hope, as he opened the pocket knife which he kept for sharpening his pencils and then (asking grace of the God in whom he did not believe) urged it towards his throat.

Other Panthers For Your Enjoyment

Highly-Praised Modern Novels

Today's Fiction

□ **Alexis Lykiard**   **ZONES**   30p
A young man's mental and erotic awakening, and his free-wheeling
swing from London to Paris to Spain. 'Bursting at the seams with
vitality' — *Sunday Telegraph*

□ **Donald Barthelme**   **SNOW WHITE**   30p
The novel with the big underground reputation. 'A wised-up story
of our time' — *Newsweek*. The lady is a tall dark beauty. She lives
with seven men who, to earn their daily bread, do various odd jobs,
and in between make love to the tall dark beauty in the shower —
more or less one at a time. 'No matter what you look for in a
book you can find it here' — *Boston Herald*

□ **Colin Spencer**   **ANARCHISTS IN
LOVE**   30p
They were young, and unattached — and *very much* uncommitted;
and passionate love-making on the night beaches of summertime
Brighton was their be-all.

□ **Julian Gloag**   **MAUNDY**   40p
Maundy is a young man starting on a banking career . . . but his
fate is hallucination, rape and final destruction. 'Fantastically
clever; it illustrates a case of obsessive sanity falling to bits in
slow motion: coldly erotic' — Kay Dick, *Queen*

□ **James Leigh**   **THE RASMUSSEN
DISASTERS**   35p
Rasmussen is a second — maybe third — generation American in
southern California where he runs a liquor store. Rasmussen is
by no means an eccentric, but the mob that suddenly home in on
his rather staid life by god are. Order is finally restored by a local
fascist and his thugs and — hold it — a bowling team. Only
California could be like this.

□ **Ivan Gold**   **SICK FRIENDS**   40p
Not since Henry Miller has any writer explored so frankly the
limits of love and sex. Its outspokenness may startle, but it is not a
'shocking' book — simply an honest one.

Some British

☐ **Piers Paul Read** **THE JUNKERS** **30p**
An exciting and important novel about love and danger in today's
divided Europe by one of Britain's finest young writers.
'Dazzling' – *Financial Times.* 'Compelling' – *The Observer*

☐ **James Plunkett** **STRUMPET CITY** **50p**
All big city life (Dublin is the city in the case of this wonderful
novel) is here – from saints (?) to sinners. The sinners need no
question mark – they're precisely what they're described as. A big
novel if ever there was one. Reviewers hailed it as the greatest novel
since DR. ZHIVAGO.

☐ **Philip Callow** **THE BLISS BODY** **30p**
Colin was young and wanted a woman – then he met Leila,
attractive, sexy, experienced. She was also married; which didn't
stop either of them. But there's always a price. *The Observer*
described the author as a 'confident successor to D. H. Lawrence'.

☐ **Colin MacInnes** **WESTWARD TO
LAUGHTER** **30p**
MacInnes sails westward in splendid style to murder, rape, piracy and
rebellion in the 17th century Caribbean. It's a novel that's got
something for everybody, and it 'takes the reader by storm' –
Spectator

☐ **Thomas Wiseman** **THE QUICK AND
THE DEAD** **40p**
The Europe of the Nazis – from the ultra-sophisticated sexual
Viennese scene to the brutal battlefields of Yugoslavia. The
author's teeming characters are people corrupted beyond all
hope. *Time* Magazine wrote: 'An extraordinary novel . . .
Brilliant'. *The Observer:* 'Comedy and stark atrocity. Life crackles
on every page'.

☐ **Simon Raven** **THE JUDAS BOY** **30p**
Ambiguous sex, possible danger, final betrayal – Fielding Gray goes
to Greece on a TV fact-finding mission and is there seduced – quite
literally seduced – by a corrupt, golden boy who's the paid agent
of an American undercover man. 'Cynical and civilised' –
Evening Standard

People

☐ Robert Tressell   **THE RAGGED-TROUSER-ED PHILANTHROPISTS**
                                                50p

The miserable reality of working class life during the Edwardian Golden Age. The first English socialist novel and as passionately alive – and relevant – as ever.

☐ George Eliot   **FELIX HOLT THE RADICAL**   40p

From the great period of English novels, the story of conflict between a noble-minded young reformer and a typical 'corrupt for the best reasons' Victorian politician, and of the heroine Esther, torn between them both.

☐ Arthur Morrison   **A CHILD OF THE JAGO**   35p

A masterpiece of social fiction set in the boisterous, brawling East End of last century's London. H. G. Wells reviewed it on publication and praised it highly. The author is the nearest we have to an English Zola, and by no means suffers in the comparison.

☐ Edward Blishen   **THIS RIGHT SOFT LOT**   30p

A 'Blackboard Jungle', London style: a secondary modern where most of the pupils have abandoned lessons in favour of fisticuffs, thieving and girls. Most of the teachers have given up. But one of them is convinced that the kids are *not* beyond hope. 'There isn't a dull page' – *Sunday Mirror*

☐ Krupskaya   **MEMORIES OF LENIN** 40p

Lenin's shadow looms immense 47 years after his death. Millions of words have been written about him – but never anything as intimate as this moving book by his widow and lifelong companion. 'A portrait of a great and honest man' – Arnold Bennett, *Evening Standard*

☐ James Agee and Walker Evans   **LET US NOW PRAISE FAMOUS MEN**   75p

One of the most famous of all twentieth century books. The 'poor whites' of the American Deep South during the Depression of the 1930's. Agee and Evans, his photographer, were sent there on a journalistic assignment, and the rare result is this masterpiece account.
'Magnificent and convincing, because Agee's involvement is so complete' – *The Guardian*

Unconventional

☐ **G. T. Wilkinson**   **THE NEWGATE
CALENDAR 1**   35p
The first Panther selection from the gruesome chronicle of crime
and punishment in 18th century England.

☐ **G. T. Wilkinson**   **THE NEWGATE
CALENDAR 2**   35p
A further selection from the same gruesome source for the numerous
readers of the first book who want more.

☐ **G. T. Wilkinson**   **THE NEWGATE
CALENDAR 3**   35p
The final Panther selection from the infamous record.

☐ **Pietro Aretino**   **THE RAGIONAMENTI 40p**
Subtitle: The erotic lives of nuns, wives and courtesans.
Probably the most plain-speaking piece of European erotica ever
published – banned more often than not since it first appeared in the
16th century. This lucid English translation doesn't miss a trick
of the Italian original.

☐ **Ovid (trans. Paul Turner)**   **THE TECHNIQUE OF
LOVE/REMEDIES FOR
LOVE**   25p
Advice for the gilded youth of Imperial Rome – a sort of seducer's
handbook. Augustus Caesar was not amused. Ovid was exiled for
life to barbarian Danubia.

Obtainable from all booksellers and newsagents. If you have
any difficulty please send purchase price plus 6p postage per
book to Panther Cash Sales, P.O. Box 11, Falmouth, Cornwall.

I enclose a cheque/postal order for titles ticked above plus 6p.
a book to cover postage and packing.

Name ————————————————————————

Address ————————————————————————

————————————————————————